THEY SAID THAT I WAS BRAINY

R V Turner

This book is a work of fiction.

Any persons who resemble the characters in this book are purely coincidental.

First Published 2018

Copyright 2018 Rachel Turner

ISBN: 9781793292018
Imprint: Independently Published

All Rights Reserved.

No part of this book can be copied without expressed permission from the author.

*Dedicated to my family whos
support has been invaluable.*

To Jan and Malcolm

It is a pleasure for me to sign my book for two people who have shown keen interest in reading it.

I hope you enjoy it as much as I have writing it.

Rachel V Turner

1

September 1990, Six Years Old

"Who knows what five plus four equals?" Asked the teacher on a bright morning in September.

It was the beginning of the new school year and she was testing the abilities of her new year two's. No one put their hand up. Paul was sat on a plastic chair, which was pushed back from the table. He held his hands in his lap and sucked his bottom lip, as if he wasn't really paying attention. The teacher looked around the room at the blank faces and gave up waiting for one of them to answer.

"It is nine." She concluded writing this information on the white board to ensure the students understanding, she shook her head as she did.
"I knew that." Said Paul without thinking.
"Sure you did." Replied one of the other students who had quickly grasped the understanding of sarcasm.
"Now children." Said the teacher trying to calm the scene "Paul, if you know the answer I would be grateful if you put up your hand when I ask the question, Simon please refrain from the use of sarcasm."

The teacher asked more questions which the other children began to answer whilst Paul stared blankly out of the window. The class moved on to English and then Geography. Paul didn't notice this really and was only thankful when the bell rang and he could go home. He was the first one out of the classroom, forgetting his rucksack. He didn't care, it would be there when he went back tomorrow. Why did he want to bring it home with him just so that it could remind him that the following day he would be back there?

"It isn't pointless Paul." Said his sister who picked him up from the school like she did everyday "School is a place to learn things." "But I already know them!" He exclaimed frustrated "I know all my times tables up to twenty times twenty and I know how to spell shelves and fifth."

He commenced with spelling them, adding that he could spell tyrannosaurus rex and Hippopotomonstrosesquippedaliophobia. His sister was a little shocked at her six year old bother spelling things even herself at fourteen years old couldn't spell. She was very mature for her age serious and methodical in her thinking, and she had only just started to begin to understand Paul.

"Joan." Said Paul quietly.
"What sweetie?" She replied looking down at the little boy who was trying to hold her hand but wasn't sure how to go about it Joan helped him out taking his little hand in hers.
"Thank you." He said.
"You're welcome." Replied Joan "Now what do you not know?"
"I don't know about a lot of things." He replied modestly "I am sure I will though very soon." He continued not so modestly.
"Library then." She said changing direction and walking towards the local library which was close to the school "I am sure there is something you can learn in here."
"I have been to the library you know." Replied Paul rolling his eyes.

Joan noticed and scolded him, "I won't take you then if you know all about it."
"No please!" Pleaded Paul trying to pull his sister back into the direction of the library as she had turned around and started to head in the other direction "I will behave!"

Joan agreed and they entered the small library together. It was full of the children from the first school, most of whom were being told off for running around. They were all reading the books with the large words and big pictures. Joan looked at the books they were reading and remembered when she enjoyed reading them herself.

"Are you sure you wouldn't like to read one of those books?" Asked Joan pointing to the children's section of the library.

"No." Was the short reply as Paul released his sister's hand and made way towards the non-fiction books. He looked up at the shelves and had to move backwards so that he was able to see the books on the top shelf.

"The children's section is over there dear." Said the librarian concluding that he was probably lost.

"But the Paul section is right here." Said Joan forgetting that the librarian didn't know that was Paul's name. The librarian frowned showing up the wrinkles which surrounded her mouth, she left them alone to choose their books.

"Maybe I should try one of those books." Concluded Paul moving away from all the books with words towards those with pictures.

"No Paul." Said his sister "You read what you want and you don't worry about what other people think."

Paul stood in limbo for a while and realised how bored he would be with only five words to a page. He chose a book on the universe, which was aptly named 'The Universe'. There were a few books with this title but the one Paul wanted to borrow was the largest of them all. Paul didn't have a library card, so his sister borrowed the book on hers as she wasn't old enough to get Paul a card of his own.

"You will have to ask mum and dad if they will get you your own library card." Said his sister as they walked up to the librarian who took the book with a raise of her eyebrows, before handing it over obviously to Joan instead of Paul, who had his arms outstretched ready to receive his first library book.

They walked out with the book being carried happily by Paul. Their mum usually picked them up once she had finished work and this was around 4pm, an hour after they finished school. Usually they would walk to the park and sit on a bench in the fields, but Paul had decided that he wanted to go to the library every day now. His sister didn't mind, as long as Paul was happy she felt that if he was progressing in life the way he was comfortable with, he would excel in the world, and be himself rather than listen to the

R.V. Turner

opinions of others.

2

February 1990, Six Years Old

Paul liked to play with toys, he had a few on his shelves which were bought for him on his birthday or for Christmas. He only ever asked for presents, and didn't like it when someone bought him something that he didn't ask for. He had organised them in height order and in groups of different toys, such as action figure or soft toy. He was proud of his set up, but his cousins didn't seem to care as they rushed in his room one day in half term just as he was admiring his achievement. They jumped up and snatched up handfuls of the action figures, before looking at them and throwing the ones that they didn't want on the floor. Meanwhile Paul just sat on the end of his bed not knowing what to think or to say. They were out of the room in seconds and downstairs before Paul had a chance to even think of what to say. Joan was in her room talking to Jessie. She was a bit younger than Joan but unlike her brothers she asked before she started playing with anything in Joan's room. They heard the commotion and came into Paul's room who was beginning to pick up the remaining toys.

"Did they take your stuff?" Asked Jessie folding her arms.
"Yes." Replied Paul not looking up.
"Don't worry about them Paul they are just two rats." Replied Jessie helping Paul to pick up his toys.
"Rats are actually surprisingly smart animals." Said Paul "They are sometimes referred to as mini dogs."

Jessie didn't take offense and just smiled supportively, Joan started to place the toys on the shelves but once she had done so Paul immediately moved them around to the correct way. Jessie went out of the room and when she returned she was holding the toys that had been 'borrowed' from his bedroom. Paul thanked her greatly and hugged the action figure and soft toy monkey before placing them back on the shelf.

"My pleasure." She replied.

They went back to doing whatever it was that they were doing. Paul closed the door and went back to the tranquillity that he was enjoying. He was thankful now that he would have two people to stand up for him, something which he knew would be useful.

The 'cousins' as Paul called them usually came to stay, along with Paul's aunt and uncle around four times a year. They lived just below Scotland and the children always complained about the traveling. Paul's family didn't go to their house. Paul only remembered going once and that was only for a brief visit. To think of it Paul's family never left their village if they could help it.

This time Paul thought that the behaviour of Mike and Owen had deteriorated since he had last seen them. They didn't understand the phrase 'indoor voices' and whether you were sitting next to them or if they were down the other end of the garden they would still shout at the top of their voices, usually in a whiny tone. Usually because they were being either told off or told that they couldn't do what they wanted. It was strange really, because their parents tried to give them discipline but they just wouldn't listen. In the end they stopped talking about them or to them, unless they were telling them off. However, they always praised Jessie. Jessie was their 'good child' and they did not let that one go. It did get on the nerves of Paul and Joan's parents, although they would smile and nod politely.

The last straw was drawn when Mike and Owen started to throw food at each other when they were eating dinner one evening. A lot of shouting took place during which Paul made his escape. Bedtime was next on their list, and because they had been told to be quiet the only thing that they wanted to do was to be loud. No one in the household got much sleep that night. The morning continued the same but the other way around. They had worn themselves out staying up all night so when everyone was getting up, they were complaining that everyone was making too much noise when they wanted to sleep.

Paul had refused to share his room with either of them, unlike Joan who had welcomed Jessie with open arms. His room was his little piece of solitude that was all his own no matter how hard his parents tried to persuade him to share, he was not going to budge.

"Let's go for a walk." Said Jessie positively.

It was early morning, the sun was shining over another cold winter day. The rain was set to come in later that afternoon, and Jessie especially wanted to get outside before it reached them. Jessie, Paul and Joan made their way to the front door and were just putting their shoes on when the two whirl winds came flying passed. Their shoes were already on their feet and their coats were quickly swung around their shoulders. They leapt outside and ran part way down the path. The rest of the party strolled along not wanting to rush.

"You are copying us!" Exclaimed Owen.
"Yeah!" Agreed Mike "We went outside first."
"So was Owen copying you?" Questioned Paul.
"What?" Said Mike confused.
"When you went outside." Started Paul "Because you went outside first, didn't you? Was Owen copying you?"
Mike thought about it for a while, "Yeah, yeah he did!"

He turned to Owen and they immediately started squabbling. The rest of the group slowly walked passed not wanting to be part of the scene.

"Quick thinking Paul." Said Jessie holding up her hand to high five him.
Paul looked at the hand and didn't touch it so she lowered it slowly.
"It was logical." Said Paul.

Jessie turned to Joan and shrugged her shoulders. She liked her cousin but didn't think that he was her type of person to be friends with. That is how she put it.

Joan and Jessie wanted to sit down and talk but Paul got bored so decided to go home. The rain clouds had come over earlier than expected and Paul was in a hurry to get home. As he reached the door two heads popped around the corner.

"You are banned." They said in unison.
"From my own house?" Questioned Paul.
"Yeah and you are not allowed in unless you know the password." Said Owen.
"Ok, I am sure that Joan and Jessie will move you away when they go through the back door." Said Paul.

Owen and Mike looked at each other before racing to the back door. They didn't think and for a moment they turned and realised that the front door wasn't guarded. They rushed back to find that Paul had snuck in.

"Idiots." Said Paul when he reached his room he closed the door behind him and wedged a chair under the door handle for good measure. As he did, he looked out of the window where the rain had started to come steadily down. He wondered if Jessie and Joan were sheltered enough sitting underneath those trees.

3

September 1991, Seven Years Old

Paul reluctantly went to the play park after school; he never went there unless he was with Joan. He said that there were too many people and all of the good things to play on had gone. His parents both couldn't pick him up and Joan was at a club and the library was closed on Wednesdays. It wasn't a good time to be Paul. As much as he liked being alone he didn't like that type of alone. His parents had assumed that he would stay at the first school in one of the after school clubs that they held, but none of them appealed to Paul. It was a cloudy day which felt like rain making Paul uneasy as he started to walk to the park. He did think about wandering the paths instead but there was a small shelter at the park. When Paul arrived there were actually no other children there to his delight, and he ran over to one of the swings. If he had to do something at least sitting on the swing he could ponder the laws of physics. He was happy for a while gently moving through the wind. He never went very high on the swing as he got dizzy very easily. He was soon joined by a rowdy looking lot of year four's, they ran up to the swings where Paul was sitting, a whole gang of them.

"I want to use that swing." Said one of the girls.
"I am using it at the moment." Replied Paul seriously.
"But I want to use it!" She argued.
"Just because you want to use it doesn't mean that you get to." Started Paul "Anyway I was here first."
"But I always use that swing." She complained "I am going to tell on you."

She ran off, but Paul wasn't upset by the thought of her telling on him, because whoever she told wouldn't have any power over him. Clearly her parents thought this too as moments later he heard the girl wailing about how it wasn't fair. Paul decided to be the bigger man and told her that he was finished.

"I don't want to use it if you have been using it!" She spat at him to which her parents told her off and they thanked Paul who smiled weakly and began to walk away from the park.

He decided to walk to the school where Joan was, because soon she would be coming out from her club where their parents would be picking her up before him. He knew exactly where it was so getting there wasn't a problem but getting there before his parents got there was. There was no one there when he arrived and realised his mistake. Rather than staying where he was he decided to get help from his school instead. He wandered back to the first school straight into the reception area.

"I need you to ring my parents." He said peering over the top of the desk
"Paul?" Questioned the Receptionist the first school only had one class to each year group and all the staff knew all the students, "School finished hours ago."
"I was going to play in the park but there were children in there." Replied Paul.
The Receptionist understood Paul, "Ok I think Mrs King is still around."

Just as she said this Mrs King walked through the door laden with her bags ready to go home.

"Paul?" She questioned just as the Receptionist had done before hand "You should be at home."
"Joan had a club and I was going to play in the park but there were children in there." Repeated Paul.
"Ok Paul." Said Mrs King sounding tired and worried at the same time "I will ring your parents."

His parents were telephoned, Mrs King was surprised at how calm Paul's parents seemed to be. They were a few minutes away so Mrs King and the Receptionist supervised the seven year old whilst they waited for them to arrive. Paul didn't understand what the fuss was about, he had been out by himself before, why was now any different?

"He does this all the time." Said Paul's mother when his parents arrived to pick him up, she always seemed to find a way to blame Paul.

Mrs King was a bit astounded with the fact that they let a seven year old wander around a town where the only way to get home was to get a lift or walk, and it was a few miles to where he lived. Mrs King nodded and smiled nervously as Mrs Westwood talked.

4

October 1991, Seven Years Old

The tree house, as Joan always called it, wasn't more than a small lean-to shack at the base of one of the trees in a small copse between some fields. Paul still wouldn't go in it because of the stigma that tree houses were in trees, even though theirs was firmly on the ground. Joan used to play in and around it with her friends for years. When Paul gained the courage to explore it, the tree house was falling down. There was fungi growing in and around the boards which were lent up against the tree. The floor which consisted of a few small sheets of wood, had ants nests in a few corners and there were wood lice coming up around the edges. This was about the only thing which Paul found interesting about it. It was long after Joan stopped playing there, that Paul came close enough to the bundle of wood to just sit outside and look at it. He imagined how he would move it into the trees and what he would need to complete this project. He never intended on building it, but found an interest in structural engineering and decided to have a go. He enjoyed working out the mathematics behind it but then it came to the materials which were more difficult to find. He tried to think logically about the issue but didn't want to touch anything that he considered 'dirty'. This made the material hunting a little harder. He decided that the wood shed would be the best place to look and after he put on the thickest gloves that he could find, he took a deep breath before he took the first steps into the wood shed. There were a few old boards in there and around the outside. He struggled with moving them to the building site, he tried dragging them but he tired very quickly. Instead he found a sack truck and carted all the wood on wheels.

By the time that he reached the tree house set up with all the materials that he needed, he was tired and bored. He wasn't interested anymore and pretended that it was about to rain, so he made his way back home. He was disappointed at the thought of not completing the tree house, he had set it out on paper so easily it almost seemed to him that he couldn't stop now, now that he had come so far. He didn't think about the fact that he didn't enjoy climbing trees and sort of got on with it without thinking at all. He had designed another plan of what he was going to do, and went back to the tree house the following day. He held the first plank of wood in his hands and knew that he would have to climb it up the branches to where the platform was going to be. He chose one of the smaller pieces of wood which would make up the foundation of the floor. He struggled as he tried to climb it up the tree and instead, made a pulley system to drag the wood up. The only thing was that he wasn't strong enough to pull it up so ended up attempting once again to drag it up the tree himself, this time he had tied the plank to his waist so that he could use his hands to climb with.

He had almost reached the branch where he was going to lay the foundation of the structure. There was a slight change in balance when Paul tried to pull himself up onto the tree branch. He scrambled for the branch but it didn't seem to want to hold his weight and Paul followed after the plank which tumbled down to the ground. He lay there for a while, he was dazed and confused but knew that he needed to get home. His parents were less than pleased when they had to take him to the emergency room, and were more annoyed about the fact that their son who was afraid of literally everything would drag himself up a tree to build a tree house.

"I thought you wanted a normal child?" Questioned Paul's father. "Yes I did." Replied his mother "I was just getting used to this one!"

He tried to build the tree house in a tree and instead of those endless childhood memories, he ended up with a broken arm. It was the last time that Paul played around that shack and he never thought about structural engineering again.

He spent four hours in the emergency room with his parents, minus the forty-five minutes, that it took them to get there and get back and at the end of the day. He was waiting a long time before he was seen, and the whole time no matter how much it hurt he didn't want to touch his arm. It lay beside him on the chair limp. When he was seen, the doctor started to poke and prod it making Paul scream. He was tired and ready to snuggle down in his bed to dream it all away. He cried the whole way home, he felt very stressed and anxious, not to mention worried about the giant brick that was now attached to his arm. He had been given some mild pain killers which helped him drift off into that dream world that he wanted, only to wake up a few hours later sweating and crying. It was a long night.

"Let me draw something on it." Said Joan looking at Paul's cast the following morning. Paul was sat in the lounge, he wasn't very responsive to anything that was said and tried to avoid eye contact with people much more than he normally did "I promise that it will make you feel better."

Paul gave in mainly because Joan said that she would tickle him if he didn't let her, and Paul hated to be tickled. Slowly a string of musical notes began to appear up the white hard structure that engulfed his pale limp arm. Paul giggled as Joan tried to cover all the cast and he watched the shapes emerge. It gave some structure to the blank canvas and Paul did smile at the art work. He started to act like himself again and was demanding because he couldn't use both hands, which was tiring to his parents. Those were six long weeks for his parents. Paul also complained when it was time for him to go to school on the Monday. He said that he couldn't write notes so it would be pointless.

"I thought that you had a photographic memory?" Questioned his mother.

Paul didn't respond and instead huffed and walked away, he was the one who was injured shouldn't he have sympathy?

When it was time for Paul's cast to be removed everyone was

They Said That I Was Brainy

happy about it, except Paul. Paul was nervous when he got sight of the tools that they were going to use. They opened it gently but Paul continued to protest, even when the cast was removed revealing the repaired arm. Paul wasn't so sure even though everyone was telling him that it was fine and ready to be used again, but Paul refused to move it properly. Even when the Doctor told him that if he didn't exercise it the muscles would deteriorate. Paul replied with 'I know *that*.' The Doctor gave up after giving him the exercises that he needed to do, so she told them to go home. He sat around the house complaining as he had done when his arm was in the cast. He didn't move it and raided the first aid kit to fashion himself a sling. This continued for a few days, and his parents were on the last straw for how many times Paul wouldn't do something for himself. He was torn when his glass was accidently pushed off of the table when they were eating dinner. He couldn't let it smash on the floor and had no choice as it began to tumble he reached out with both hands and caught it. Not only was it a great catch but was the best sporting achievement that he would ever have. The ordeal was soon forgotten by the little boy who had much more important things to fill his mind with, than remember that time when he hurt himself. He went around the house like he usually did and never made any attempt to not use his arm, to the relief of his parents.

5

March 1992, Seven Years Old

"What are you playing?" Asked his sister sitting on the crumb covered floor by Paul.
He was holding an action figure and was waving him about in the air.
"He is trying to avoid all the strings in the air." Paul exclaimed quickly moving the action figure to avoid one of these 'strings'.
"What?" Questioned Joan resisting the temptation to roll her eyes wondering what strange idea her brother had come up with.
"I read about it in the library." He stated continuing with his game.
"What book was it?" She asked.
"A blue book I think." Replied her brother.
She laughed, "No silly! What was the book called?"
"Physics." He replied "There were all kinds of things in there not only about the strings, but on the 'Big Bang', the different planets, something about loops, black holes." He continued to list almost every item in the book until his sister stopped him "Tomorrow I am going to read about dinosaurs."
His sister breathed a sigh of relief, "At least that is more normal for kids of his age." She thought.
"The palaeontologists say that the Argentinosaurus was the largest dinosaur." He continued to list facts about dinosaurs.
"Maybe not." Thought his sister.
"But you have to go to school tomorrow." She stated "When are you going to go to the library?"
"I was thinking that I would retire from school." He replied in all seriousness and placed his action figure on the floor amongst the tiny particles. He began to carefully pick up each individual

crumb to which his sister said that she would get the vacuum cleaner but her brother wasn't impressed.

"I like doing it like this." He said "I don't like school."

"I know sweetie." Replied his sister.

"School is boring." He stated.

"But you have to go." She said trying to comfort him.

"Why?" He questioned "I am too old for school. I want to learn the important stuff."

"Like what?" Joan asked wondering what was going on in his little head.

"Like." He started trying to think of something "Like space. Maths harder than adding, dividing and subtracting. Music which involves me actually reading the notes not just shaking a maraca about."

"You can read music?" She questioned continuing to ask if he just wanted to read music or if he had already taught himself.

"Sure I have." He replied picking his action figure off of the floor and brushing him down forgetting about all the crumbs he had picked up and they scattered gently back over the floor again.

Paul was getting increasingly bored with school and all the teachers knew it. There was nothing that they could do because they had to follow the syllabus set for year three's. They encouraged his parents to get a tutor for Paul, so that he could be challenged and have something to aim for. His parents were not best pleased when they found out that to ensure their child's happiness they would have to fork out some more money, but they did it despite their objections. Paul wasn't sure that he would enjoy being tutored, it seemed like a lot of effort to him. As he thought that he could probably learn all that the tutor was going to teach him by reading books from the library.

"So Paul I hear that you need some more challenging material." Started the tutor.

They were sat down at the kitchen table, it was after school on a Monday and on Monday afternoons Paul had scheduled in time for him to play with his toys. He thought about that a lot through the next hour that he was sat there.

"Yes." Replied Paul "But that is obvious really otherwise you wouldn't be here."

The tutor looked at him for a moment long enough for Paul to look behind him to make sure that it was him he was looking at.

"Anyway I have brought over some key stage three material to share with you." Continued the tutor.
"I have already done that." Replied Paul "Try GCSE level."
The tutor shook his head with a smile, "Paul you are not ready for GCSE level. Key stage three is going to be better. Let's just start with that and see how we go."
"I would like to see your qualifications." Said Paul.
"I have shown them to your parents and they seem satisfied so you don't need to worry yourself with that." Replied the tutor trying very hard to stay calm.
"You are not qualified to tutor GCSE students are you?" Questioned Paul.
"No I am not but we are lucky because the last time I checked you weren't a GCSE student." Replied the tutor annoyed.

Paul was also very agitated, he hated when people assumed that because of his age he wasn't as intelligent as he was. He started to quiz the tutor, he said different questions mostly to do with maths and when the tutor refused to answer them Paul did just to show that he did know the answer.

"I don't think that there is anything that you can teach me." Said Paul getting up from the table "You may go."
"Paul where are you going? I have been asked to tutor you." Replied the tutor pretending that he cared.
"It is Monday afternoon." Replied Paul "On Monday afternoons I play with my toys."

Paul left the bewildered tutor sitting at the kitchen table wondering what he had got himself into. He didn't know what to tell Paul's parents, but did his best in explaining that he wasn't qualified enough to handle Paul's intellect. Paul's parents tried to persuade him to stay and all he kept saying was that it wouldn't be fair on Paul.

The next tutor that they hired was an A-Level tutor, and was more expensive than the key stage three tutor. Paul sat once again at the kitchen table, this time it was a Thursday when Paul researched quantum mechanics. There was no other topic that he wanted to discuss. It helped that the tutor had studied physics somewhat but she was astounded by Paul's intellect on the subject.

"Have you ever thought about taking a GCSE now?" She asked "I am sure that you would sail through it."

"No thank you." Replied Paul getting up from the table "This was fun we should do it again sometime."

The tutor returned the next few Thursdays, every one she was being drained by Paul's increasing knowledge on quantum mechanics. Very soon after the fourth Thursday a letter was received through the door stating that she couldn't tutor Paul any longer.

"That is a shame." Said Paul "I was almost beginning to like her."

6

July 1992, Eight Years Old

"Mrs Round taught me a new piece today." Paraded Paul as Joan and him walked home.

Joan listened intently as she steered the boy through the people who were walking the other way. It was a Thursday evening and Paul had just had his piano lesson. It seemed to have taken over from his quantum mechanics evenings. Ever since he was six years old he was encouraged to pursue music by Joan. She used to play the piano and had passed a few grades. They had an old piano in their house which stood in the hallway, it was mainly used as an ornament since Joan had become disinterested with it. Paul had approached the instrument first after having a conversation with Joan. It was a challenge, and at six years old he begun to think that there were no more challenges for him. Some old music was set out on the stand where it had been left for all the months that Joan hadn't played it. Every time she walked passed she would look over and think, "I really must play that sometime." But she never 'got around to it'. Paul fancied that he could play the music by the end of the day and by the end of the morning, he had mastered the simple piece before him. The house was empty, other than Joan who was in her bedroom listening to music through her headphones. It was only when she felt hungry and decided to go downstairs to the kitchen that she realised that the piano was being played. She carefully and quietly opened her door and sneaked around the banisters peering through them. She saw Paul with his little legs dangling from the piano stool, and his tiny fingers carefully and precisely pressing the keys. His face was serious as he scrunched it up to read the music before him.

"You play beautifully Paul." Said his sister when she finally came downstairs to find out more about this hidden talent.
"It really isn't me honest." Paul started "It is like doing an experiment, if you do it right it will always come out the same way."

Joan chuckled to herself about Paul's rationality. Paul was clearly bored with that piece and since talking about experiments he decided that he would do that instead. Joan tried to persuade him to stay and play some more but Paul wasn't interested.

"I have mastered that now. What is the point in playing music it is all the same notes just in a different order?" Replied Paul before running upstairs to his room.

Joan admitted defeat and continued on her way to the kitchen thinking about how arrogant her brother could be.

Joan remembered this as they walked along back to their own house. He had only started lessons when he was seven, up until that point he thought that music had been done and there was nothing more that it could teach him. The trees were beginning to get the green fullness back and the flowers had already began brightening up the green spaces, there were few people still wandering around the streets. Joan would take Paul to his piano lessons after school on Thursdays and wait whilst he was having his lesson. Mrs Round was happy to accommodate Joan, and allowed her to use her dining room table to do her school work whilst Joan waited. The house was old but comfortable and not only did Paul look forward to his piano lessons, but Joan looked forward to them too as she was eager to find a place where there was calm all around her, and the faint noise of the instrument in the next room comforted her. She always said that she did the best work whilst sat at that dining room table.

"Why don't you take some exams Paul?" Encouraged Joan as they entered their house.
"No." Replied Paul shortly as he took of his shoes absentmindedly throwing mud onto the hall wall before placing them neatly in the shoe rack and going to his room.

"Why?" Called Joan up the stairs.
"I don't want to." He replied before she heard the click of the door close.

The next day Joan pursued the fact that Paul should take his piano exams, she tried to encourage him to. She said that he was only eight years old and could achieve his grade eight in a few years easily with his talent. Paul was not impressed and stated that he would never play the piano again. Joan felt a tightness in her chest she was sure that Paul meant it, no matter how much she tried to convince herself that he didn't. She tried to believe that he was just going through a phase and that it wouldn't last for very long. Paul's parents didn't really mind if Paul continued with his lessons or not, they were in some respect happy that he actually did something other than read, but then they thought of the money they would save.

"It is the only normal thing that he does." Stated Paul's dad putting down his paper suddenly. It was late that evening, Joan and her parents were watching an episode of their favourite series on TV. Between the adverts Mr Westwood picked up his paper. Joan and her mother both turned in sync to look at him.
"That was a bit of a random thing to say." Stated his wife.
Her husband took some time to gather his thoughts before continuing with his argument, "He doesn't play sport, he doesn't do well at school but he does play an instrument."
"Actually he plays four." Stated Joan and now it was her parent's turn to look at her in sync.
"What?" Questioned her mother "Four but how are? What? Who is paying for it?"
"It is the same lesson just with a different instrument it doesn't cost anymore." Laughed Joan wondering what her parents thought, that Paul was sneaking out to have secret music lessons.

Her parents were astounded by the fact that their son could play four instruments at the age of eight years old. They didn't really mind which ones although Joan continued to tell them.

"He can play piano, violin, cello and flute." Said Joan proudly.
The moment passed very quickly when her father added, "He has

given it up though, never mind."

Her parents seemed to forget all about the subject, their programme had just come back on the television and they sat intently watching the last twenty minutes of it. Joan sat through it, but she couldn't help thinking of Paul and how he should continue to play music and how she could persuade him to. She didn't know whether she should persuade him but he was so fantastic at it. She kept thinking of if she could play half as well as Paul how she would play every day, and learn as much music as she possibly could. It was 11pm when she went up to bed, and as she walked to her room she noticed that there was a strip of light coming from Paul's room down the small gap, that Paul always left in the door. She sneaked across the floor avoiding where she knew there were squeaky floor boards. She peered through the gap but it was no use Paul wasn't in view. She opened it slightly and put her head around the door. Paul was sat on the floor playing with his dinosaurs or sort of playing. He was moving them about but didn't really put any effort into it.

"Paul what are you doing? You should be in bed." Said Joan entering the room and sitting on the end of Paul's bed.
"Playing." Said Paul taking no notice of the fact that he should be in bed.
"It is late." Said Joan "Please get into bed otherwise mum and dad are not going to be happy."
"I thought they wanted me to be normal." He said continuing to place his dinosaurs in different positions.
"Oh Paul." Said Joan "There is no such thing as normal. You are you, and you shouldn't try to be anyone else."

Paul was silent but did begin to pack away his dinosaurs into a little plastic box with a clip on lid. He stood up and placed this box on a colourful open cabinet shelf.

"Promise me Paul." Started Joan "You won't try to change?"
"I promise." Said Paul drearily before he clambered into bed.
"Good." Replied Joan with a smile getting up from the end of the bed and walking to the light and turning it out. She went through the door leaving it ajar which pleased Paul before he closed his

eyes and drifted off into his dreams.

Joan continued to try and persuade Paul to go back to playing the piano, but it was no use. Paul had made up his mind. Joan felt like it was her fault that Paul had stopped playing, had she pushed him too far to achieve his grades? Paul tried to convince her that it wasn't her fault and that he had been becoming bored with music just as he had when he first started to play but Joan still felt a twang.

"Really it was nice of you to try to get me to experience music." Said Paul "But I really don't get it."

Joan looked at him sideways she looked at his face and it showed no emotion. He was looking straight forward at the outside. Joan was sitting on one of the garden chairs in the summer sun but Paul sat inside looking out.

"You're lying." Accused Joan putting her head back and closing her eyes. She didn't notice but Paul's expression stayed the same he didn't make one movement of his face, "Come on admit it. You love playing music."
Paul continued to say nothing so Joan opened her eyes and turned around to look at him, "There must be a reason that you quit?"
"I was bored." Replied Paul.
"I know you have said that but there must be a reason for you getting bored." Said Joan.
"I don't like exams." Started Paul.
"You have never taken an exam." Said Joan confused "How do you know what they will be like?"
"When you took your GCSE exams." Said Paul "Now I know."
Joan was still finding it hard to understand him so asked him to elaborate.
"You started to get sad." He said "You didn't play with me or help me with my experiments. You stopped going out with your friends and you didn't sleep much."

Joan was speechless for a moment how did her little brother know so much? Understand so much about human emotion when he showed none of his own?

"How do you know that I didn't sleep?" Questioned Joan when she had found her voice.
"Your light was on." Said Paul.
"But you must have been in bed?" Replied Joan.
"I was but through the gap in the door there was a slight deviation in the glow from the landing light." Said Paul.
"What was that?" Asked Joan expecting some elaborate explanation.
"It was brighter." Replied Paul standing up.

He looked as if he was about to do something or say something. His thoughts were almost articulated through the way he swayed slightly backward and forward, scrunching his fists and screwing up his face slightly. You could see the wash of tenseness that covered him as he swayed. Joan thought that he was about to go outside but no, he lift his leg and sat back down on the floor and sighed.

"I will carry you?" Suggested Joan "If you like."
Paul thought about this idea for a while looking out into their small back garden. It did seem a vast expanse to him though.
"To the fence and back again?" Stuttered Paul.
"To the fence and back again." Repeated Joan confidently nodding her head.
"Don't touch the fence though." Replied Paul as he clambered onto Joan's back.
Joan agreed, "Ready?"
"Ready" Said Paul quietly.

Joan slowly paced through the small garden passed a pile of rubbish and a compost bin on her left, and a small gap with the garden gate in on her right. Paul clung on more tightly when he noticed the pile of rubbish. It moved in that way which he remembered, the ants nest wasn't so fun when they were crawling all over him. He had decided that he wanted to study insects, and tried to look inside a red ants nest. As he moved the rubbish around with a stick he found a swarm of them. He was so excited that he span around tripping over an old bike that was laying down on the floor. Ever since then he had never wanted go out in the garden again. The thought that ants live in other places and not only their garden, didn't seem to enter his head.

"Back now!" He exclaimed.
"To the fence." Replied Joan continuing on her way.
"Back!" Screamed Paul wriggling.

He wriggled so much that Joan lost her grip on him and he fell to the floor. He wasn't hurt but he didn't seem to want to move. His eyes were wide and he was gasping through forced tears that trickled down his cheeks. Joan looked at him there, he was stuck on his back like a turtle that was afraid to roll onto its feet again, rather than it couldn't. Joan sat on the floor beside him and pulling him up to a sitting position put her arm around him. He stopped crying shortly afterwards and started to jabber on about nothing. Paul could feel them crawling all over him but was petrified to move. They heard a call for dinner and Joan got up whilst Paul continued to sit on the grass.

"Are you coming?" Asked Joan.
Paul shook his head they were still around him.
"Suit yourself." Replied Joan pretending to walk off knowing that Paul would stop her. When he did stop her he slowly got on to his feet and grabbed her hand. He was trying to clamber onto Joan's feet but Joan refused to let him.

"Paul you can do this." She said "I believe in you."

Paul wasn't so sure, but as he looked around he saw that there were no ants and they were all in his imagination. He took little steps towards the patio doors that led into the lounge. Once on the patio he jumped into the lounge gasping but smiling.
"There." Said Joan.
"I will only go outside if you come with me." Said Paul.
"Sure." Agreed Joan "That is absolutely fine."

Joan felt happier and this achievement glazed over the mistake of the piano lessons. She told her parents who seemed disinterested, but were pleased that Paul would spend some time that summer in the garden.

"Like a normal boy should." Said her father.

7

November 1992, Eight Years Old

Paul really admired his grandfather, as he listened to him intently when Paul told him what he had learnt from the books that he borrowed from the library. Paul always thought that he listened because his grandad enjoyed listening to him talk, and he probably did, but his grandad mostly didn't remember. So when Paul would say 'I know I told you about blah blah, today I learnt that actually they discovered blah blah' his grandfather wouldn't remember what Paul had told him so instead of saying so, would listen patiently asking the occasional question that he could manage. This realisation didn't occur to Paul until he was eight years old. He was going round to his grandparent's house but when they got there his grandfather wasn't there. His grandmother was frantic trying to locate him and his mother and grandmother went phoning all their friends, in hope that one of them knew where he was. Paul sat in the lounge looking up at the large chair where his grandad always sat. He didn't look at the books that he had brought to show his grandad, because now he wasn't in the mood. They found his grandfather, or rather he found them, as he sauntered into the house with a green groceries bag on his arm and a smile on his face not knowing what all the commotion was about. His wife scolded him, as did his daughter in law.

"You know that we don't go to *that* greengrocer anymore." Said his wife taking the bag off of him.
"Yes we do Smith and Son, we always have." He replied reaching to look in the bag but his wife pulled it away from him.
"It hasn't been Smith and Son for years." Said his wife but her

husband didn't want to listen so she continued to persuade him "It was twenty, no, twenty five years ago since they moved out of that shop to a bigger one nearer the town. We go to Lodgers now, don't you remember?"
"Of course I do." Lied her husband "I just wanted to see how that one was doing that is all."
"Sure." Replied his wife beginning to hand him back the bag before she pulled it away from him again "What's in the bag?"

Of course he couldn't remember, the next day he did the same thing again and the next. His wife decided to question him before he went, to find out what he was going to buy. He said that he was going to buy a punnet of grapes, a lettuce, cucumber and two large tomatoes.

"But you haven't bought that shopping list for ten years, why do you feel you need to buy it now?" Asked his wife.
"I have always bought that." He replied and as he did his wife went to show him the piles of food in their cupboard.
"We don't need anymore." She replied closing the door to the cupboard.
"Right I better get some more grapes." He replied and walked out of the house.

Paul was sitting in the lounge and reliving the day his grandfather went missing, but this time Paul started to read his books as if to escape from the reality of his emotions. His grandma came into the lounge and sat on the sofa looking down at him. She sighed heavily and asked what he was reading, Paul tried to explain but it just wasn't the same telling her. His mother came to pick him up later in the afternoon, which was when they realised that grandfather had been at the greengrocers a long time. They found him half an hour later wandering down the wrong street. He was confused but didn't admit it, but he recognised his daughter-in-law as soon as he saw her.

It was late that evening when they finally arrived home. Paul had been sat in his grandparent's lounge by himself whilst his mother and grandma talked and talked. Paul felt like he had been there longer than he ought to have, he felt funny and decided the best option was to fall asleep on his grandparent's sofa, which was when his mother decided that it was the right time to bring him home. His mother was tired when they got home, and she said goodnight to Paul before she walked wearily into the lounge. Paul could hear his parents talking in the lounge downstairs, he didn't want to listen to what they were saying so started to hum to himself to make sure that he didn't. He didn't realise how loud he was humming, until his sister quietly opened the door.

"Paul?" She questioned as she let herself into the dark room "Are you ok?"
"Fine." Replied Paul shortly.
"Then why are you humming?" She asked standing as a silhouette in the doorway.
Paul sat up in bed, "Can't you hear them?"
"Hear who?" Asked Joan walking over to sit on the bed.
"Our parents." He replied looking down "They are talking about grandad but I don't want to listen so I hum."

Once Joan got over how good Paul's hearing was she tried to comfort him, but her comfort was no good. Paul didn't accept her kind words and certainly didn't accept any hugs. He snuggled back down in his bed and rolled away from his sister, who took this as a cue to leave, so she walked out of the door and back to her own room. Once he heard his sister's door close Paul turned to face the door to his own bedroom door. It wasn't right so he got up and went over to the door slightly opening it. As he did he heard his mother say, "He has got to go in a home, your mother can't cope with him anymore."

Paul physically jumped when he heard this and ran back to his bed not caring how much noise he made. It must have been a lot, because soon he heard the footsteps of his mother coming up the stairs. She opened the door and peered in, making out the shape of her son sound asleep she closed the door and went back downstairs.
"Oh great." Said Paul aloud as he turned to look at his door again, it was wrong.

8

May 1993, Eight Years Old

"What is your favourite word?" Asked one of the girls in Paul's class.

It was break time, usually Paul would ask if he could stay inside but the teacher always said no. Then Paul would sulk and sit in the shade under the pergola, which covered a hop scotch game. He used to sneak a book outside and sit and read until it was time to go back in again, but Paul wouldn't want to because he was interested in his book and would sulk for the rest of the day. It wasn't often that the other children would talk to him, especially if he was reading because he would say things that they didn't understand and think that he was being mean to them.

"Paul!" Exclaimed the girl shaking the book that Paul was holding to get his attention.
"What?" Questioned Paul annoyed.
"What is your favourite word?" Repeated the girl.
"Words are just words they are all the same." Replied Paul.
"No words are different." She said "I have a favourite word."

The girl prompted Paul to ask her what it was but Paul didn't, so she continued to tell him anyway.

"It is rainbow." She said "It is made up of rain and bow."

She smiled pleased with herself.

"That word is just like shoelace or football." Replied Paul.
The girl huffed but continued to argue her point, "You cannot compare a rainbow to a football because a rainbow is pretty."

"I quite like different." Said Paul thoughtfully "It is the easiest word to type on a computer and it means everything."

The girl didn't understand what Paul meant, and was happy when another boy joined the conversation.

"I like throughout!" He exclaimed proudly "It is the longest word I know."
"Try Argentinosaurus instead." Replied Paul going back to reading his book.

The girl and boy just looked at him for a second, before they realised that they had better things to do and forgot about the conversation entirely. Paul hadn't, he went home and questioned his parents but they didn't have a favourite word and thought that it wasn't worth thinking about. Paul agreed and explained the playground conversation. Joan was interested when she heard and was proud of Paul's answer, she herself hadn't thought of having a favourite word but was eager to find one of her own.

9

August 1993, Nine Years Old

Paul never liked the dentist, he didn't like sitting still for that long with his mouth open and someone prodding at his teeth. He always asked them where they got their gloves from, and if they were new and sterilised. If the instruments they were using were stainless steel and if they had been sterilised also. It wasn't until he was nine years old when he realised how much he didn't like the dentist. He was sitting happily in the grey waiting room looking at all the posters on the wall, the reason he was happy was because he wasn't the one who needed his teeth checked but rather those of his sister. He just had to go along because there would be no one to look after him otherwise.

His mother handed him a bar of chocolate as an incentive to be quiet and not to quiz the dentist. Joan was soon called in, so they all went to a small room down the corridor. He sat on his mother's lap and could feel the chocolate bar in his pocket. He was excited to eat it and was bored at looking at the different things in the room. Also it made him feel funny to watch Joan have her teeth prodded so he decided that he needed a distraction, so out came the chocolate bar. When he opened it the waft of the sweetness made his mouth water. He began to munch merrily away.

"Don't you know that chocolate is bad for you." Said the dentist noticing the chocolate bar.

Paul looked at her with the chocolate square that he had just broken off between his fingers. He was a bit taken aback by being told off by a dentist. The square of chocolate started to melt between his fingers and he wasn't happy with the sticky feeling.

"It is bad for you teeth." She continued "You shouldn't eat it."
"Do you eat it?" Replied Paul.

The dentist looked at him bewildered for a moment she didn't think that he would respond in this way. All the other children she had told about sugar had quietly listened with a small sense of uneasiness and a glazed look over their eyes. Paul being Paul, was not going to back down that easy he knew he was going to be right. He couldn't imagine that she would not eat chocolate when there are so many holidays celebrated by it.

"So you are being a hypocrite." Stated Paul with a blank expression on his face.
"Paul!" Exclaimed his mother annoyed with what her son had just said.
"It is ok Mrs Westwood." Replied the dentist smiling then turning to Paul "I am just saying that you should watch what you eat."
"Do you?" Questioned Paul raising his eyebrows he wasn't going to let this one go.
"Of course I do." She smiled.
"I don't think that it is working." Said Paul with a straight face.

His sister, who had her mouth wide open, was clearly laughing but trying not to move about too much. She was jiggling around in the chair clutching at the sides of it whilst the dentist went back to her work. Paul realised that his sister found it funny, so was about to continue but his mother was not pleased. She tried not to shout at him and instead sent him to the waiting room. As he reached the door he turned around and the dentist was looking at him. He spitefully took a bite of the chocolate bar before making his escape.

"Paul you should be respectful to your elders." Said his mother as they were walking away from the dentist.
"Even if they are wrong?" Questioned Paul.
"Even if they are wrong Paul, otherwise it is impolite." Scolded his mother.
"That doesn't make sense at all." Replied Paul "How can you not correct someone when they are wrong."
"It is easy." Replied his mother "Just nod and smile and say abso-

lutely nothing."
"But they are wrong. I can't not correct them otherwise they will start believing things which are wrong and telling other people who don't know any better and so the rumour will just spread." Said Paul "Isn't it better if I correct them now so that we can save time later?"
"No." Replied his mother shortly.
"I do get very annoyed when people try to tell others what they should and shouldn't eat." Said Joan "At school the teachers tell us that we shouldn't eat crisps and when we see them at break time they are gobbling them down."
"That is not a nice word Joan, don't use it again." Said her mother.
"Shouldn't it be our choice what we eat and when we exercise? It is not their fault if people want to eat junk food all the time and just sit and watch TV." Continued Joan "If you have all of these things in moderation then surely it is ok."
"I am bored of this conversation now." Said their mother who swiftly changed the subject.

10

September 1993, Nine Years Old

"But Paul doesn't have any friends. I have told you that boy is not normal." Said Aunt Bess as she gently rocked in *her* chair.

Paul was sitting by the window engrossed in a book about quantum mechanics. He was nine years old and had just started middle school. New school meant new rules, new people, and new teachers, new spot to each his lunch, new everything. When Paul read a book he became unaware of the goings on that would happen around him. It worked at school and home. Although, he was usually told off if he was reading a book that wasn't related to the subject in lessons. He didn't hear the mean things that his aunt said about him. Even if he had heard them, he probably wouldn't have particularly reacted, he may not have even understood.

"Paul is just Paul." Was the simple answer that his sister gave, she was happy with Paul being exactly how he was, why wasn't everyone else?
"He is not normal." Repeated Aunt Bess.
"He is his own normal." Said his sister trying not to turn their conversation into a dispute "Anyway no one is *really* normal. How would you even define normal?"

Their aunt huffed loudly as if she was trying to make Paul notice her, he didn't. He kept on reading his book looking at more than just the pictures. Joan rolled her eyes and quickly checked that Aunt Bess hadn't noticed. Aunt Bess had closed her eyes and was clearly pretending to sleep, as when Joan got up to join Paul Aunt Bess opened them wide again.

"I thought you were here to keep me company?" She retorted.

Joan took her seat not being able to talk otherwise her aunt would scold her for keeping her awake, and she couldn't sit anywhere else otherwise her aunt would accuse her of leaving her alone. She was stuck for another hour until it was dinner time. Every Tuesday they were told by their parents that after school they had to visit their poor aunt. It was only really so that they didn't have to visit her themselves. Dinner time came quickly, and Joan made the usual excuse of the fact that it was school the next day and Paul needed his sleep.

"Hopefully he will make a friend then." Said Aunt Bess before absentmindedly slamming the door in their faces.

Paul hadn't noticed he was still reading his book as they walked down the path of the middle terrace house. Night had covered the street that was usually busy with the rush of traffic and bustle of people heading for town. Most people had drawn the curtains, and there was only a faint glow from the windows. Paul struggled to read his book in those conditions, and would spend a few minutes standing under each lamp post before his sister moved him on. They reached Joan's car which was parked a little way down the street. Joan almost had to push Paul into the car as he stood under the lamp post which was by it. The drive home was quiet as Paul continued to strain to read his book. Joan pulled up in their drive, before they had even got out, their mother opened the door. The beam of light which extended from the hall way to the outside world looked very inviting.

"Paul put that book down now." Pleaded his mother as he walked in the house almost tripping over the step to the door.
Paul ignored her making his mother impatient, "Paul!" She exclaimed making him jump.

She pulled the book out of his hands and pointed to the dining room. Paul had a quiver in his lip as he went with his arms drooping and his head down.

"That boy needs to do something useful." Said his father "He

needs to go out and play. Play a sport, football. Just do something!"
"He is doing something useful. He is doing what he loves, and it is his life so let him live it." Stated Joan trying not to shout.

Nevertheless, she was told off by her parents so she too sulked into the dining room. They all shared a quiet dinner together. It was the awkward silence when you are so annoyed and angry that you try not to laugh. There were a few giggles from Paul who found the silence especially amusing and once again was told off. Joan didn't wait to be excused by her parents and as soon as she had finished her dinner she stormed up to her room. Paul sat outside her bedroom door with another book that he had, dinosaurs. He started saying the facts through the door thinking that Joan would like to talk, but Joan told him to go away as she was busy with school work. She had her A-level exams coming up, and studying for her was also an escape from the frustrations that her family life caused. It was the same as with Paul and his books. Her room was covered with sticky notes and posters that she had made. Her desk had all her books neatly lined up and she spent hours looking at them when she came home from school. She picked up one of her past papers and looked at the grade 'D'. In her frustration she threw it down and it landed neatly in the bin.

"Where it belongs." She thought with tears in her eyes she huffed "Grade D."
"Grades don't matter." Said her brother through the door still listening "I am nine and I haven't got a real grade and I know more things than anyone in my school."
"Then why do your school reports say that you don't try hard enough?" Questioned Joan talking back through the door.
"School is boring, it is more interesting to do other things." Continued Paul "I fail on purpose."

He seemed to be pleased with that aspect. He also tried to make a stand on the fact that just because he didn't get 'A' grades and that he was nine years old didn't mean that he didn't know as much about certain topics. Especially when it came to people older than him, who always tried to make him seem insignificant.

Joan opened the door, "You mustn't do that Paul. You need to try

your best in everything because then you will get the best support."
"Support for what?" Asked Paul confused.
"Support for your future." Replied Joan vaguely.
"The future is a long time away now isn't it." Said Paul in a grown up tone "I am off to bed now. Good night sister."

Joan said good night to him, and watched him as he wandered to his bedroom carefully leaving his bedroom door ajar just so a stream of light would trickle in.

11

May 1994, Ten Years Old

The elderly peoples home wasn't a place that Paul liked to go, but sometimes if needs must. He felt like all the elderly people were always looking at him, as if he were someone else and he didn't like it. He felt happier when he was in his grandad's room so they could talk. Grandmother brought Paul to the home, this time grandad could recognise them, but thought that he was still living at his house and would often say that he would fetch something from the front room to show him, or get a picture off of the office wall or something. Grandma would always have a trick up her sleeve to get him to talk about something else or remind him of something. Paul was there for a reason this time he wanted to ask his grandad an important question, which would cause him to go in one direction or another. He thought that he knew the answer, but wanted to hear him say it.

"Do you think that I am smart?" Asked Paul.
His grandad had to think for a moment to absorb the information, "Yes." He said slowly "I think that you are a very intelligent boy."
"How about for my age?" He asked wanting more information.
"Yes for your age certainly, more intelligent than the other six year olds I know." He replied.
"But I am ten." Said Paul.
"Yes dear." Interjected his grandmother "He knows that he just said the wrong number that is all."

Paul seemed to accept this idea with relief from his grandma, shortly after they left his grandfather and wandered into the wintery world. Paul buttoned up his coat and shivered as they stepped outside. His grandmother put her arm around him more of a comfort than to keep him warm but Paul liked it all the same. Paul always had strived for his grandfather's approval which is funny really because whatever he did, whether he was academic or not, his grandfather would have approved of him. Everything Paul said, his grandfather tried to agree with. It was only when Paul talked about older people, he corrected him a few times but his views on adults he agreed with.

"Grandad doesn't tell jokes like he used to." Said Paul as they were on their way home.
"I know." Replied his grandma vaguely.
"Why?" Asked Paul.
"Because he is getting older." Replied his grandmother even more vaguely.
"So are you and you still tell jokes." Responded Paul.

His grandma laughed rather than get annoyed about him calling her old but she didn't say anything else on the subject, which was ok with Paul as he didn't really want to talk anyway, it was just that sometimes his thoughts came out aloud.

12

June 1995, Eleven Years Old

His mother looked at his summer report, she raised her eyebrows as she scanned the pages flicking through each one. She looked up at Paul who was sitting on one of the breakfast bar stools looking at his feet.

"Paul." Started his mother slowly "How did you improve this much? I mean you never have showed this much progress."
"I haven't?" Questioned Paul "I read books every day I know all of the current theory of string theory. I know how mechanics work I can work out the maths to any problem and I certainly am academic."
"Now Paul, no one likes a boaster." Said his mother "It sounds arrogant."

She handed him the report before diving in the fridge to find something for dinner and then realising that she might as well get take away pizza instead. Paul knocked on Joan's door, but there was no answer so he slowly opened it. She was sat at her desk looking serious, Paul sneaked in and quickly peaked at her laptop screen.

"University!" He exclaimed aloud making Joan jump and turn around "But you can't leave!"
"I am not, I am just looking." Said Joan softly she noticed the report in his hands and used it to change the subject Paul handed it to her and she looked through it with a beaming smile on her face. "Well done Paul I knew you could do it."
"So did I, but I just decided not to." He said "When the other kids found out that I got full marks in the science test they called me

brainy, but I don't think it was a nice thing."

"I am sure they were just saying that you were smart and that is a good thing." Said Joan.

"Does that mean people who are stupid are bad?" Asked Paul.

"No." Said Joan trying to find a way to explain "No one is stupid everyone knows something that someone else doesn't know or doesn't understand. People who don't know as much as you are not bad. They had the same chance of being bad as a genius does."

"The teachers are taking notice of me now." Said Paul "It doesn't seem fair."

"What doesn't?" Asked Joan "They are just proud of you like we are."

"But I can do the work, why don't they spend time with those who can't?" Questioned Paul.

"I don't know Paul." Replied Joan "But if you or I were teachers we would ensure that everyone gets their fair chance wouldn't we?"

"Sure." Replied Paul not really gathering what Joan was rabbiting on about "I am going to go play now."

He left her with the music still blearing loudly from her headphones she pulled them back up to her ears and sighed loudly. Paul heard this and a shudder went through him he turned around and went back into the room.

"Joan." He said.

Joan knew he was there and turned around pulling her headphones back off of her ears she asked him what the matter was.

"If you want to go to university I don't mind really, if you want to go." Continued Paul.

Joan just smiled before Paul retreated back to his bedroom, he was sure that he was going to cry but when he got to his room he sat on the end of his bed. He didn't have any tears roll down his face, he didn't feel anything really. He realised that he wasn't going to cry so smiled to himself before he sat down on the floor to play with his toys.

When Joan eventually announced that she had been accepted to her chosen university and was to start the following summer.

She seemed ecstatic with the prospect of learning something that she cared about and becoming someone that could make a difference. Paul suddenly felt a twang of emotion but he held back the tears that attempted to well up in him. He wanted to be happy for her but the smiles didn't reach his face. Her parents congratulated her, they always wanted one of their children to go to university mostly to show it up in Aunt Bess' face as she didn't believe that their children were good enough. Secretly they would have been pleased if they got a job in the corner shop in town.

"I am going to be back for Christmas and Easter and then summer." Said Joan understanding that Paul was upset.
"Can I visit?" Asked Paul looking up from the mackerel and peas that was laid on his plate untouched.
"Probably, but not very often." Replied Joan "It is a long way. I don't think mum and dad would want to go all that way just for the weekend."
"Joan is right it is a long way to go for two days." Said his mother "By the time that we get there on the Saturday it would be late afternoon and we would have to leave again by lunchtime so that you can go to school on the Monday."
Paul looked down, "Ok." He replied "I am going to university too someday and you can tell me how it is, at least there is a highlight I suppose."
"You don't have to go to university." Started Joan "You could get an apprenticeship or just go straight into work if you wanted to."
"No if you go to university so do I." Replied Paul that was a decision that he was set on.
"If you ever do got to university." Started his father "You have to study something which you want to do as a job, something which you are going to use otherwise it is a waste of money."

13

July 1995, Eleven Years Old

"Why do you keep tugging at your curtains Paul?" Exclaimed his mother in frustration.

It was bedtime and she had been standing in the doorway for over ten minutes whilst Paul corrected his curtains a number of times. He kept tugging at them walking part way back to his bed and then turning round to tug at them again or getting into bed and just as his mother was about to turn out his light, he would get out go over to his curtains and tug at them once more. Even when his mother had gone to bed Paul would lie in the dark for a while glancing briefly at the curtains, until he decided that he needed to get back out of bed to go over and tug at them again. Sometimes he would do this until it was 2am when he would be too exhausted to do it any more times and just fall asleep thinking about it. This happened for a few months until it developed by him tugging at them four times and stopping. His mother was weary by this point and just let him get on with it without question for fear that if she interfered he would have to do it all over again. Paul did like a routine but this was more.

Everyday Paul would get up at 7:20am whether it was the holidays or term time. When it was a school day he would get dressed, eat his breakfast, brush his teeth, put his shoes on, then his coat and then put his bag on his back and stand by the front door until the rest of his family were ready. On the weekend or holiday time once he got to the point after he brushed his teeth, he would go back to his room to read a book or something. He used to go outside but his parents didn't think that this was a good idea whilst they were still asleep in bed. Mainly due to the number of times he would get scared and come back into the house crying, waking up his parents who would think that he had broken his arm again.

Joan would hear Paul get up and rummage around the house for a while, before she would hear soft footsteps tiptoe passed her bedroom door when Paul was making his way to his bedroom. She would naturally wake up at the same time every day without an alarm clock, whereas Paul set his alarm clock every day for the same time. His mother moved it once accidentally when she was changing the time on the clock and Paul was so upset when he found out. He refused to use that clock again, which his mother thought was a bit of an overreaction. Paul wanted another clock but insisted that he needed a clock that was exactly the same as the old one. His parents pretended that his old clock was a new one. They didn't want to have to buy another clock when this one was perfectly fine to use, and the main reason was the fact that the shop they bought the clock from didn't sell them anymore. Paul was happy enough with the clock, and didn't even question why it didn't come in a box. When he reset the alarm on it he spent a while changing it slightly to the left and a little bit to the right so that he could wake up at the exact right time.

Time was another thing that had started to bother Paul instead of his usual routine everything was timed down to the minute, with five minutes to get dressed, ten to eat his breakfast, five to brush his teeth and twenty minutes to put his shoes coat and bag on and stand by the door. If he was ahead of schedule he would wait the extra minutes before starting his next task. When he got home from school it was the same process too. Between 4pm and 5pm he would do his homework, 5pm and 6pm he would practice the piano, 6pm and 7pm he would eat dinner and if his mother or father were slightly early or late in cooking it Paul refused to eat anything and would exclaim how he was wasting time.

"It is not a waste of time if you enjoy doing whatever you are doing." Said his sister when Paul had stormed off to his room when dinner was prepared at 5:30pm "If you eat dinner now you will have an extra hour when you could be doing something else."

Paul thought on this for a while, and came to the conclusion four days later that she was right, so stopped his 'routine' for the most part and started to try to let things bother him less. If his school books were moved when his room was being cleaned then he would take a deep breath and replace them the way he liked instead of shutting himself into his room and refusing to come out until they were perfect. He still tugged at his curtains, but it didn't seem like such a struggle to him anymore.

"It is easier doing that than thinking of certain things when I tugged at them." Said Paul vaguely when his mother waited for him to climb into his bed.

His mother didn't have any time to ask any questions because as she was about to, Paul stated "I am done you can turn the light off now."

Paul did suffer with more than just being a perfectionist. OCD entered his life when he was eleven years old and failed to leave it. There were times when he was so frustrated he would be in tears all day, but whenever someone mentioned going to the doctors he would use all the will power he could muster to conquer what had taken hold of him. He began coping better and better, and became oblivious to the things that he would do over and over again. He wasn't necessarily happy but he was coping. Surviving isn't the same as living but Paul almost felt like he was doing just that.

14

November 1995, Eleven Years Old

Mrs Summers was Paul's favourite teacher at his middle school. She was sweet polite and always talked about her family. For some reason for Paul, it made her seem more real and less like the teacher who lived in the storage cupboard at the end of the school day. She talked about how her husband didn't know how to use the TV remote which made the kids in the class giggle. She told jokes about how he struggled to use the computer at the library even after he had read the instruction manual. All of the students that she taught looked forward to her lessons, for the very reason that she made them smile.

Her children were younger than Paul but he identified with them nevertheless. It seemed like Arthur and Susan were often up to adventures kayaking and swimming down the river, climbing trees and fishing, riding their bikes around the woods and all which Paul dreamed he was a part of. Although, if it actually came to him kayaking in the river he probably wouldn't do it, but he liked to think that he would. Susan was seven and was a keen dancer she loved to do ballet and tap. Arthur was ten and was in the football team and the rugby team. They were at a different school to the one Paul attended and he wished that he could go to their school so he could become friends with Arthur who would teach him about sports and having adventures. Arthur was the only friend that Paul wanted, but would prefer to be taught by Mrs Summers than go to a different school and have a friend. Paul never thought about friends, much to his parent's annoyance, and often wanted to spend more time alone so it wasn't very hard for Paul to accept that he would probably never meet Arthur.

"I don't understand Miss!" Exclaimed Paul when Mrs Summers was going around checking that her year six's were doing ok.
"What don't you understand?" Asked Mrs Summers sweetly (all the other teachers would usually exclaim 'the great Paul doesn't understand! I can't believe that!' or something similar) whereas Mrs Summers would listen to every word that Paul said, and tried to help him understand. She would never state that he was too smart to understand or be derogatory to the few times he didn't.
"Fiction." Stated Paul.
"As a whole?" Asked Mrs Summers "Well it is usually away of an author expressing themselves to tell others of a story that they have dreamed about or embellished."
"But why do we have to write one, when there are other people who do that sort of thing?" Questioned Paul.
"Because it is nice sometimes to imagine a different outlook on the world." She replied smiling encouragingly "Paul I don't like it went teachers say 'I know you can do it' because it sometimes makes you feel upset if you struggle with something. I certainly felt that way at school I knew I couldn't run 400m and in the end my teacher and I came to the agreement that I would run the 100m. I felt much better after that."
"I will write one page then." Said Paul "Instead of the two."

Mrs Summers agreed that this was the best course of action for the moment. As an English teacher she loved to get the students to think of stories to write, even if they were meant to be studying a book she would ask them to re-write certain passages so that they could better understand why the author wrote certain things in certain ways. Paul didn't really understand this way of thinking and instead thought the author wrote a book in a particular way because that was the way that they wanted to write it and that there was no other way of looking at it.

Mrs Summers only graded official papers or work so that she could check their progress for their school reports. Instead of grades she would use an effort rating system based on smiley faces and she never used a red pen. Paul was very proud of the four out of five smiley faces that he got on his short story, it showed to him that he had tried his best and that was good enough. Mrs Summers never gave any of the student's five smiley faces because she didn't want them to stop trying to achieve them. All the students tried harder than ever to get five smiley faces which pleased Mrs Summers. Her students were trying the best that they possibly could and that was good enough for her. Joan put the work that Paul did in a plastic art portfolio as he was so proud of it.

"There you go!" She exclaimed handing it back over to Paul.

He looked at the shiny page with a big grin on his face until his smile turned into a glum frown. He wondered about the times when he would have to change teachers all over again. He had finally found a teacher that he liked in Mrs Summers and would be sad when he was no longer taught by her. When he came home he showed Joan his work she was pleased and then noticed the frown on his face and asked why.

"It will be a shame when I am not taught by Mrs Summers anymore." Said Paul "Never mind."
"You have a few more years of being taught by her yet." Said Joan.
"Not if I go to the grammar school." He said.
"Are you thinking about it then?" Asked Joan surprised.
"Yes some of the other boys are trying out and almost all of the girls are." He said looking at the piece of paper in his hands.
"You do whatever you want." Said Joan "It is totally up to you."
"Ok then I think I will try out and see what I get." Started Paul "If I get high enough then I think I will go if I get on the waiting list I think I will stay where I am and not bother waiting for a place to open up."
"Ok." Said Joan as supportively as she could "If that is what you want."

15

January 1996, Eleven Years Old

Paul decided to take the exams for the boys' grammar school. All those taking the test had gathered outside the school hall ready to try their best. He looked around him at the worried faces and was sure that he should feel worried too. He didn't. He was calm and collected, which surprised him. To him, it showed that he wasn't that interested in changing schools. He sat in the hall with some of the other boys from his year and some from different schools that he didn't recognise. The test began and all the heads went down. Paul looked around the hall at the things that he knew, the posters which hadn't changed, the old green curtains which were around the stage and the old wooden bench that everyone tried to get a space on during assembly. He started to wonder if the change of scenery would be too much for him, but as he started answering the questions on the test paper he began to smile. The tests were harder than the ones his teachers had been setting. The questions were on topics which were not on the syllabus, but knew them because he had read about the topic. He felt good when he had the 'I actually know that!' feeling. He was determined to pass and as he sailed through the next few questions he was sure that he was going to pass with top marks. He looked at the rest of the students they all still had their pen in hand and there was thirty minutes left to complete the test. Paul clasped his hands pleased with himself and placed them on the table, he was finished and had checked through his work. Twice.

"How do you think you did?" Questioned his mother when she picked him up after the test.
"I aced it." Said Paul using what he usually described as 'urban

slang' but his overwhelming sense of achievement over took all his usual thoughts.

"Aren't you going to miss your friends?" Questioned his mother.

"Friends? It is like you don't even know me." Said Paul annoyed "Are you trying to make me not want to go because it is not on *your* way to work?"

"Of course I would never do that." Said his mother lying.

"I heard you and dad arguing about the fact that the grammar school isn't on your way to work." Started Paul "What is twenty minutes out of your time to help me!"

"Button your mouth mister!" Shouted his mother "You don't talk to me like that when we get home go to your bedroom without any dinner."

"That punishment was for back in the dark ages!" Complained Paul before thinking further "What was for dinner?"

"Cottage pie." Replied his mother more calmly.

"Good." Said Paul "I don't like cottage pie."

His mother could feel the smile on her sons face, she was proud of him but she didn't want him knowing that. She would have been proud of him no matter what he did as long as it was good and made him feel proud of himself.

Paul was more mentally exhausted than he thought he was going to be. His mother did relinquish the punishment but Paul didn't feel that hungry anyway, and after picking at his food he went up to his room. He lay on his bed only planning to stay there for a few minutes, reluctantly he fell asleep on his bed without changing into his pyjamas or brushing his teeth which was very unlike Paul. He woke up very confused as if he had missed a day rather than just slept the night in his school clothes. He didn't go to school with his usual attitude towards learning. Lasagne was on the menu that evening it was cooked because it was Paul's favourite meal, his mother didn't like to see him moping and did it in an attempt to cheer him up.

Paul loved lasagne, he loved all the different layers and usually named them the different layers of the body, different layers of the Earth or different layers of a maths problem. It annoyed his parents somewhat to see him playing with his food but they never said anything.

Going to school until the results of his test were released were exhausting. Every day he would wait patiently until school was over and he could find out if his parents had received anything. Even though he was sure that he had passed, he was still worried at the thought that he might not be as smart as he thought he was.
The results came through on a Monday morning.

"Do you want to read them?" Asked his mother handing Paul the envelope.
"No." Replied Paul calmly "Please can you?"
His mother smiled and carefully opened the envelope she started to read out the content of it before the important part came, "You needed to achieve 120 marks out of 200 to get in and you achieved 194 marks."

His place at grammar school was confirmed, a slow smile came over his face until he was overcome by the excitement and he began bouncing around the lounge where his mother and him were sitting. She laughed at the sight of him being so happy.

He rushed around the house preparing his pencil case with all the new pens and pencils he could find and tidying his bag, as if it could get any tidier. He was excited for the first day already he now was sure that he wanted to go.

"You have the rest of this year to go first." Said his mother when she realised what he was doing.
"But that isn't so long now." Said Paul "I better finish off packing!"

To Paul it felt like he was going away to university or to go to a boarding school. He really was excited and couldn't contain it. For the next few months he was coming home eating dinner and going to bed just so that it would be tomorrow as soon as possible, so then he could start the process again and be ever closer to his first day at the grammar school.

16

September 1996, Twelve Years Old

Paul was excited for his first day, although when he got there he was having second thoughts. Everyone seemed bigger than him and they all seemed to look at him, as if they were going to have him for lunch. He ducked and dived between their legs before finding the solace that he needed in the library. He didn't know where his classroom was and he had missed the assembly in the hall, because his grandmother had taken him to school as his parents had decided that they were both going into work early. The librarian gave him a few sideways glances, trying to figure out if he was lost or not, as he seemed to make himself quite at home nestled in amongst the books. It was also odd to her that it was soon lesson time and Paul made no move to get anywhere else. She decided to quiz him on his form tutor and what his first lesson was. In the end his form tutor emerged and had to escort him to class.

"You know that you could have asked any member of staff and they would have directed you to where you needed to go." Said his form tutor.
"But I wanted to go to the library." Said Paul "At my old school before lessons I was allowed to go to the library if I wanted as long as I told my teacher and gave the librarian a signed card from her."
"Here we don't have that." Started Paul's form tutor more slowly this time "But during lunch and break you can go to the library as much as you want."
"Oh, ok." Replied Paul glumly as he was led into his Maths class.

All of the other students didn't look very happy to be there. Not like the brochure at all. Paul wanted to go there, one because it would be more intellectually stimulating and two all the other students looked like they were eager to get to school. In reality it was more like his old school with the student's only thinking about break, lunch and home time. Paul did his best to just get on with his work, but they seemed to not want to let him and started to pick on him. Paul was impressed with the B grade that he got on his first test. Usually he would have got an A but blamed this on his change of scenery.

"I am so much smarter than Paul!" Exclaimed one of the boys.
"We all are, stupid." Replied another laughing.

Paul begun to feel down and the year started to drag and drag. The lessons were no longer fun and he stopped being interested in learning. At 9am when he arrived at school he began wishing to when it was 3:30pm and he could go home. He had never thought this way before, always wanting to go to school so that he could learn something new or just consolidate what he already knew. Joan realised how much Paul was hating it and tried to persuade him to leave the school and re-join his other school, but Paul didn't want to. He said that he couldn't bear to face the people in his year group. He was insistent that they would all tell him 'I told you so' and say things like 'I knew Paul couldn't do it'.

"Then just stay for two years and join the upper school." Said Joan "I am sure that lots of students do that."
"Do you think so?" Questioned Paul "Maybe I could I don't know I will think about it."

17

January 1997, Twelve Years Old

The towel scenario of Paul Westwood was a period in time that no one really wanted to remember, but then they didn't know why really because to them it seemed pointless. Paul refused to use a particular towel when he was twelve years old, his parents couldn't work it out and many times Joan asked him why he wasn't using the towel. To them it looked the same as any other towel but to Paul it was a whole new ball game. He preferred to wash his hands at the bathroom sink and then run through the house dripping the water all over the floor to the kitchen where the next available towel was. Things got trying when Paul refused to use either towel, and instead would sit on the floor and wait for his hands to air dry. He wouldn't wipe his hands on his trousers or shirt or go to the airing cupboard and find a different towel. Even when the towels were changed he examined each one and began to not use any of them.

"Why don't you just use a towel?" Exclaimed his father when he found him sitting on the bathroom floor.
"They don't have any tags in." Replied Paul as if it was obvious.
"I don't see how that would make any difference." Replied his father.
"You can't read what material is used, what the wash instructions are and where the towel came from. For all I know I could be drying my hands on a towel mum found on a table outside someone's house with a 'free' sign taped to it." Said Paul getting up as he realised his hands were dry.
His father shook his head but didn't want to get into an argument before he went to bed, "Then why don't you use the towel you use

for your bath?"

"Because that is my bath towel." Stated Paul walking out of the room "I can't use my bath towel to dry my hands that is what the hand towel is for."

He walked away from the bathroom leaving his father with his jaw dropped slightly and eyebrows raised. He shook his head as he went into the bathroom and closed the door behind him. He spent a few days thinking about how to resolve this episode. There were a few things he thought of, such as getting angry at Paul and punishing him if he did it again and try to condition the behaviour out of him, or he could resolve it in another way. The towel saga upset him more than he thought it would, and decided that the best way to resolve it was to come up with a compromise to ensure that everyone was kept happy. He bought a few towels from the home shop. They were the cheapest that he could get and ensured that they all had labels on them. He even chose Paul's preferred colours as a personal touch. Paul was very excited about his new towels, his father smiled seeing the little face light up at what he considered a very small thing. His son was now happy which made him happy, mainly because he didn't have to deal with the stress of not being able to use the toilet when he wanted.

"You do realise that the towels were the same towels as the ones that you have always used?" Said Joan to Paul a few weeks after Paul got his new towels, Paul hadn't held up a queue of people waiting for the bathroom since.

"No they were not. The towels I had been using had labels in them." Argued Paul who was convinced that the towels were not the same ones the ones he remembers were bright vivid colours where as these ones were dull and faded.

"But the labels wore off." Said Joan "That is what happens when they have been in the washing machine so many times."

"I suppose that is a logical reason." Replied Paul slowly nodding his head "But then again whether they were the same towels or not you could no longer tell what material they were made out of."

Joan decided to not push the discussion any further so left her brother playing with his toys in his room. Sometimes she didn't even try to understand how her brother's brain worked she didn't seem to get it at the best of times and usually just went along with whatever ideas he had about the world that he lived in.

"For someone so smart he couldn't figure out why the towels were faded or why they didn't have labels in anymore." Said Joan to herself as she walked to her bedroom "Who would have figured."

18

August 1997, Thirteen Years Old

Paul waved a teary goodbye to Joan when they left her at the university. It was pouring down with rain and the droplets hid his tearful face. They had unloaded all of her things, although Paul only carted a small bag across to her room before he refused to go back out in the rain again. He sat on the desk chair which was made of hard wood. The room was painted the cheerful colour of beige and some graffiti had been etched into the bottom of the wardrobe. It didn't seem like a place he would want to live, but Joan seemed happy with it. She waved back to them eagerly before she went back inside to organise her room.

Paul was quiet as they went the rest of their way home, he stared out of the window watching the scenery go passed. It went so quickly that he couldn't focus on what was in front of him. He tried to make out the shapes, but as soon as he thought he knew what it might be, the scenery had changed and the process began again. They reached their own town and Paul knew where he was, finally there was something that he recognised, he knew what all of those shapes were. He turned his eyes to look inside the car. He had seen that a thousand times and was now etched into his mind. The town wasn't one of Paul's favourite places but it felt like home and he was glad to be back there. They got out of town and made way towards their lonely house.

As soon as they reached their gate Paul instantly felt as if the house was missing Joan too. He wandered about and although his parents were milling around downstairs, he could hear every foot step that he made and they seemed to echo about the hall. She was four hundred miles away from here, four hundred miles away from home. It was a cloudy day in Cornwall the rain had reached there earlier in the day, and so it was still wet underfoot but the clouds overhead were just passing. Paul new he had to get outside, he felt claustrophobic cooped up in the house that no longer felt whole. He changed into his wellies and reached for his rain coat. He hadn't even finished buttoning it up before he ran from the house, across the fields towards the hills and the trees beyond. He travelled far for a twelve year old finally stopping by a small wood. The ground was drier there. Taking his coat off and laying it down on the floor, he sat under one of the trees that looked out towards the coast. He closed his eyes and listened to the waves rush against each other. They too had been affected by the storm that had been. Swirling about they gently eroded more of the cliff face away and washed it under the ocean.

"How am I going to do this?" He said to himself opening his eyes.

His mind was full of his future, his past and the things he hadn't understood and still didn't understand about life. Joan had always been his support and had always given him hope and got him to look at situations in a different way. As he thought about the fun they used to have, he had a wave of inspiration and leaping to his feet he ran all the way back home. It had grown dark, although his parents didn't seem surprised about his return or anxious that he was so late. He leapt inside the house where they were watching television, and didn't even move when he came into the lounge. They were obviously so absorbed in the screen of little moving pictures.

"I want to take my piano exams." He blurted out stomping his foot.

His parents turned around to look at him, they stared for a while until his mother looked down at his feet.

"Paul!" Exclaimed his mother making Paul jump backwards "Go and take those boots off now!"

He had brought mud into the carpets it was in little clumps where he had stepped. He immediately ran back into the hall took his boots off as quickly and as carefully as he could. He ran back into the lounge and stood in front of the television, this time he wanted to be listened to and wasn't going to take no for an answer.

"I want to take my piano exams." He repeated trying to block as much of the television as possible so that his parents would listen to him he was waving his arms about out stretched by his sides.
"You have never wanted to take them before." Replied his mother looking at Paul with a blank expression on her face, she didn't understand why he now wanted to take his exams when he decided that he was never going to take them a few years ago.

His father was leaning over the sides of the chair that he was sitting in, to try and see the corners of the television that Paul was not covering. He didn't succeed so slumped back into his chair with a grumpy look on his face as he listened to Paul speak.

"I want to take them now!" He exclaimed.
"I want never gets." Replied his father becoming grumpier by the minute.
"Please, they can be my birthday and Christmas presents." Pleaded Paul knowing how much the exams cost he didn't want to be unreasonable.

His mother looked at his father they gave each other a look that Paul didn't understand, his mother turned to look at Paul, "Ok if that is what you want." She said with little effort at all.

Paul leaped in the air swinging his legs about, he thanked them as if he had never thanked anyone before and ran into the hall and started to play happily. His mother smiled and his father shut the door. The sound still echoed into the room, the happiness of Paul spread to his parents even if they didn't know it.

Paul took his first exam before Christmas it was grade one and he passed with flying colours. He spent all his spare time, when not at school, practicing the pieces but he didn't need to as he was already good enough. He started learning the new pieces for the next exam as soon as he had received the certificate for the last exam.

19

July 1997, Thirteen Years Old

Paul's parents were not very happy with Paul's fickleness. They said that a school is a school no matter which one you go to, it is still a school. After much debating they had all agreed that it was better if Paul left the grammar school, once his feelings were taken into consideration it was an easy decision to make. Soon after his parents put in an application for Paul to start year nine in the local upper school, namely the one he would have gone to if he hadn't decided to go to the grammar school. The thought of leaving the school which he despised so much changed his mood completely. He was happy all the time, and even though he had to go back to that school every day for the rest of the academic year, just the thought of leaving made him smile and he couldn't stop smiling. His mother began to smile through her weary eyes as she looked at him with that beam on his face. She was hopeful once more for Paul mainly because she thought that he might get a different outlook in regards to friends.

Paul stopped complaining about things that usually annoyed him in his grumpy mood, like having to eat vegetables. He munched them down now and the bitter taste of the green leaves turned sweet in his mouth. His spare time was spent learning as many new songs on the piano as he could, something that he hadn't done in the whole time that he had been at grammar school. Another thing that he hadn't done was play with his action figures. When he mentioned this to the other boys at his school they would laugh and taunt him. Paul felt this deeply and stopped playing with all of his toys entirely. He looked at them longingly but it was as if the other students would know if he made up some fantasy game involving the inanimate objects sat on the shelf in front of him.

There was an open day for the upper school which Paul dragged his mother too. She didn't understand why Paul wanted to go. He had already been accepted to the school, and there was no other options but Paul wanted to go anyway. It was a little taster before he actually opened the doors on the first day of school. As they wandered around Paul got a little waylaid looking at the GCSE and A-Level information. He started to choose which ones he would do and humoured the teacher and some of the sixth form students by answering the hardest questions that they could think of.

"Now let me ask you some." Said Paul with a smirk as he began to ask questions which even the teacher struggled to answer.

Feeling pleased with himself Paul announced to his mother that they could go home.

"But didn't you want to go to the year nine talk in the hall?" She questioned.
"Why would I want to do that?" Queried Paul not really wanting to go to a talk with a load of children.

That evening the family sat down to dinner it was a regular meal of chicken and vegetables which Paul would always complain that it was bland, other than today when he was too happy to notice.

"It has been an emotional rollercoaster." Said Paul thinking over the time that he had tried to decide what school to go to.

The rest of his family smiled and laughed kindly, Paul noticed the joke so smiled with them.

"Honestly though." Started Paul seriously "It is going to be nice going to a school where the students don't constantly compete with each other for top grades. It was beginning to get on my nerves."
"There is competition between students of an upper school Paul." Said his mother.

"Yes I am sure, but it probably isn't as much at the grammar it was constant unless you always got 'A' grades you were not good enough." Started Paul "I want my best to be good enough, whether it is an A or not."

20

July 1997, Thirteen Years Old

Paul was now determined to pass all his piano exams as soon as he possibly could. Every minute that he could spare he was playing the piano, the same songs over and over again so that they could be the best that he could do. By the time he was thirteen he had passed four grades, all the certificates were placed in frames that were neatly put up on the wall in his bedroom. Not only did Paul like to play the piano, he liked the idea of constructing music and playing different instruments as well. Music was becoming his best subject at school the teacher was impressed with the ability that he displayed in lessons. It was a little daunting for him when it was time for him to move to the upper school. He was pleased to leave the grammar, but he had just found a teacher and a subject that allowed him to push the boundaries on what he could learn. He was the best in the class and he liked that feeling. He didn't think that it would last when he changed schools. It wasn't just the fact that he would have to get use to new teachers, he knew that there would be other students that he would have to get used to, and hoped that they wouldn't notice him at all.

"But the lessons will be harder." Explained his mother "You would like that wouldn't you?"

Paul only stated that the grammar school had challenging lessons but that didn't mean that he enjoyed it. He kept thinking that if he hadn't gone to the grammar school Mrs Summers would have still been teaching him, all he could think about was the missed years that he could have enjoyed somewhat at that school. He also thought about all his lovely times in the library and how his routine changed when he moved to the grammar school.

R.V. Turner

He hid in his room on the transfer day, he didn't want to leave the house and was determined that no one would get him out. His mother wasn't taking no for an answer and dragged him out of his bedroom and made him leave the house. She took him straight up to the gates of the school where all the students who were coming up to year nine in September had gathered ready to be taken off to taster lessons. His mother left him there looking lost in the crowds of people who gathered around the teachers who were there to greet them. She didn't want to cave in and take Paul home so she decided that the best course of action was to just drop him and go, but Paul didn't know that.

There were a few teachers from his old middle school which put him a little at ease and ran off to greet some of them. They all showed that they were happy to see him and they all remembered the little boy with the big brain. To his disappointment, Mrs Summers was not one of the teachers there but Paul was only too happy to have a familiar face to greet him. They were all gathered in groups, where sixth form students led them through the maze of the school to their first taster lesson of the day. Paul's anxiousness returned as the leader showed them the way through the corridors to their classroom. She pointed out other classrooms along the way, a few of them were ones which they would visit later in the day. Paul chose a seat at the back of the classroom. He thought that he would be excited to go to the school he had waited so long to attend. He didn't understand why he wasn't feeling this way. He struggled to concentrate on what the teacher was saying. He saw her lips moving up and down but didn't hear a word of what she said. He was sat in a science lesson, and instead of looking forward showing his attentiveness to what the teacher was writing on the white board, he was looking out of the window to the summer's day outside. The pretty blue of the sky contrasted with the grey white of the clouds as they drifted across making shadows on the green grass below. His focus was far away from the lesson, and he didn't notice at first when the teacher tried to attract his attention.

"What have I been saying?" Asked the teacher to which Paul didn't answer she continued "What is a better absorber of energy a dark matt surface or a light shiny surface."

She expected that Paul wouldn't know the answer, but she didn't know Paul.

"Dark matt." Replied Paul still looking out of the window he wasn't satisfied with his answer so turned to look at the teacher "Houses are often painted white in hot countries as it reflects off of them meaning that the houses will be cooler."
He wasn't satisfied with that answer either and was about to continue. He didn't get very far as the teacher was happy with the very first answer that he gave.

"Well I was wrong you were listening." Replied the teacher admitting defeat.
"No I wasn't listening." Said Paul happily "I already knew the answer."

This time the teacher wasn't very happy but said no more about the subject. She set an activity of a few questions to answer on energy transfer, the subject that they had just learnt about. Paul looked at the paper with a frown. The teacher noticed this and raising her eyebrow reached for something a bit harder.

"You could have a go at this if you want?" Asked the teacher handing him a GCSE test paper.

Paul happily nodded his head he had always wondered how knowledgeable he was, and maybe this was a way of him showing it. He completed the test in no time and whilst the other students were getting on with the next activity Paul was working his way through an A-Level paper. At the end of the lesson the teacher asked to speak to him.

"You do realise that I don't go to this school yet?" Questioned Paul "You can't give me a detention."
The teacher smiled, "No Paul I was going to ask if you had thought of taking a GCSE or A-Level exam whilst you are in year nine." She started Paul didn't say anything "When you come to the school in September I am sure that we can cater towards your abilities."
"No thank you I am trying to focus on my music." He said and

walked out of the classroom.

He ran a short way to try and catch up to his group but he couldn't find them, he was surprised that they left without him. Instead of panicking he breathed deeply, it didn't work and decided to ignore those feelings instead. He began walking down a corridor looking in the different classrooms he found himself becoming interested in what the students were learning about. Some were Maths and others were Biology, Geography and French. He went down another set of stairs and found that he had started to follow his ears. He walked along a corridor which was covered in orange, it was a bit bright at first but he soon got used to the colour. The floors and walls were both orange with a white ceiling and white doors to the different rooms. As he wandered he gazed into some of the classrooms and he realised that he had found the music department. He smiled to himself as he pressed his face up against the window of one of the classrooms. It was full of students, and when they started to stare at him he left to find another classroom. The next one he came across was empty, apart from a few instruments, one of which was piano. He opened the door and walked slowly up to it, looking around before he decided to sit down and play. He chose a piece that he had memorised and particularly liked from the grade five exam that he was taking. It was one of his favourite so far, he played it over and over at home making his parents agitated. Here he could play to his heart's content, for the moment anyway, shortly afterwards the teacher from the next classroom found him there.

"You shouldn't be in here." Said the teacher sternly.
Paul jumped up stuttering, "I um er I lost my group."
"I thought as much." He said ushering Paul out of the room "I will take you to reception and they will look after you."
"Thank you, Sir." Replied Paul trying to be as polite as possible.

The music teacher began asking Paul about his playing and how he learnt to play so well. Paul didn't know any answer other than it is just maths. This seemed to be his favourite answer when it came to talking about music. He was very excited and started to explain how this was true, to which the teacher listened to show his support. Paul felt more comfortable as the teacher softened and Paul didn't stop talking until they reached the reception. Paul was met there by his group leader along with the rest of his group who trailed behind. They had just been to a taster History lesson, Paul was relieved as History was one of his least favourite subjects. He didn't like looking into the past he found it boring, the idea of the future was much more appealing to him. Next the group was led to the food technology department, where Paul enjoyed trying the cakes and biscuits that some of the other students in his group had helped to bake.

Lunchtime was the part of the school day that Paul always dreaded, to most other students it was their favourite time of the day, but Paul didn't enjoy lunchtime much. He was almost always alone, not that he minded this but rather preferred it. He was still anxious as he sat on his own on one of the steps outside in the shade. He was hoping that all of the other students wouldn't notice him and just leave him alone. Lucky for him as transfer day was one of the hottest days that summer meaning that most of the other students were in the sun on the playing field. So he was left alone most of the time to his relief, until the bell rang. What Paul hadn't noticed was that the school was actually quieter than normal and this was because the school gave the transfer students an early lunch so that they could find a place to sit. Swarms of the older students began pouring out of the doors walking over to where they usually had their lunch. Paul hurriedly got up from his seat way before any of the students could reach him. In his panic he rose quickly dropping the half of sandwich that was balanced in his lunch box on the floor. Paul stared at it for a brief moment before reaching down to pick it up. He skipped down the steps towards the bin and dropped the sandwich reluctantly down the dark pit. He found his hand gel and applied it generously before dodging through the people to find the meeting point for his group. It was way before the students were due to gather there, but to Paul this was the safest place for him to stay for the moment. He sat there for a while looking around himself trying to figure out everything and anything. The other students seemed to ignore him as they walked passed, Paul felt completely invisible and protected. The group leader eventually came along and slowly the group began to grow with students. Paul was grateful for the early lunch as he didn't know how he would compete with the older students for a good place to eat, but knew that when he started school in September he would have to eat his lunch surrounded by the older students. It was a daunting prospect as they already had *their* spaces to eat. Paul would have to take whatever was going.

In the afternoon the group took part in some Drama, which Paul started to do reluctantly but then when they had to do a performance in groups. He refused to join in, the teachers tried to persuade him that he would enjoy it, but this made him even more agitated. The students were told to bring their PE kits with them as almost certainly they would be trying out some of the sports equipment. Paul refused to take part from the start. He didn't even change into his PE kit, he sat on a bank in the sports field watching the others who were playing team building activities, such as egg and spoon races and a relay race. Paul was annoyed that he didn't get to go back to the music department again but knew that he would live there when he got to the big school.

21

October 1997, Thirteen Years Old

Paul started to soar to the top of his classes during the first term of year nine. He was determined to be the best no matter how many times his parents told him he didn't need to be the best at everything, he made this his goal. All the teachers seemed to like his attitude towards learning, but all agreed on one thing, that Paul should stop correcting them. They would gather in the staffroom and chatter about the 'disrespectful' skinny intelligent boy who tried to be smarter than them. The other students began their *nice* task of finding the person that they could make fun of for the rest of their school life, and that person happened to be Paul. Paul was picked on for being smart and for doing extra work for the classes he liked, for always being alone and not having any friends (they didn't take any notice that this was by choice). The teachers did begin to notice, but decided that it would be best if they didn't get involved. Paul was saddened by being picked on but decided that he wouldn't let it bother him. He started sitting in the library for break times and at lunchtimes. The only issue was that he wasn't allowed to eat in there so he found an indoor clubs to join. As much as he didn't like people he loved learning and this is what he headed for. He figured that they would be the least popular clubs, so most of the ones he joined were academic clubs like the physics club or biology club.

He decided to step out of his comfort zone to try something that involved interacting with people and that was the chess club. There were five of them in total, two girls and three boys but Paul didn't take much notice of who they were, only in the games that they played. He decided to detach himself from the people in the group and didn't think of emotions, only of facts. He was winning most of his games, a little smirk grew on his face when he won. When he lost, he didn't get annoyed but took it as a fact and shook the hand of his opponent gracefully. Paul had grown to really love chess and started to learn some of the famous moves that could be used. His bookshelf was filling up with chess books, all with a slightly different idea surrounding the game. Paul started to play with a stratagem, whereas the rest of the students played for fun. They understood the game perfectly but didn't plan their move in their head before they played it like Paul did. To his parents amusement another club Paul joined was a creative writing club. He joined mostly for the parts when everyone was writing and they were all in silence, and in the new school there was some comfort of taking part in something that Mrs Summers had taught him. There were some discussions before they started the club and as the year progressed Paul actually started to join in. He spoke his mind even if he knew that other people would disagree with him.

"It is creative writing." Said Paul "It isn't meant to have rules."

By far the chess club was Paul's favourite and as the year progressed Paul actually began to build a sort of friendship with those in the club. They all seem to be interested in the things that Paul liked. They didn't seem to be like the other students in Paul's year, he could relate to these people and it made him happy. The two girls were friends outside of the group but the two boys had separate friend groups, but they all met once a week for half an hour and it was one of the best school memories for Paul. One of the boys spent his lunchtimes and break times playing table tennis on the table tennis tables outside of the PE department. Paul had often watched them and tried to figure out the scientific principles behind the game, and whether there was a way that he could win every time. The other boy sat in the library with a group who seemed to be into comic books but Paul wasn't sure, just because they had them open in front of them didn't mean that they were reading them. They were told off many times by the librarian as they talked loudly, which was another reason that Paul didn't believe their façade. The two girls went about by themselves, Paul would often see them in one of the Geography teachers' classrooms. She was their favourite teacher and always let them study in her classroom. Paul was impressed that they spent their spare time studying, what he didn't know was that they also spent most of that time talking.

"Do you like reading science fiction books?" Asked one of the girls who was playing a chess game against Paul.
"No." Replied Paul as he focused on the chess move he was going to make.
"What about fantasy books?" She asked.
"No." Said Paul.
"What do you like to read?" She asked.
"Non-fiction books." Started Paul "Have you read the series on the universe?"
"Yes." Replied the girl now focusing on her chess move.
"Interesting." Replied Paul.
"What is interesting?" She asked.
"That you have read them." He replied.
"What because I am a girl?" She questioned.
"No because you are only thirteen." Replied Paul.
"I read them when I was twelve but who is counting." Said the girl.
"If it is a competition then I read them when I was seven." He said.
"Good move." Replied the girl raising her eyebrows.

Paul didn't know whether she was talking about the chess game or their debate. They talked about different things that they enjoyed and Paul started to ask her some questions. She played a lot of sport, but only because her sister was a tennis player and her parents wanted her to be one too. The girl didn't actually like sport and enjoyed reading and writing more. She wasn't as intellectually intelligent as Paul but she certainly knew a lot more than he did.

22

November 1997, Thirteen Years Old

The chess club had become more than just a club to the students who went to it. Even to Paul. Friends, or acquaintances as he called them, did mean something to him. He didn't know what exactly but he felt different around those people slightly more confident, and yet when he was in a crowd he often longed to be alone and when he was alone he felt lonelier now, than when he was in a crowd. There is a difference in being in a crowd and being lonely, and being in a small group of people who all acknowledge you existence. As the students talked over their chess games they decided that they would try to find out as much as possible about each other by playing games that they made up. Most of them were on the basis of a certain amount of questions and each person got to ask a question but it had to link to the previous one. It had another set of more complicated rules and even they struggled to remember them all.

"Do you have a favourite colour?" Asked one of the girls.
"That isn't a very good question." Stated Paul.
"Just answer the question!" Pleaded the other girl.
"No I don't have a favourite colour." Replied Paul "In the spectrum of light with is your favourite wave length?"
"That has nothing to do with colour!" Complained the boy that Paul's question was directed at.
"Yes it does." Replied Paul.

The boy looked over to the sporty girl. She seemed to be the adjudicator of the group and they all seemed to listen to what she said.

They Said That I Was Brainy

"Answer the question." She said.

The boy reluctantly tried his best to choose a favourite wave length and the conversation went on from there. What they found out about each other no one else would probably find interesting, they didn't ask the usual questions. Although Paul thought that they understood each other better because they knew the things that others wouldn't find worthwhile to know, and that was why it was important to him. He never thought that he would find another person interesting, it turned out that he knew four new interesting people.

Chess club became his favourite club, there was a teacher there but he only sat in to make sure they were not messing about, rather than to teach them about playing chess. It was not as if any of them needed teaching because they all seemed to be playing at the top level. It was probably a bit intimidating to those who didn't know much about chess and wanted to join the club, but the group liked the club how it was and didn't want anyone else to join.

"There is a chess match against other schools!" Exclaimed one of the girls coming into the classroom holding the poster.
"Did you take that off of the notice board?" Questioned Paul.
"Sure I needed to show you guys!" Exclaimed the girl even more excited.
"You shouldn't have taken it." Replied Paul.
"I am going to put it back." She said.
"You shouldn't have taken it." Stated Paul.
"We are the chess club no one else is going to look at it." Replied the girl now getting annoyed "Are you in or not?"
"Sure." Replied Paul.

It was the most laid back that he had been since he had joined the school. He didn't understand why they didn't stay a group on the other days when they didn't have chess club, but then thought how he wouldn't look forward to going to chess club if they did, and they wouldn't get on so well either. Then again Paul didn't think much about other people's thoughts.

23

December 1997, Thirteen Years Old

The chess competition was entered by the group, Paul was looking forward to it before he finally entered the large hall covered with tables and chairs and most of all people. He froze for a moment as the rest of his team walked straight to the registration table. It was packed with the other teams all ready to play the chess games. They seemed eager to get started, they all had badges with their team name written on them. Paul's team had decided to call themselves 'The Kids' it was mainly the girls' idea but all the boy's went along with it. Paul had forgotten all about the team name and about the chess match, it was overwhelming seeing all the competitors wandering around and acting intimidating as if they owned the place. He looked at his friends, one of which handed him his badge, Paul put it on proudly and seeing his friend's excitement he decided to pretend to be excited too. The rules of how the matches were played were explained to them and so the matches commenced. They each played games against the other team's players taking turns to play each one. The chess matches were over a few days as many different teams had entered. The matches were held in town which was easy for travel to and from home, which his parents were glad for because Paul would not have stayed in a hotel. Paul greatly enjoyed the games, he liked the strategy and trying to figure out what his opponent's next move was going to be but mostly because his opponents didn't talk to him. They were so focused on playing chess Paul wondered why other people weren't like this.

"We are so going to win!" Exclaimed one of the girls in Paul's team.

The days' matches were over and they were on their way home, one of the girl's parents had a minibus and was doing the rounds dropping them all off. It was the Christmas holidays, there were two weeks where they didn't have to think about school putting the whole team, even Paul, in a better mood.

"I don't know." Replied the other girl.
"I think we can!" Said one of the boys.
"No." Said Paul surely "We can't win."
"Don't be like that Paul." Said the first girl getting annoyed "You are always like that."
"It is the truth." Stated Paul "We are seventh on the leader board even over the next two days we can't make up that many points."
"Yes we can." Said the girl "You just have to believe."
"That still won't make up the points." Replied Paul.
"Paul it doesn't matter we just have to believe that we could win and we are more likely to do better." Said one of the boys.

Paul didn't say anything else he just wanted to get home, he wasn't use to not winning arguments. He had never backed down either, it might have been because deep down he knew that pessimism wouldn't help him and being optimistic would at least mean that they tried as hard as they could have done. He went straight to bed and tucked himself under his covers, it was late and he wasn't hungry even though his mother had kept him back some lasagne. As he was enjoying the darkness there was a bright flash that shone through the curtains. Paul jumped turning to look in the direction of his window which was now in darkness once again. Paul began to think nothing more about it until the crackle of thunder echoed through the sky. That time he scooted back so he was sitting upright with his back against the wall. He dragged his duvet up to his nose and waited. It felt like ages before he saw the bright light and was welcomed once again by the crackle. He was frozen whilst the thunder and lightning continued to conquer the sky above. His eyes became droopy and he slowly slipped back down into his bed and once in dream land the event was forgotten, for the moment.

"Did you hear the thunder and lightning last night?" Questioned his mother when Paul came down for breakfast in the morning.
"No I didn't hear a thing." Replied Paul as he sat upright in his

chair at the kitchen table he munched on the cereal that he had in his bowl.

It was his Thursday cereal. Monday's were toast with jam no butter, Tuesday's were porridge with little pieces of banana, on Wednesday's it was toast with butter no jam, Friday's were rice cereal, Saturday's were the cooked breakfast that his dad made and Sunday's were fruit cereal with a cup of tea. This is just one of the reasons why he didn't like going on holidays. The others included using an unfamiliar bathroom, sleeping in a bed where even though the sheets were clean someone else has slept there before, and the door to the room didn't have that perfect gap to let the light shine through to just the right place on the carpet.

"Are you excited for you chess matches today?" Asked his mother sitting down with her breakfast.
"No." Replied Paul.
"Why?" Questioned his mother "Are you nervous?"
"No." Stated Paul "We are not going to win. What is the point pretending that we are?"
"You should always try Paul." Explained his mother "It doesn't matter whether you win or lose as long as you try your best to succeed."
"Why should we always succeed?" Asked Paul feeling thoughtful again.
"What other point in doing something is there?" Said his mother.
"You enjoy it." Said Paul thinking back to what the girl had said on their way home "Whether you are good at something or not it doesn't matter. I play chess because I enjoy it but if I was not good at it, does that mean I should quit?"
"No but you should always try to be better than you are." Said his mother.
"No I am ok thank you. I am happy being me." Replied Paul getting up from the table and putting his bowl by the kitchen sink.

His mother watched him as he walked out of the kitchen with his fists clenched by his sides. She smiled to herself before looking into her cereal and making shapes with the floating pieces of banana and berries. It was the first time that Paul had shown real confidence in himself, she wondered how long it would last.

They Said That I Was Brainy

The chess matches went as Paul expected them too, but he did enjoy himself even if it appeared like he was bored. He didn't want his team mates to know that he had changed his mind about being optimistic about winning. The last day of the chess matches revealed that their team placed fifth, the team wasn't very happy.

"It is all Paul's fault!" Exclaimed one of the girls in his team.
"Yeah it is your fault Paul." Agreed one of the boys.
"Come on guys it isn't Paul's fault." Said the other girl trying to keep everyone happy.
"If Paul tried harder we would have won." Said the first girl.
"No we wouldn't have." Said Paul trying hard to not get annoyed.
"There you go again." Joined in one of the other boys.
"What if this is as good as I am going to get?" Asked Paul meaning the statement to be a rhetorical one.
"It is clearly as good as you are going to get." Said the first girl "Otherwise we could have won."
"I just played for fun." Argued Paul.
"Fun is for losers." Replied one of the boys not really thinking about what he just said.
"Yeah!" Agreed the other boy.
"Then I am a loser." Concluded Paul.
"Right you are." Said the first girl.
"It has been nice being friends with you but I am not coming to chess club anymore." Stated Paul.
"Why?" Asked the second girl.
"Clearly I am not good enough for chess whether I enjoy it or not." Said Paul "If you don't think that I try hard enough then obviously I shouldn't play anymore."

Paul left the conversation without an answer from his friends, he was tired of arguing for once and didn't want to explain because he believed that they wouldn't understand.

"Did you enjoy your chess match?" Asked Joan.
"I suppose so." Replied Paul trying hard not to rethink the day over again.

He was reading a book and decided that he wasn't in the mood for talking so continued with short answers no matter what Joan asked.

"You are not going to go to chess club anymore?" Questioned Joan "I thought that you really enjoyed it."
"I do." Replied Paul.
"Then why don't you keep going?" Asked Joan.
"To enjoy something whether you are good at it or not when compared to the usual standards is not acceptable apparently." Said Paul putting down his book.
"If you enjoy it." Started Joan before Paul interrupted her.
"If you enjoy it you should carry on?" Said Paul "Is that what you were going to say?"
"Yes and I believe that you should carry it on it doesn't matter whether you are good at it or not." Replied Joan "I love to dance but I wouldn't say that I am good at it."
"You are not." Replied Paul honestly.
"Thanks." Said Joan sarcastically but Paul didn't get this.
"You are welcome." Stated Paul "I am not going to stop you dancing because you enjoy it, but my friends didn't think I was good enough and I don't want to be around people."
"People like that?" Questioned Joan not understanding.
"People in general. Most people think that way." Said Paul.
"I am sure that you are wrong." Replied Joan.
"I don't want to get into an argument before I go to bed just admit that I was right and we can continue." Said Paul.

Joan didn't accept it and started an argument which continued as they were both in their rooms lying in their beds. They kept thinking of an argument which they would call to each other down the hall. They parents told both of them off multiple times, but they decided not to listen and just let them get on with it. Even when Joan had fallen asleep Paul smiled to himself happy with their argument whether he was winning or not didn't matter. It was the Christmas holidays and Paul was just happy to have Joan home. Joan was half way through her third year of her English degree, she was studying to be an English teacher and was thoroughly enjoying it, not to Paul's liking because he wanted her to come home permanently. Then again he was a little pleased that she enjoyed it, because that would mean that he might enjoy it if he ever decided to take that route.

He hadn't decided what he wanted to be when he grew up but then again does anyone at his age? Most people don't know what they want to be in their late twenties let alone their early teens. Anyway Paul had thought and thought and the only thing he liked was music and then the possibilities narrowed for him as he didn't think beyond musician, and he didn't want to do that. He thought that it didn't give him much of an option but he still kept thinking for a solution. That was one thing that he was going to stay optimistic about.

24

April 1998, Fourteen Years Old

On Paul's fourteenth Birthday the present that he always wanted arrived in the post, he had been waiting days for the results of his grade eight piano exam and today he would find out. He ripped open the envelope clumsily, opposite to his usual behaviour but he was in a hurry. He didn't even need to read the letter which came with the certificate that he proudly held in his hands. He beamed from ear to ear as he danced about with it. He ran up to his bedroom, he proudly looked at the other certificates on the wall before taking an empty frame that was already with a pin in the wall. Paul carefully dropped the certificate behind the glass before putting it back on the wall. He stood back and gazed upon it.

The rest of his birthday was like any other, his parents gave him the few presents that he asked for and they insisted on giving him cake even though he never really ate cake and didn't like candles. He had requested that his aunt didn't come round and without much persuasion his parents agreed that it was his birthday so they should respect his wishes. Paul saw his grandma the previous day which he enjoyed and only wished that his grandad was there too. Paul wanted his sister to come home for his birthday, but she was still at university and both his parents and Joan felt that it was a long way to come for the weekend. Paul looked around him at the loosely decorated room, the balloons had started to deflate and the cake was slowly beginning to melt away making the icing drip on to the plate. Paul had read the books he was given and although it was only 9pm he was tired and went to bed. He lay there awake not realising how long for until he heard the bathroom light click on and off as his parents were getting ready to go to bed. Their door shut softly and Paul felt the whole house go quiet, he didn't know quite what he was thinking of but he suddenly felt a lot older than he should have done as he gazed upon his certificates on his wall.

Paul was still feeling a little down that weekend, it was sunny, bright and cheerful but this didn't spread to Paul who dragged his feet along the floor as he moved about with his head down. His parents were talking when he came into the lounge on Saturday morning and he didn't want to interrupt. Mostly because he didn't want to talk and somehow for a brief moment he didn't want to be alone so decided to endure it. Paul sat on the sofa in silence, he was still in the birthday mode that everything should be about him, after a while he began to feel a bit ignored and decided that he wouldn't be missed at all if he left. He stood up and walked out of the room closing the door softly behind him. He waited a moment but they didn't seem to want to ask where he was going so he continued to go outside. The warm air greeted him kindly as he stepped out into the fields. He wasn't in the mood for walking far but just wanted to walk with no direction and no purpose. He flicked a piece of grass in his fingers as he walked along, and as the stem became limp and squashed he dropped the remains on the ground and rubbed his grassy hands on his trousers. He had a lot of ideas about want he wanted to achieve when he was older and like a lot of teenagers they were big dreams that he wanted to fulfil as soon as possible. Joan had told him about university and now Paul knew that was what he wanted to do. He knew he would have to be patient and wait for four years before he could go and another four years before he would have, hopefully, achieved his degree. He was smiling as he entered the house, his parents were still talking eating some of the nibbles that they had bought for Paul's birthday that Paul hadn't touched.

"Paul!" Exclaimed his mother shaking her head "You have grass stains on your trousers."

Paul's smile was wiped of his face for a moment, but then he realised this was just one moment so why should it effect all the others? He wanted to be happy so didn't let this ruin his mood, he thought about the ideas that he had and now everything seemed possible. His patience's for things doubled in a few minutes and he was prepared to work as hard as possible to achieve what once seemed so intangible, and he was only fourteen.

His piano teacher was impressed with his distinction on his grade eight exam and joked by stating that there was nothing more to teach him. Paul kept going to piano lessons he knew that there was more to learning an instrument than just getting grades. He wanted to get better and better, he wanted to learn new pieces of music and pushing himself to try pieces that were difficult because he knew how good it would feel once he conquered them.

"Next the violin." He said eagerly his secret dream was to get as many grades in as many different instruments that he could.

He was eager to pick up the previous instruments that he had been learning before he decided to put all his focus into playing the piano. His piano teacher smiled at his enthusiasm, she had listened to him speak about music and playing instruments and she was sure that he was a promising music prodigy. Although this wasn't Paul's motivation, he had discovered that music was something that he enjoyed even though he knew that the pieces were the same notes but just in a different order. It was something which had a mathematical principle behind it and showed both his creative side and intellectual side.

25

May 1998, Fourteen Years Old

When Paul told the music teachers at his school about his grade eight achievement, they were all very pleased for him. Paul had never been very comfortable with sharing his achievements or come to think of it sharing anything with other people. He never told people what he was really thinking and tried to hide his feelings as much as possible, although there were times when he just had to speak his mind and would usually end him up in trouble but to him it was always worth it.

"I am so proud of myself." Said Paul wearing a beaming smile.
"That is good you should be." Replied one of the teachers smiling supportively "Are you going to study for another instrument?"
"Or are you going to continue enjoying the one that you can already play." Chirped in another teacher.
"Violin." Replied Paul happily.
"Violin is very difficult to play." Said the second teacher.
"So is the piano." Replied Paul "I learnt to play that one."

The bell rang and Paul being satisfied with the conversation felt that there wasn't anything more he wanted to say and walked away leaving the teachers standing in the hallway. They all had been proud to call Paul their star pupil, although Paul didn't like it very much. He hoped that they would spend time with the students that were struggling with the lessons, instead of asking him what he was doing. He never understood why teachers would do that and he didn't like it. It was like in his food technology or art lessons Paul never understood what the teacher talked about and they would always spend time with those who could, rather than explaining to him what he needed to do. He also didn't like the names that the other students called him because of his star pupil status. But, as Paul would he sucked it up and thought of something else refusing to be bothered by it. It reminded him somewhat of the grammar school but there he was made fun of because he wasn't smart enough and here it was because he was too smart or because he actually enjoyed learning.

Paul was often allowed to use one of the sound proofed practice rooms to practice his instruments, this was his escape from having to go outside during morning break and lunchtime. He wasn't allowed to eat in there, and would stuff a sandwich in his mouth quickly as he was walking across the quad to the music building. He was happy in his own world, instead of those of his peers. He enjoyed his own company which the other students found weird, so even if Paul had wanted to make friends it would have been likely that he would still be sitting in his own company. Paul figured out that it was best for everybody if he tucked himself away. The other lessons weren't that easy for him, not in the academic sense, because since he talked with Joan he had never failed a test on purpose again which meant that he tried his best and because he usually got high marks he not only got unkind words from those in his class, he also felt a lot of pressure to do well all the time.

"Paul what did you get?" Asked one of his classmates.
"Fifteen." Replied Paul.
"Yes!" They exclaimed "I got Seventeen."

He heard them go and boast to their friends how they got a higher mark than him. He felt like giving them the 'grades didn't matter lecture' but understood that may look like he was a 'bad looser' so didn't bother. He felt this all the time even though he was very proud with his mark he could tell that no one else was around him, it made him feel incredibly down inside he didn't want to have to please other people. He had never done something to please other people before, his best was always good enough why wasn't it good enough now?

26

July 1998, Fourteen Years Old

It was the day of the whole year group photo. Paul dreaded any day when he had to have his photo taken. He always felt awkward when he put on a false smile and felt it didn't look very good either. Traditionally the photos were taken outside and they were lucky with the weather once again as it was a beautiful day. The sun was shining and just a few clouds drifted across the sky, every now and again blocking out the sun before it started streaming through again when the clouds departed.

Paul had pleaded with his mother to let him stay at home but she didn't understand why it was bothering him so much, and didn't understand the fuss he was making so decided to ignore it. She took him to school and dropped him off like she always did and a disheartened Paul sat in the back wishing that he was home.

The photographer was all set up and staging that was placed just in front of the school, using the building as the backdrop. The photo wasn't until morning break and all through his lessons Paul felt a tightness in his stomach. It was agonising and he didn't want to have to sit through the anxiety that he was feeling. He made several attempts to ask to go to the medical room, but the teachers got wise to Paul and what he was trying to do so all refused. As the bell rang for morning break Paul froze, he thought about the line that he would have to stand in as the photographers would try to arrange them all in a particular order. He remembered in his middle school, being shouted at by the photographers for him to move to a particular space on the stand when they were trying to take a photo of the whole school. It didn't leave a very good memory for Paul of photographers and he just tried to keep his head down as he shuffled onto the stage.

It felt like ages whilst the rest of the year group was arranged. The sun was getting hotter and he looked at the red and sweaty faces around him. Finally, to the relief of all the students the photo was taken and they were allowed to leave.

A week later the final photo was published and a sample was sent to all the parents.

"We have got to buy this one." Said his mother squinting to find Paul on the tiny sample photograph.
"You can't even see where Paul is." Replied his father knowing how much the photos cost.
"We bought Joan's one." Replied his mother "It only seems right to buy this one and anyway if the individual photo doesn't come out great then at least we have one of Paul having finished his first year at upper school."

Paul raised his eyebrows, it sounded like an insult.

"It is ok you don't have to buy it." Replied Paul "I hated having it taken anyway."
"No Paul we are going to get a copy." Replied his mother smiling.
"Thank you." Replied Paul slowly and disjointedly.

The photo arrived in a tube, his mother was eager to take it out to find where he little boy was amongst all the other identical looking students.

"I have found him!" Exclaimed his mother triumphantly waving the magnifying glass in the air "You look lovely dear."

She showed Paul his photo to which Paul promptly replied, "That isn't me."
"Are you sure?" Questioned his mother who placed her face even closer to the picture.

Paul quickly scanned the picture and pointed to himself.

"Ah yes." Said his mother looking carefully at it "That is very nice."

27

September 1998, Fourteen Years Old

Paul was waiting in the queue of all the other year tens who were waiting to have their photo taken. The individual photo was always the worst, at least with year photos and class photos he could hide at the back and no one would really notice him. Everyone seemed to come out of the hall with a smile on their face, so Paul relaxed a little. He didn't really like the attention that he felt when he sat on that stool in front of the photographer, hearing the other students laughing and giggling. It wasn't directed at him, but he felt that it was. When it was his turn he sat on the stool in front of the camera, the lights were shining all around him and in his face which wasn't very comfortable.

"Now just sit there." Said the photographer positioning the camera he didn't seem phased by a new face and just got on with his work without speaking, for once Paul thought that some words on what he was doing would have been comforting.

Paul was looking away from the camera he didn't like to watch people it made him feel awkward. He avoided eye contact when he could and right now he was studying the bricks on the walls. He looked back when the camera man called his name, there was a click.

"That is perfect thanks." He said "Next."

Paul asked to see the photo but the photographer said it was fine, Paul decided to believe him but was disappointed and so were his parents when they received the preview of the photo through the post. They stared at the photo shining on the photographic paper.

They all didn't say anything for a while until his mother broke the silence.

"Oh." Said is mother "Maybe if we frame it."
"It is rubbish!" Yelled Paul "I hate it now everyone else is going to see it and it is horrible."
"Why is everyone else going to see it?" Questioned his mother.
"The photos of the top students are going to go on the wall." Explained Paul calming down a bit "I don't want you to buy one."
"We weren't going to anyway." Said his father looking at him and then back at the photo.

Paul didn't know whether to be pleased or offended, so decided that because he was in a bad mood anyway to be offended and ran to his room. They tried to comfort him at dinner but Paul was not happy, he just kept saying that he asked to look at the photo but the photographer said it was fine. In the end his mother just rolled her eyes. She was going to buy one to keep Paul happy to show that she liked it and now she wasn't going to bother. She didn't want the hassle that it might cause so expressed this fact to which Paul replied.

"You just don't love me even if I did look like that in real life you wouldn't love me!" Exclaimed Paul before again running to his room.

His mother replied with just another of her eye rolls.

28

May 1999, Fifteen Years Old

One of the things that Paul really didn't want to do was the year ten work experience week. It was the one week in the year when students in year ten could go and experience the world of work. Paul didn't want to. He was happy at school learning, he was only happy with the education and not so much the fact that he had to go to a school to achieve this. There were some students who didn't want to or couldn't find anywhere to complete their work experience so they could take part in some workshops at the school. Paul didn't want to do either really but his parents wanted him to do the work experience week because they thought that it would give him an outlook into what career he wanted. Paul didn't want to think beyond going to university. Music was all he ever really wanted to do but he couldn't decide what job would suit him.

"There is a music school just outside of town." Started his mother before she realised that Paul wasn't listening to her "Paul? I really think that you would enjoy it you might want to teach piano when you grow up."

Paul continued to ignore her, and instead he carried on thinking. He was in the garden, his fear that he had now overcome. He lay on a blanket that was placed on the grass, he looked at the sky. It wasn't a particularly sunny day but the clouds drifted slowly over the vivid blue sky and Paul liked that. He could watch the clouds as they transformed into different shapes.

"Fine Paul." Said his mother "I am not going to wait for you to answer me, I am going to get you work experience there."

His mother stormed off, Paul noticed this and had truly not heard a word that she had said. He didn't even notice that she was talking to him. He thought that it wouldn't be important so lay back down on the blanket to continue his cloud watching. Paul wasn't very impressed when he found out that he had to do work experience at the music school. He thought about refusing to go but then that would probably be more trouble that it was worth.

His mother walked in with him on the first day. He was greeted by an elderly looking lady who shook his hand eagerly.

"We do need a lot of help here at the moment." She said "I am sure that you will be of great assistance."

Paul's mother was polite but Paul was not, he didn't speak and when his mother went off to work he wished that he could go with her instead. The lady took him through to the office which was messy with paper laying everywhere. There were two desks one of which looked abandoned and unlike everywhere else was the only place which was tidy. It didn't conform and Paul didn't like that.

"The person who worked there has just got another job." She said pointing to the clear desk "You can sit there if you like."

Paul did sit down but tentatively, the chair was set at one height and it was too low for Paul his legs were awkward trying to fit in the limited space that the desk allowed. He wasn't very happy.

"Now." She said "I will just do this and then I will be right with you."

Paul made a noise to show that he understood rather than say anything with actual words. He waited patiently sitting on the annoyingly low chair, every now and again looking across to the computer screen that the lady was looking at. She was slow on the computer, but then again a lot of people were, thought Paul. He then tried to work out the possibility of a person growing up in a particular area, and whether that correlated to if they were slow or fast on the computer. He didn't think that she was doing anything productive and after an hour Paul was beginning to get bored.

"When do I get to sit in on a music lesson?" He asked.

The lady either didn't hear or didn't want to hear as she ignored what he said and carried on talking to herself quietly. Paul asked his question again to which the lady replied, "I will just finish this off and will answer your question then."

Paul started tapping on the keyboard to the computer but the lady didn't notice which annoyed Paul. At 11am Paul hadn't done or learnt anything.

"Coffee time." She exclaimed with a beam on her face "Would you like anything?"

Paul shook his head.

"I will only be a moment." Replied the lady picking up her mug on her desk and leaving Paul in the office.

He breathed heavily and put his hands on his forehead, he was beginning to get stressed. He thought if this was work, then he didn't want to get into it. It was not organised enough, not structured enough and there was no time table for his visit. He took out his work experience question book that he had to fill in for his school. He finished it before the lady returned. It was getting on for half an hour she had been making a drink and Paul was refraining from kicking something.

"Now then." She said coming back into the room.
"When am I going to do anything?" asked Paul.
"You must be getting bored." She said "Let me just go and check with the music production officer."

She left the room again and by the time she got back it was lunchtime. Paul did think about walking home but it was a long way. After lunch the lady told him that the music production officer didn't know if he could do anything.

"Then why am I here for work experience?" Asked Paul.
"I don't know the answer to that." She replied "I will check with the music production officer."

This time Paul thought that there was no use in him being there and packed up his bag, he was about to leave when a man came in. Paul assumed that it was the music production officer but it wasn't.

"Are you Paul Westwood?" He asked.
"Yes." Nodded Paul.
"I thought that Sally would tell me when you arrived." He muttered to himself "I do apologise I was in my office before I had a meeting for the rest of the morning. I thought I was going to be told of your arrival."
"There isn't anything for me to do." Said Paul "I am going home."
"Doesn't surprise me." The man said "They always do this sort of thing I am Linus by the way I am the manager of the music school."

Linus logged Paul onto the computer and showed him a timetable that Sally was meant to have printed out ready for Paul's arrival. It was printed and various parts were highlighted. Paul was beginning to feel better until Sally came back.

"Owen said that there isn't anything for Paul to do." She said.
"There are plenty of things for Paul to do." Replied Linus in a friendly tone "I have written here that he can design that poster for the music concert that is being performed."
"Ok." Replied Sally stressed "Can you explain that because I just don't, I just can't."
"Yes I am here to explain it to him." Said Linus stopping Sally's sentence knowing that she was trying to find an excuse to why she couldn't explain the task.

Linus spent the next ten minutes explaining to Paul what he would like him to do and Paul was happy. Paul wasn't sure whether he was going to enjoy designing a poster but once he got into it he discovered that he actually liked it. He designed a few so that Linus could choose which one he thought was the best. He spent the rest of the day completing this, the next day he presented his work.

"I think I like the first one." He said.

"Really?" Questioned Paul.

"Why don't you like that one?" Asked Linus.

"No I do, but it is the first one that I did and I didn't think that it would be good enough." Said Paul.

"It is certainly good enough and I am glad that you included it in the ones that you showed me." He said "The fourth one is good also if you ask Sally to choose between the two then get back to me that would be great."

Paul was very pleased with himself he felt proud of what he had accomplished and was so excited with the thought that it would be published. He showed Sally when she appeared from wherever it was she went to.

"I think I like this one." She said pointing at the first one "I will check with Owen as he is the one who usually does the design of the posters."

She went off came back and didn't say anything to Paul. She started clicking on the computer before turning briefly around to him.

"That wasn't what he wanted." She said.

Immediately Paul felt unhappy again.

"I don't know why you were asked to do that, Owen always does the design." She said "This is what we needed you to do."

She handed Paul a piece of paper which showed the poster divided into different sections.

"It is always done on A5." She said to him, because Paul had designed it on A4.

"It is being emailed it doesn't matter whether it is on A4 or A5." Said Paul.

"It is always done on A5." She said "That is what Owen does."

Linus wasn't very impressed with Sally or Owen. He spoke to them both briefly about it and asked Paul to change a few things to keep them happy. The following day Paul was unhappier than he was the previous day and became more so as he listened to

Sally speak.

"Owen is going to design it." She said "He always does I don't know why Linus asked you to do it."
"I will tell him." Said Paul who knew where Linus' office was.
"No if you don't for a moment, don't design anything else before we get back to you." She said.
"You just said that Owen is going to do it." Replied Paul.
"Owen is going to do what?" Questioned Linus walking in the door.

After hearing what had been said Linus called Sally and Owen in for a meeting concerning Paul's poster. Linus understood how proud Paul was to have designed it, and yet it was dismissed as if it couldn't be an achievement.

"Did you want to sit in on the music lessons instead?" asked Linus.

Paul smiled and nodded, "Yes please that is what I thought I was here for."

"I must admit it would have been better." He replied "I only deal with the administration side of things there is a different manager for the music lessons and the like."

Paul was happier now that he was in the music part of things. He sat in and listened to the music and how it was being taught, he enjoyed it but would much rather be playing the instrument. He decided that he might get too annoyed if a particular piece was not played to his liking, but he enjoyed watching all the same.

"I hope that you enjoyed the last couple of days better than the first." Said Linus.
"Yes I apologise if I was a nuisance, thank you for your support and I think that you should tell the next work experience student what they should be expecting before they turn up." Replied Paul "Other than that, it was an interesting experience thank you."

Linus didn't have time to reply because Paul was out that door as quick as the clock struck 5pm, home time.

29

November 1999, Fifteen Years Old

Paul was fifteen years old when he first cried in a lesson at school, for a year eleven it was a life sentence to be picked on but Paul wasn't thinking about that. It was either the fact that all his emotions finally got the better of him or the fact that the teacher was picking on him, again. Exams were coming up and they were soon, there was only a month to go before Paul's first exam and the pressure was getting to him. His teacher was staring at him trying to get him to answer all her questions. She was very annoyed at the intelligence of Paul, even though Paul didn't flaunt his gift at all. She thought him arrogant when he absentmindedly corrected her. He had only done this a few times but the first was enough for her, and from that moment she never liked him. Even though Paul had tried to explain that he tried to stop himself she didn't take any argument from him. Paul didn't really like history very much anyway, he didn't like the idea of looking backward he wanted to look forward to the future. He tried to explain this fact but his opinion didn't seem to matter to her. That or because he opened his argument with 'I don't like history because'.

"You arrogant boy." She snarled "Detention!"

She gave no explanation to why she did this the rest of the class knew but Paul didn't. His mind immediately raced to what his parents would think, how would it affect his future, and what would his sister think? He obviously was thinking irrationally because he knew that deep down that Joan would never be angry with him. It was his first detention and he didn't know how to react, clearly to him it was a big thing and that was made obvious to the rest of his class. The emotions that he was such a stranger from all at once overwhelmed him. Two steady tears rolled down his pale cheeks and landed in two splodges on his notebook. He looked down as she continued to belittle him he began to rub the page where the two splodges were. He rubbed them and rubbed them until the two holes that he had made merged into one. She started to get angry over this too, so Paul looked up at her his face had now turned red and the tears started to flow more freely now covering his collar with wet patches. She didn't notice how he was feeling and Paul didn't think that she really cared. She wasn't paying attention to the fact that would someone who was provoking her deliberately wouldn't act like this when given punishment. Not one of Paul's classmates stood up for him, then again why would they? They all stared at him and the teacher enjoying the little debate before things suddenly got real. Paul would have sat there in a blank bubble of confusion trying to figure out the jumble that made knots in his head for all the time the teacher felt like she wanted to talk to him.

He was rescued by his geography teacher who was walking passed the classroom and noticed the display that was occurring on the inside, so she decided to intervene. She pulled the teacher out of the classroom which caused a hum of voices between Paul's peers they all obviously looked over to Paul when they were talking about him but Paul didn't notice this. His face was still squarely looking down at his greyed out notebook with the blank page looking back at him. He didn't want to look around him. He wasn't ashamed of crying as such, and he shouldn't have been. He was just the type of person who started to worry about the consequences down the line. Whether real or irrational Paul thought of them all. The geography teacher came into the classroom and told Paul to gather his books and to leave the classroom. The history teacher waited outside until Paul had left before she rejoined her class. Paul and the geography teacher briefly heard her yell at her class to be quiet before the door closed softly.

"Paul what do you think you should do now?" Asked Mrs Flick walking Paul down the stairs, she was the type of person who tried to get to the bottom of the emotions of her students without putting an impression on their views. She took this approach with teaching her geography students too.

"Home." He mumbled his tears had now dried but had stained his face he didn't look up when he spoke to her but kept his gaze fixed on the carpet.

"Speak up Paul." Encouraged Mrs Flick she was smiling the whole time to show how much she thought that he shouldn't be sad, but it didn't work Paul had his mind set on what he wanted to do and in this moment it wasn't being happy.

"I need to go home." Said Paul this time looking up at her "I am not coming back."

Mrs Flick didn't show signs of complete shock, it was obvious that she was experienced with dealing with students who were upset. She took it all in her stride before composing an answer with the intention of keeping Paul in school.

"Why don't I take you to Mrs Thee?" Asked Mrs Flick walking him outside and across the courtyard in the direction of the learning support department, she wasn't giving him a choice really. Now she was putting a plan into action she couldn't wait for Paul to make the decision as he was clearly irrational, but to Paul he was thinking as straight as he had ever done.

Paul said nothing which Mrs Flick had assumed he would do so she opened the door into the building, which was all a light blue colour, and they went straight into Mrs Thee's office. Mrs Flick whispered to Mrs Thee before motioning for Paul to sit down, he didn't really take any notice so she asked him instead and Paul sat on the edge of the chair. He was ridged and his fists were clenched dangling down beside him, he stared at a spot on the wall and didn't want to move his gaze.

As Paul sat on that chair he began to feel nauseous, his face was pale and Mrs Flick thought he was going to faint. Paul was taken to the medical room where he lay motionless on the sick bed.

"I am going to ring your parents now." Said Mrs Flick softly she was reluctant to send him home but Paul didn't look very well, whether it was psychosomatic or the shock of being told off, she didn't know but all the same Paul wouldn't be able to attend any other lessons that day.

Paul's eyes, which were closed, widened, "No." he said sternly "Ring Joan."

He wasn't really sure why he said this but he knew exactly what his parents would say his dad would say 'stop being a wuss, man up' and his mother would say 'stop making such as fuss you are such a melodramatic if you don't get your way.' In fact it was nothing of the sort he was genuinely overwhelmed with the whole situation it was out of routine for him, and it didn't make him feel good he just needed someone to understand this and listen to him, even if he didn't know it. Mrs Flick smiled gently at him she opened her mouth to say something but Paul interrupted her.

"Please." Said Paul "Phone my sister please!"

Mrs Flick just looked at Paul and smiled before looking down and leaving the room. This left Paul in a state of panic. He didn't understand who she was going to contact. He didn't understand social que's at the best of times and this time he was very unsure. He was shifting on the bed, twiddling his thumbs sometimes tapping the wall which was beside him. He didn't know what to do or what to say.

Paul suddenly used all the energy that he could muster. He slid off of the bed, the medical nurse went over to him but the time she got there Paul was out of the door. Mrs Thee's office was just down the hall and he knew that he could make it there.

He burst in, Mrs Thee looked up and asked him to take a seat. She could see that he was nervous as he shifted in his seat. He still didn't look very well, but didn't say anything when Mrs Thee asked him how he was feeling and decided that she would take a different approach.

"Now Paul could you explain to me what happened?" Asked Mrs Thee calmly her hands were clasped on the desk with a pen wedged between them.

"Who is she going to phone?" Asked Paul "I don't want them knowing!"

"Why is that Paul?" Asked Mrs Thee coolly trying not to show any emotion which actually unnerved Paul a bit after seeing that everyone around him usually showed something that he didn't understand
"I just don't!" He exclaimed very annoyed getting up off of the chair and walking out of the room. Mrs Thee was a bit astounded so paused briefly before she got up off of her chair too. She thought Paul was going to try to walk home but she was wrong. Paul was heading for elsewhere.

"Who is that?" Asked Paul bursting in on Mrs Flick in the department staff room. Mrs Thee wasn't far behind and came up apologising quietly as Mrs Flick was on the phone.

"Thank you Mrs Westwood." Said Mrs Flick before putting the phone down "I had to call your parents Paul as they are responsible for you. I didn't think you were well enough to continue the days' lessons. Are you feeling better?"
"Joan is twenty two years old." Said Paul quietly ignoring Mrs Flick's question.
"You don't just need to be over the age of eighteen Paul." Started Mrs Flick but she didn't get to finish because Paul had walked out and sat down at one of the chairs in the workspace outside the staffroom.

He put his face in his hands and sobbed. Mrs Thee tried to get him to move as she noticed some of the faces from the classrooms turning to look. Paul didn't want to move he stayed there until his mum arrived. The teachers ushered him down to the reception where she was waiting for him. She looked a bit dishevelled as if she had rushed from work, as she was in the middle of something and was eager to get back there before she forgot something important.

"What have you done now?" She started before changing her tune to a comforting one "Come here sweetie."

Paul was awkwardly hugged by his mother, he slinked off to sit in the car he was at the point where he just wanted to go home and hoped that he would soon. He waited for what felt like ages and pressed his face up against the glass and tried to spot the signs of when his mother was finished talking, but he was sat there for a long time yet. Mrs Flick explained the situation in more detail, although left out part about being pressured by the history teacher. She told his mother that Paul didn't want them to let either of them know and that he wanted them to ring Joan.

"That would have been of no use." Said Mrs Westwood laughing "Joan is in America."

30

May 2000, Sixteen Years Old

The teacher asked the question again but Paul still didn't say anything, his mouth was slightly open. He didn't know the answer. The corridor was a bustle of students moving to their next lesson, but Paul was stood facing the teacher who handed him back his homework. The question was asked again and Paul really didn't understand. He stood there bemused and not sure how to prompt the teacher to explain what they meant.

"Paul it is a joke." Replied the teacher smiling "Don't you understand."

Paul stated that he didn't, slowly saying his words and choosing them and the order as wisely as he could. The teacher didn't believe him. He started to say the joke again and then explain it to Paul as if he was a child. He said every word individually then explained each one.

"It doesn't matter Paul." Said the teacher as he began to move back down the hall "You are not expected to know everything."

Paul didn't want to go to lessons anymore, he wanted to walk forever and just keep going he didn't want to be around those people. He wanted to just get away from everyone who made him feel bad, and not have the worries that he did have every day, his emotions began to pile on top of him again. This time he didn't let it phase him, and on the outside you couldn't tell that anything at all was going on inside his brain. Instead he was thinking and thinking and over thinking about every detail of the conversation. He didn't understand what they said sometimes and they didn't understand that he didn't understand. It was a frustrating and confusing situation as Paul tried to think hard for the right thing to say. He didn't know. He just didn't know.

He sat in with Mrs Thee, she was busy typing away on her computer but was happy for Paul to sit on one of the soft chairs for as long as he wanted. She tried to be as accommodating as her authority allowed, and let many of the students who were overwhelmed come and sit with her and talk if they needed. He wasn't ready to go back to lessons, and was starting to feel like the confrontation with the teacher was an excuse to not go. Mrs Thee didn't want Paul to start making excuses to not go to lessons, as she knew how much he liked learning, but also didn't want to make Paul feel like it was his fault. He couldn't help the way he thought and Mrs Thee wondered why more people didn't accept him for who he was but she didn't want to disrupt his state by voicing her opinions.

"It is lunchtime now Paul." Stated Mrs Thee confidently "Don't you want to go to lunch?"
"No." Replied Paul shortly.
"Paul, what is really going on?" She asked not sounding impatient but she said it in a positive way that sounded as if she knew what she was doing.
"I just don't have the words." Said Paul.

Mrs Thee questioned this as she didn't understand.

"Exactly." Said Paul getting animated and jumping up from his seat "I just don't understand what people say sometimes."
"Why don't you tell them that?" Asked Mrs Thee still not really understanding.
"It is better to say nothing than get it wrong." Said Paul throwing his arms gently in the air before sitting back down on the chair in front of Mrs Thee's desk.
"You can't think that, if you answer a question and get it wrong at least you have tried, if you don't try you can't get the answer right." Concluded Mrs Thee getting up from her chair and walking to the door holding it open.

Paul understood this que and got up from his chair.

"There." Said Mrs Thee "That question you got right."
"But you didn't ask a question." Stated Paul.
"I didn't need to." Replied Mrs Thee.

She had a smirk on her face, she really liked Paul but sometimes she found it hard to get inside his head and other times she knew exactly what he was thinking.

31

May 2000, Sixteen Years Old

Paul was often in the learning support department now, he found that they made him more comfortable than just sitting in the library at break times. He never thought about it before but ever since he cried in that lesson they had been very supportive of him. They always had a chair for him just in case he needed it, which he took up often. They could have debated about whether he really needed it, but kicking him out didn't even cross their minds. He didn't want to go to the music department anymore to practice his instruments either.

Paul had his GCSE exams that summer and felt that he needed to study. He had been revising for the past few months just to make sure that he was ready, even though he really didn't need to. He didn't listen to the people who told him that it was an overload of information. Paul was intent on doing the best he could and even though everyone told him he would pass without studying, he didn't think that this was right and wanted to make sure that he did actually understand all the content that he need to. He wanted to know exactly how all the questions in the papers were asked and what they wanted him to put in his answers.

There was an isolation room which was usually used for students who had misbehaved in class and were excluded from lessons. Paul must have been the only student to actually request to be allowed to use the room to study when it wasn't occupied. There was a debate amongst the staff whether this would give Paul an advantage over the other students, but Paul wasn't interested in them. Not that this was the point but Paul pointed out that without this quiet space he might not do as well as he could in his exams, if he was always worried about being picked on by the other students.

"Everything has to be fair Paul." Said one of the staff not wanting to let him use the room on the basis that he would get an edge over the rest of the students. She was one of the teachers who wasn't exactly against Paul but wasn't on his side either, she didn't like the fact that he was smarter that a lot of the other students. She would never pick him to answer a question, even when he had put his hand up like everybody else "Some of the other students might need use of a quiet space too."
"None of them thought about it." Replied Paul motioning to some of the students who were walking around outside "Why should it matter whether I use the room or not? I thought about it first it was ingenuity to think outside the box which I must admit I don't do very often."

After what felt like a battle, Paul's request was finally agreed upon and he felt safe and calm when he was in that room. He found that he could study more efficiently and started to feel confident in himself again. He had a timetable prepared to organise his study and he actually stuck to it. He had planned to go on to the sixth form in the upper school that he was in, but they were particular on who they would allow to attend. They wanted the top grades and few to no detentions. Paul was worried, even though he was certain he could get the grades, the unknown of what could be in the exams paper made him anxious.

Paul also spent too much time thinking about when he should have had a detention, but was excused by other members of staff. He worried that this might make a difference to his future. He spent all his time studying, which worried his parents thinking that he would do worse than if he had just relaxed and used his time to do other things that he enjoyed. They always paused when they said this and thought for a moment, the thing that Paul likes the most is learning. He enjoyed studying for the most part even if it was just reviewing things he already knew it was a relief to find when he could say 'I know that' with confidence.

His exams came and went more quickly than he imagined. He sat

in the large hall, where he took most of his exams, and thought this time next month I would have finished all my exams, then this time two weeks from now I would have finished all my exams, then this time next week I would have finished all my exams, then this time tomorrow I would have finished all my exams. His last exam was Maths meaning that the hall was full of students, whereas during his other exams other than English the hall was slightly over half full most of the time which suited him, as usually he was near an empty seat due to his last name beginning with a 'W'.
He began to feel a little claustrophobic and tried hard to shake it off. He drank some water and nervously shook his leg which must have annoyed some of the other students, but he wasn't thinking about them. He was just trying to keep calm and make it through his last exam. He kept telling himself 'this time in two hours I will have finished my last exam and be home.'

Paul didn't plan on going to his end of year disco which was usually the official finish of GCSE's but for Paul this last exam was just that. When he finally put down his pencil he still had half an hour to wait before the exam was over. He started to panic and checked and rechecked his work over and over again to the point that he was worried he was fixing a calculation that didn't need fixing so he stopped. Breathed; looked at the clock. Twenty minutes to go. Put down his pencil and finally believed in himself.

He knew what he had done was right, he knew that the questions where he struggled and knew that he couldn't do anymore to try to figure them out. He knew he had done his best and now any changes he might make would be because of panic and that was worse than getting it wrong at his first instinct.

"Are you sure that you don't want to go to the disco?" Questioned his mother when she came to pick him up.
"Sure." Nodded Paul he wasn't going and no one could make him.

Paul didn't go to the disco, Joan was home for the summer and instead they went out for dinner. Paul decided that it was best if he didn't object, otherwise they might have told him to go to the disco. Paul almost enjoyed himself and thought that it was a much better evening than being stuck in a room full of people who he didn't really know.

Results day came around in August and Paul had to go and collect his results envelope from his school. He would finally find out whether he had achieved the grades to get into the sixth form. He was sweating with nervousness when his mother dropped him outside the school. Paul's legs were shaky and wobbly as he stumbled into the reception area, and stuttered when he asked for his results. The envelope was handed to him and he had to sign to show that he had received it. His hand was still shaking, his name was scrawled across the line and was only just identifiable. He brought the envelope straight back to the car and wouldn't open it before they got home. When they did he ran to his room, he closed the door and opened the envelope.

"I did it!" He exclaimed aloud even though the rest of his family were waiting patiently in the lounge for him "I get to go to the sixth form!"

They all heard him as he was shouting at the top of his voice, he was obviously excited. They were gathered watching the TV and all smiled briefly before focusing their attention back on the program that they were watching. It was nice to know that the worry of Paul and his results had come to a happy conclusion.

32

June 2001, Seventeen Years Old

Paul had chosen to study music, physics, maths and English for his A-levels. Most people had worried about him taking both Maths and English, as usually people prefer one or the other. Paul had started his lessons and was enjoying only doing the subjects which he enjoyed. The classes were smaller which also made him feel better about going to school. He felt that he was actually treated like a citizen of the school rather than an annoying child that teachers had to deal with. It felt good he spent all his spare time studying, he could spend time in the library during his free lessons and he would just stay there through break times and lunchtimes if he could.

"Are you worried about the exams?" Asked his mother after she looked through some of the content that Paul was learning.
"I suppose but right now I am worried about the mock exams." He said.
"Mock exams already? You have only done half a year." Exclaimed his mother "What can they test you on?"
"The content that we have learnt so far." Replied Paul "Obviously."
Paul's mother just rolled her eyes like she usually did before continuing, "You know what I mean Paul it seems a bit soon to be testing you already."
"I also want to complete my grade seven in violin before next summer." Stated Paul cleaning away his books from the kitchen table.
"Why can't you want to play computer games like a normal child?" Questioned his mother who began to prepare dinner "It is probably cheaper."
"Actually it is actually quite expensive thirty pounds on average

for a computer game that you can finish within hours." Started Paul "And then what? After you have completed it you are not likely to want to play it again. Whereas when I no longer have lessons I will want to continue to play the violin and I can learn other pieces of music with only a cost to my time and actually it isn't much of a cost when you enjoy it."

"Paul." Said his mother.

"Yes?" Replied Paul.

"Stop talking." She shook her head as she said this but with a smirk on her face she meant it really as a joke.

"Ok." Replied Paul sincerely and left the room.

His mother continued to shake her head and smiled before neatly putting the chicken in a pan full of vegetables.

Paul's mock exams were nothing like the real thing, as he found out when he took his AS exams that summer. They were harder and more stressful, most of the students in his year had given up on the real thing. They had spent so much time on the mock exams that their brains were frazzled with the information that they had been given. Paul was determined to not let it bother him and decided to treat it as a new challenge as much as that frightened him too.

"It is easy for you, you don't even need to try." Stated one of the students in Paul's year.

They had just finished the physics exam. Paul had stated that he thought that it went ok and then said about a particular question which he did find a bit challenging. The other students hadn't taken this so well and started stating how he was naturally smart and so didn't need to put in hours of hard work to get the grades he wanted. Paul tried to tell them that he actually enjoyed learning so read up on things and didn't treat it as study time. They didn't understand, want to understand or were so angry with the whole exam situation that they didn't have time to think.

"Sorry." Called Paul quietly after the students who were making their way to their next study session.

33

November 2001, Seventeen Years Old

Paul had decided that he was going to university and had filled out all of the applications with some help from Joan. He found them confusing as they went on and on. After the first few forms Paul began to get tired of them, so blocked all of the relevant information out of his mind to give him an excuse to stop.

"How is that boy ever going to get on at university?" Questioned his father as he looked across from his chair in the lounge to Joan and Paul who were sitting at the kitchen table with a laptop in front of them.

Paul's hands were in his head staring at the table rather than the desktop computer which Joan seemed to be clicking a load of buttons. Paul did shout at her a few times to stop, as the stress of hearing that constant click was getting annoying. However, Joan continued to persuade Paul to carry on because once all the forms were filled out and his personal statement was written he wouldn't have to do them again.

"I don't know." Replied his wife walking over to his chair to peer through the door way to watch the same scene as he was "Believe it or not I think that he will do better than we think."

Joan soon finished the forms that Paul had to fill in and his application was sent. The following summer, after he had completed his A-level exams he would know whether he would be accepted or rejected by his chosen university. Before his exams he had to attend an interview to his chosen university. He wasn't very happy with the interview process as he had to have a group interview as well as an individual one. There were going to be people there who were applying for different courses, which made him even more anxious as he would have to make 'small talk' opposed to what he called 'meaningful conversation'. He was sat on his own in the waiting room as he was very early for the interview. The clock slowly ticked on by and he waited for the others to arrive, he was surprised that they were not as early as him and started to doubt their ability already. He felt like he was the one interviewing them and that actually provided him with a little comfort. A short while later a girl came in and sat in the chair next to him. Paul looked at her and then looked at the many other chairs which were placed in the room. He then looked back at her briefly before shifting his gaze to elsewhere in the room. He was nervous and he couldn't deal with her heavy sighing so he made the decision to move to a different seat. He awkwardly and slowly got up from his chair and began to walk to one of the other ones.

"Oh sorry!" She exclaimed when she realised what he was doing.
"That's ok." He replied sitting in a seat in the other corner of the room.
"I am really nervous too." She replied smiling clearly wanting to make conversation.
"She wants to talk." Started Paul speaking quietly to himself "Oh good."
"What was that?" She asked leaning over as if to try and hear what he was saying better.
"I just said that I like the quiet." Replied Paul bluntly but added a smile to soften his speech.

The girl didn't get the message and started talking about how she liked the quiet too and of other things about interviews that she either liked or didn't like.

"My name is Stella by the way." She said randomly in the middle of a conversation that she was having with herself.
"Paul." Replied Paul with a forced smile.

Moments later a few other candidates arrived and they soon went in for their interview. They had to talk about themselves which Paul found uncomfortable especially with strangers. Then they had to do some 'team building' type exercises which Paul found completely pointless. The individual interview made Paul a little more at ease, until they asked him how the team building activities went and he lied through his teeth telling them how much he enjoyed them and thought that they would help him in the future. They asked him the normal interview questions such as 'why do you think that you are suitable for this course?' and 'if you were an animal which animal would you be?' Paul was still stressed when the interviews were over, he kept thinking about his answers and in his head he kept thinking that he should have said something else instead.

"I am sure you did fine." Said Joan when she came to pick him up she decided to change the subject so they didn't focus on the actual interview itself "Did you meet anyone nice?"
"Stella." Replied Paul.
"That's good would you be friends with her?" Pried Joan.
"I am not a child." Replied Paul annoyed but mostly because of the adrenaline rush that he was feeling "I don't have to have friends it is not a clause of life."
"But otherwise you will be lonely." Argued Joan worrying about her little brother who will be going off by himself.
"I have never felt lonelier than I did in that room full of people." Replied Paul "I am better off being alone."

Joan decided that she would be wiser to not argue with Paul so said nothing. It was a quiet journey home which took a few hours but luckily Paul didn't object to the radio, as long as it was the classical channel because it was the one with the least adverts in. Joan didn't mind as long as there was music playing so it wasn't entirely a boring journey.

Paul was both happy and nervous when he received his conditional acceptance to his chosen university. His family were pleased with him but he still needed to get the grades before he could attend. This was the biggest part for him and he relived receiving his GCSE's which wasn't a good experience to say the least. He had learned a lot from when he took them, but then again an exam is an exam and no matter how much someone says 'you will be fine' and 'I know you have done as much as you can to prepare'.

It will never be enough to take away that anxiety that he felt as he stepped into the hall to sit at the desk where he would be for the next two hours. To write about everything he had learned and try to understand what it is he was writing and tailor it to each individual question.

"Don't worry Paul." Said his grandfather when his parents explained Paul's situation "You always were a very intelligent boy."

34

May 2002, Eighteen Years Old

His exams he found less stressful than his GCSE's maybe it was because he didn't have to cram information from a multitude of subjects, and the four he had chosen seemed small in comparison even though there was a lot of information on each. The hall was not stacked full of students either, all the exams he took were in smaller rooms or rooms with a few GCSE students doing their exams too. Paul felt more relaxed about the exams, although he was delighted when they were over. Once again his mother picked him up after his last exam and again tried to persuade him to go to the disco but once again Paul was adamant that he wasn't going to go.

"But Paul it will be the last time that you will probably meet up with most of the people that you have been at school with since you were thirteen years old!" She exclaimed "I wouldn't have missed my disco if I had one."
"I am not you." Said Paul bluntly "I am not going, I don't actually know 'those people' and they wouldn't notice whether I was there or not."
"Don't say that Paul of course they would, you have got to go." Replied his mother.
"No I don't and you can't make me so I am not going." Replied Paul "Anyway it is on the same evening as my cello lesson."

His mother admitted defeat and decided not to try and persuade Paul anymore, much to her disappointment.

When it was finally time to collect his results Paul relived the GCSE scenario. This time when the envelope was placed in his hands he ripped it open as fast as he could. The results were confirmed and he was going to his chosen university. A wave of relief washed over him before a small smile spread over his face. It was a big step for Paul to leave home and now it was certain that he was going to his chosen university Paul had to have his accommodation confirmed. He had applied for his favoured room which was in the halls of residence and to his relief it was accepted. There were only a few rooms with an en-suite bathroom and even though this cost a bit more Paul was not going to share a bathroom with one person he didn't know, let alone a group of them. The building that Paul was in was one of the larger of the university's accommodation buildings. There were a few student houses dotted around the city but Paul didn't want to have to walk through unfamiliar streets to get to university every day. He soon was packing up the items that he was going to take with him, he felt a twang of sadness as he realised that this was the last time he would be a child as from now on he would have to look after himself for the most part. It was something that he had never had to do and it was a daunting prospect. Joan heard the muttering that was coming from his room, so wandered in to check on him. She also had a surprise for him, something to make him feel less lonely whilst he was away.

"I got you this." Said Joan.
"It's a fish?" Questioned Paul taking a little aquarium with one little gold fish swimming about.
"I was worried about you being lonely." She started "Now I don't have to worry anymore."

Paul could have said that he never got lonely so didn't need something to keep him company, but it made her feel better so he decided not to say anything. Paul smiled at her sister's feelings, he didn't understand why she always worried about him but he was sometimes glad that she did. The little fish was his little piece of home, he had never thought about leaving the comfort of the familiarity of all he knew in the same way before. Once he had a wave of worry he looked over at his little symbol and he was certain that we would be alright. After coming to terms with having to share his routine with a pet he was pleased that this was his parting gift. He knew that he would have to alter the way that he did things such as not sitting in his chair at the kitchen table or keeping his door slightly open. At least he could blame it all on a fish which made coming to terms with it a bit better.

"What did you name him?" Asked his mother as Paul placed the small aquarium on the desk in his new room in the university.
"Ken." Replied Paul smiling at the little orange fish who bobbed up and down happily.

The name wasn't questioned as Paul would probably go into some lecture about how it was one of his favourite scientists or musicians. It was actually the first name that came into his head and somehow had never been able to change it to a majestic or symbolic name.

The first night that Paul spent on his own in his own room in the university was a tough one. He lay in bed not daring to close his eyes lest something happened that he missed, also he could hear some rowdy voices down in the street, probably new university students who just wanted to have a good time. For Paul he couldn't sleep even though he was on the second floor he still didn't want to sleep just in case. He wanted to stay awake and was aware that he found his senses heightened as he tried to hear what the voices were saying. He kept looking over at Ken who was hiding under one of the rocks in his aquarium, but Paul could still make out his orange shape amongst the greenery and rocks and this was a huge comfort to him. All through the night there were voices outside the window, some were laughing, some were shouting and all of them loud. He got up throughout the night to ensure that the door to his room was locked, every time it was but he just wanted to make sure. It was the first time that he had worried about his door not being locked. When he was a child he used to scream if one of his parents closed his door. He had to have it open then, and now he had to have it closed, locked and bolted. He paced up and down his room back and forth tearing his brain apart trying to rationalise his situation. Once he got up the courage to peer out of the window and down into the street when there was a particularly rowdy lot outside. As he did they immediately noticed him and after a few unkind words were said about him spying on them he quickly closed the curtains again. His heart was pounding and head buzzing as he lay back down in the soft bed under the duvet cover which, although was his own it did seem the same somehow. The comfort wasn't the same and clinging to it the way he did at home didn't feel natural. He listened to himself as he breathed loudly and inconsistently eventually falling into a light sleep which was disrupted a few times as he woke himself up to check his room was fine.

After a few months of being there he did get used to the noise which usually occurred at the end of the week and the weekend. He was glad that he had persevered rather than stating that university wasn't for him and make his way back home. He made a routine for himself and Ken doing the same things in the morning in the same order. Everything he now did became his new normal and he wouldn't have wanted to revert back to his old routine.

His course was trying at first, mainly because Paul had to get used to the prospect of other people being there too. He would have much preferred to be in a class all of his own. There were not many students who were taking the music degree course, but Paul was ok with the amount which turned up for the first lesson. They were all in the different clubs which were held and his tutor tried to encourage him to join one but to no avail. Paul didn't join a single club and didn't go to a single event held by the university to encourage the students to talk to each other. He was happy going to his lessons then going back to his room to do any assignments and to just try and relax. He did miss having a piano just down the hall. There were practice rooms that he could use but they were too far away for him and somehow even though the rooms were sound proofed he just didn't feel the same solitude as he did in his room. He mostly tried to block homesickness out of his mind but found it hard when he looked at his calendar and sighed. It was a long time before he would get to go home for the holidays.

35

September 2002, Eighteen Years Old

Most of Paul's lectures were held in the same room which suited him very well. Staying in the same place meant that he could sit in the same seat, and understanding typical human behaviour most people would end up sitting in the same seat if they visit the same room regularly. Paul enjoyed listening to most of the lectures but often got bored or disagreed with the lecturer and didn't know how to keep it to himself until the lecture ended. When he heard something that he didn't agree with he would shift his weight around on his chair back and forth. He would grasp the bottom of his chair with his hands and turn to look at the other people in his class to see if they had noticed what he had. Most of the time they hadn't or if they had they would keep it to themselves and calmly wait until the end of the lecture to raise the question with the lecturer. Paul couldn't do that, he would stress about it so much so that he would have to find a way to release the tension.

"Music is just maths with sound." Paul blurted out, immediately feeling better once he did. His face had become red and now was returning to its pale colour. His palms were no longer sweating and he could feel the tension being released.

There were giggles amongst his class, feeling a wave of them wash over him. He knew that they weren't meant to be kind but it didn't quite get through to him. He built a metaphorical barrier against this sort of thing, for the most part, he would be able to detach himself from the uncomfortable feelings that were caused by other people's words. He pretended to himself that he had self-confidence and didn't need to prove himself to anyone.

Whereas in his true personality every little thing would bother him, so that his self-esteem was around his ankles instead of up to his head. The way that other people perceived it so much so that it could come across as arrogance on their part.

Paul continued to explain his reasoning, "It is true" he started looking around at the faces which were trying to hide their smiles. He ignored them and continued to explain how this was so. The lecturer listened patiently to what he had to say, by now she was used to these outbursts from Paul. She waited for him to finish and when he did so she thanked him for his contribution; continuing with her lecture. She didn't say it in a dismissive way but in a way that stated 'this is the content that you have to learn whether you disagree with it or not if you state something other than what I am teaching you then you won't get the mark'. Paul relaxed but refrained from slumping in his chair, which is what he felt like doing as he had drained his energy mentally, and continued to sit upright with his hands clasped together in his lap. He looked at his classmates for approval but he was greeted with the bored looks on their now blank faces which were looking towards the front of the room.

"Why don't you try to think of music more like a feeling and less like a calculation?" Said the lecture when Paul walked passed her to exit the room after the lecture.

He was the last one to leave due to the fact that he took a long time making sure that all of his stationary was placed back in his bag exactly how it came out. He always smiled awkwardly at her in appreciation of her taking the time to teach them, even if this time he didn't entirely agree with her but he didn't want to make her unhappy or not like him for that fact. He knew that a lot of the teachers at his upper school found him 'difficult' or 'challenging' at least that was what they said at parents meetings. He hugged his notebook close to his chest whilst he walked quickly down the corridor. There were other students walking up and down the halls heading in the direction of lectures, or to their rooms, or their friends rooms, or the outside to sit and study in the fresh air. No matter how cold it was there was always some students sitting outside, not Paul. He walked into the open air squinting as the sun was lowering in the sky. He weaved in and out of people walking in his direction doing an awkward dance with one of them as they tried to get passed each other. He reached the building where his room was and once he had reached his room, he opened the door to a small gap swiftly squeezing inside he closed the door behind him and on the world. He breathed slowly out through his mouth but not steadily. He had become out of breath from the walk. He tried his best to calm himself down but it wasn't a fast process. He carefully placed his notebook and four pens on the desk perfectly parallel with the table top. He picked up the chair and squarely walked it over to the chest of draws which were in front of the window. He looked at the fish tank that was placed in the middle of the chest of draws and Paul lent his head on his hands with fingers interlocking each other, he stared at the one gold fish in the tank. Paul watched him flit from one side of the tank to the other and round in circles. Paul took it as a sign that he was happy to see him and smiled briefly before looking more serious.

"How easy you have it, Ken." Paul started, gently poking the glass with his finger and running it along its surface not startling the fish at all "You never have to meet another fish in your life and the only way that this could happen, would be if I put one in your tank but I would never do that to you."

He smiled as he watched the fish swim up to the top of the tank and then swim down to the bottom of the tank multiple times. He took this as a thank you.

36

June 2003, Nineteen Years Old

Paul was not looking forward to yet more exams, he had survived a year of university and was given the prize of having to sit four exams. It wasn't exactly what he wanted for studying hard all year but he tried to put a positive mind towards it, even if he did have a nagging doubt that he would ever survive the next year. He was fortunate to have little doubt that he would actually pass the exams. Being his passion he didn't treat it like a chore to study, unlike some of the other people on his course. He had made a study plan and a wave of memories from his GCSE exams came over him. He stuck to his study plan down to the minute. He knew he was prepared but still kept going over the material to make sure he knew everything that he needed to know and understood all the content.

"What if you didn't have a good memory?" Questioned Paul he was in his allocated break which he had timetabled for himself.

He had found Stella sitting outside in the sun and had joined her. Not so much for the company but mainly because she was sat on the bench that he always sat on. There were a few students wandering around, a few of them were packing up ready to go home excited by the fact that they chose a coursework based degree. They all had happy looks on their faces of achievement that they had survived. The few that were left had serious looks on their faces, most of them ready to give their exams their best shot and some who decided that there were better things to do than study.

"What do you mean?" Asked Stella not really following Paul's train of thought. She was trying to prepare for her exams too, although

she seemed to get distracted a lot and Paul wasn't helping.
"If you don't have a good long term memory then how will you perform well in exams?" Continued Paul.
"Study I guess." Replied Stella who had her nose in one of her study books, she wasn't very interested in what he was talking about. It all seemed like meaningless chatter to her which is ironic because no one loved to talk more than Stella.
"No matter how hard you study some things some students just won't remember. I don't think that we should have exams because they are tests of you memory not your knowledge." Continued Paul "When you work you are not expected to remember chapters and chapters from text books."
"You are only saying that because you don't want the anxiety of having more exams." Replied Stella looking up from her book "Paul I am trying to study and I think that you should be too."

Paul didn't bother telling her that he had timetabled in the time for a break and instead left her in the quiet that she wanted. He walked around the courtyard for a while before making his way back to his room. It was almost time for him to start studying again.

The exams went to the expectations of Paul. He performed as he thought that he would and it was confirmed that he still had a place at the University for the next year. It was also a relief to find out that the floor his room was on, was going to be allocated to second year students. In which case this meant that most of the students staying there now could keep their rooms. Paul was more optimistic now that he didn't have the worry of having to find somewhere else to live for the next year.

37

October 2003, Nineteen Years Old

Paul kept looking at the clock on the wall it was ticking at its usual regular pace but somehow seemed to move slower. He didn't listen to the lecture, he was focused with a fixed stare on the clock that eventually struck 4pm. Paul hastened, rushing out of the door only to remember when he was outside the university that he had left his notebook on his desk. Paul gave a tiny squeal whilst frowning before brushing his hair down with his hand and turning around to go back and collect his notebook. As he reached the room one of the students on his course was still sitting down at their desk. Paul stopped at the door briefly and with his head down rushed to his desk picked up the notebook and was almost out the door when the classmate decided that he wanted to exchange pleasantries. Paul tried to quickly think of things to say but he just wanted to leave the room. He didn't try very hard to make conversation, but the classmate didn't seem to notice and he kept chattering on. The student didn't seem in any rush to be elsewhere, and even Paul had beaten him out of the room after the lecture had finished. Eventually Paul was allowed to leave the room and he raced out of the confines of the university.

It was reading week and he was exhausted, he didn't realise how much he needed more than just weekends off and time to think about other things. Studying music all the time almost made him not enjoy it as much. He hadn't played the piano in a while and was beginning to miss the actual sounds that you could make with a musical instrument instead of just learning about the parts that make them up. They had spent too long this term on the theory of music, and Paul wanted to get back to the first two terms where he had actually played the different instruments in accordance with the portfolio that he was building up. He was nearly back to his room when he couldn't hold it in anymore the relief overwhelmed him as he broke into a thousand tiny glistening drops of water. He stumbled the rest of the way to the sanctity that was beyond one door in a row of hundreds. He shattered as he entered his room closing the door softly behind him. His notebook and bag just fell from his body as he dropped to his bed and lying amongst the sheets weeping. Only for a few moments he allowed himself to feel all the feelings which he had bottled up for so long before stopping himself. He sat up wiping his face gently with both hands. He took a deep breath and stood up, it was only late afternoon but Paul was drained of all meaningful energy. He changed in his pyjamas and didn't even brush his teeth liked he usually did, instead he sighed whilst he turned off the light, crawled into his bed and tried to think of anything else other than lessons, people and life.

He woke up in the morning feeling refreshed and ready to do something that he enjoyed. He was going home. He sat on the edge of his bed and rubbed his face as he yawed loudly. He stayed there for a moment with his hands either side of him clutching at the mattress. Once he had gathered his thoughts he got up and greeted a good morning to Ken. Paul changed his clothes and went about his business still being thankful that he didn't have to share a communal bathroom. Outside, the world looked bleak with the clouds greying at the edges and the blue sky hidden between them. Below there were people dragging along small suitcases and waving goodbye to their friends as they headed home for the week. Paul would have been happy to take the train, and had planned to, but Stella offered to take him part of the way and she wouldn't take no for an answer. Paul still wasn't in the mood for talking but when she knocked on his door he opened it with a forced smile and some kind words. She was beaming with the excitement of getting to go home she hadn't planned on doing any of the reading that she was meant to, and Paul tried his best to convince her to do all the work that she was told to do. Stella ended up promising that she would although Paul didn't believe her.

Stella had spotted Paul on the first day that they arrived at the university. She had remembered him from their interview, whereas Paul had tried to forget it. It just so happened that they were signing in at the registration desk at the same time. She was ecstatic to see him again, but Paul was surprised that she remembered him at all. She wouldn't leave his side for the first few days, always making sure that they met up and talked whether Paul liked it or not. She was a complete extrovert the exact opposite to Paul. She tried to get him to go to parties or nightclubs but Paul still refused, and wasn't going to be persuaded. Since then Stella had decided that Paul was now her best friend and stated this fact to anyone even if they hadn't asked. It was sort of embarrassing but Stella was good company most of the time, apart from when she would talk for hours even when Paul was virtually kicking her out of the door she would still start up new conversations.

Paul and Stella set off in a pool of happiness; soon Paul was beginning to feel better. It was either that, or he had masked his feelings so well that even he couldn't tell that they were not real. Even Stella's constant chatter was less annoying than it usually was, and sometimes even found himself listening to what she was saying. As they went down the country the weather seemed to get better and better. The clouds weren't so grey and the blue sky peered through the gaps trying to break out altogether. The little rays of sunshine made it all the way to earth and this made the ride easy, as Paul gazed out of the window at the world outside. Paul was still eager to get home and kept saying to himself 'only two hours to go' and 'only one hour fifty minutes to go'. It felt like a life time before he actually reached his house where he stepped in the door greeting his parents briefly, made an excuse to exit and went up to his room where he shed another few tears. His bedroom was dark because the curtains were closed against the afternoon outside. If he had opened them he would have seen a rainbow, as well as the sun which was proudly in the centre of the sky. Paul quickly got himself together took a few things out of his suitcase before he slowly went back downstairs. He was wearing thick white socks with no slippers or shoes, something that he hadn't done in ages. When he was in his room at the university he made a point of wearing shoes on his feet, not wanting his clean socks to acquire any of the dirt that may have gathered around from the previous occupants who would have stayed there. Now the smooth wood felt good under his feet and the carpet in the lounge comforted them as he sunk his toes into the plush fibres.

His parents were very pleased to see him even though sometimes he did get a bit much for them. They particularly were beginning to get more and more annoyed when he corrected them for the way they said something or the use of the wrong word. Paul had tried to curb his quick tongue that seemed to upset people. He didn't mean to, it was just the way his mind worked, it made him stressed to think that someone was saying something wrong or didn't understand the correct meaning of a word. It just frustrated him too much to think that someone was going around spreading wrong information like 'the stars are little planets' or when people say 'pacific' instead of 'specific'. His sister got annoyed when he corrected her too but unlike everyone else she tried not to show it. Although there was one time when during one conversation about styles of music Paul had corrected her five times, not just because she incorrectly defined a style but because of the grammar she used and the way she said specific words. The annoyance bubbled up inside of her and in one angry burst she yelled at him. She was so annoyed that they couldn't have a conversation without him thinking that he knew better. She had exclaimed how people say things differently and he just had to accept it. Paul must have been only about eleven years old and for the first time Joan made little tears run down his face. They pooled at the end of his chin before dropped like little globes onto her soft bedroom carpet. She didn't feel sorry for him at first, but after she had slammed the door in his face she suddenly wanted to hug him and say sorry. Paul's bedroom door became the barrier, and sitting outside it for a while she composed her speech to try and mend their friendship. She tried to calmly explain to him how sometimes correcting people made them feel bad. She spoke through Paul's bedroom door but couldn't be sure whether he was listening or not. Paul *was* listening he just wanted to appear as though he wasn't. He didn't make a move towards the door and just lay on his bed with his face turned towards her voice.

He didn't like being wrong but this time he started to wonder whether he was.

Now Paul had learned to never correct Joan. He still got annoyed at things that she did, such as when Paul deemed that she was too slow on the computer and would snatch the keyboard out of her hands. As annoying as this was it wasn't nearly as annoying as when he would correct her.

His parents were sat around the beloved TV set when Paul entered the room. He smiled at the springiness of the carpet before joining his mother on the sofa. Paul was quietly thinking to himself and not taking an interest in the TV programme which his father kept shouting at for some reason. Paul had brought in with him one of the books from his reading list, and started to study the cover before opening it to the first page and began engulfing every single word.

"Did you make any friends?" Asked his mother softly trying to change the subject from why the player missed the goal or why the referee had to 'talk' to his father's favourite player.
"One." Replied Paul shortly trying to read his book.
"Finally." Said his father under his breath before adding louder "What is he like?"
"She." Replied Paul trying to make it clear that he was more interested in reading his book than talking.

This made his mother blush a little, she clasped her hands close to her chin before exclaiming, "Oh Paul that is wonderful."

She had clearly miss understood and Paul noticed this, he took no time in correcting her, before clearly not wanting to be disturbed again and turned away from them with his nose in his book. He was saved by Joan coming round to see him but Paul wasn't really in the mood for talking to her either. Instead their parents asked her a lot of questions about her own life nearly all of them implementing a man called Hugh. Joan quickly got bored of the conversation so said that she would like to go for a walk.

"But it is dark outside." Replied Paul not wanting to move from his comfy spot on the sofa

"So?" replied Joan "Come on to the first oak and back again."

Paul reluctantly agreed and put down his book neatly on the side of the coffee table and they escaped the questioning mouths of their Parents. Joan tried to get Paul to talk to her, but he only used short words. Joan knew that Paul was upset and she didn't want to make him more upset by talking, so they walked along in silence. The dark velvet sky washed over the pale blue of the daylight. The stars were beaming in all their shiny glory, trying to make up for the lack of sun in the sky. Along the path they spotted a badger and a fox who were both trying to catch something in the bushes. It was sometimes more interesting to walk in silence because then it would make them look at the world around them. Every now and again Joan would look at Paul and try to make out his facial expression by using the moon as light. Neither one of them had brought a torch with them. Paul kept most of his emotions to himself as he believed that there was nothing anyone could help him with. They were his emotions how could someone help him understand them? He knew why he was upset he just needed to push it all to the back of his mind and forget about it. Anyway he only had three more years to go, he could stick it out until then.

38

November 2003, Nineteen Years Old

Paul was tucked up in his bed in his small room at the university within the four walls where he usually felt safe. It was a cold night and there was a light wind blowing that gently rippled across the window. Paul had left his curtains open as he believed that Ken liked to see the sun rise in the morning, otherwise Paul would have been adamant that the curtains were to be closed. He had grown used to a lot of different things since Ken had been introduced into his life. Not only did he keep his curtains open, but he also didn't use the night light that his parents had bought him. He didn't like to disturb Ken when he was sleeping. He realised that he might be being a bit irrational but Ken gave him an excuse to do things differently. As he was lying with his face pointing towards the wall there was a crack and a thump before a loud whistle of wind started. The noise woke up Paul with a start clasping at his duvet cover with both hands hurriedly. He slowly looked towards the window, still in a daze, but even in his daze he still noticed the little shards of glass that were protruding out of the edges of the window frame. There were little shatter marks drawn around the remaining glass. He found his bearings before swinging his legs out of his bed and placing them on the floor. He got up to walk towards the window. He had started shaking and his hands and feet were numb he almost didn't notice the crunching under his feet.

"Ow!" He exclaimed aloud, before falling back on his bed clutching one of his feet.

He felt that it was wet and held his hand up to the light of the moon, he quivered. He hugged himself through his loud irregular breathing and absentmindedly rubbed his hands dry on his pyjamas. His eyes began to water. He ran his hands through his hair suddenly stopping with his hands on his head. His eyes became wide and he quickly scoured the floor with his eyes, finding what he was looking for he knelt down on the floor forgetting about the glass that lay scattered about. His hands were shaking as he scooped up the golden object that began to move as soon as he touched him. He placed him carefully in his glass of water that was beside his bed. Paul stroked the glass with his finger before brushing through the glass that was on the floor to find an oxygenating plant. He found one and dropped it carefully into the glass of water eagerly watching as his little fish began to move more steadily. He smiled through his tears and carefully picked up the glass of water clasping it with both hands never looking away from the little fish.

When the sun began to rise Paul was still hugging the glass. He didn't move all morning, and when he missed his lecture Stella knocked hard on his bedroom door. Not waiting for an answer she walked in.

"I tried phoning you." She started before looking around the room her tone lowered "Oh Paul, what happened?"

His face was tear stained and he was curled up in the corner of his bed. He shook his head avoiding eye contact with her. She noticed his feet and quickly walked over to his bed avoiding the glass to the best of her abilities. His clothes were covered in red stains which had dried into his blue pyjamas. She sat down and touched his arm tentatively to comfort him, but Paul shivered.

"Paul, I am going to get the nurse, ok?" She asked though she was meaning to do this even if Paul objected but Paul nodded slowly.

The nurse looked at Paul's feet and declared that there was no glass stuck in them but his left hand was worse off and he would need to go to the emergency room. She patched up his feet and knees with some loose bandages, not once did Paul let go of his gold fish. The glass was held firmly in his hands he didn't care that they hurt he just wanted to make sure that his little fish was safe and the only way he thought to do that was to hold him.

"Come on Paul. I will take you to the hospital." Said Stella passing him his shoes. He didn't take them "Paul you can't take Ken with you."

"Then I'm not going." Replied Paul sternly with his eyes fixed on his fish.

"Stop acting like a child Paul you are nineteen years old just suck it up." She exclaimed before her face softened, she looked at him with a gentle smile "You must be the only person who loves his goldfish as if it were a person."

"Please." Begged Paul quietly he wasn't going anywhere without his fish.

Stella, Paul and Ken made a detour passed Stella's room and she dug about in her bag and found a clear water bottle. Once Ken and the oxygenating plant were carefully transferred they went to the hospital. On the way there Paul started to complain how his feet and knees were sore but was adamant that his hands were fine not letting anyone hold Ken.

The doctor studied Paul's left hand carefully before she determined that it was safe to remove the glass and pulled it out as delicately as she was able to. She also checked on his feet and knees bandaging them again making sure that absolutely no glass was stuck in them. She was very thorough, and cleaned all his cuts to sterilise them. He also had to have tetanus jab which he wasn't very happy about but did endure it.

"Who knew someone could get so many cuts from a fish tank." Said the doctor smiling at Ken who was held carefully in Paul's right hand. Since the left one had now been bandaged right up to his fingers.

"Paul, please trust me with Ken. The doctor needs to look at your right hand now." Said Stella as she held out her hands to take the bottle, but Paul refused placing it between his legs instead.

Paul was patched up and said a quiet but meaningful "thank you" to the doctor. The doctor gave him some pain killers as Paul was sore and he was quiet thankful for them too.

Stella worried that Paul would drop Ken as he attempted to hold him with one heavily bandaged hand and one lightly bandaged hand. He looked very clumsy trying to balance the water bottle between his hands. In the end Stella insisted that she must carry Ken, she pleaded her case as they walked from the consultation room. She was especially worried about Paul dropping Ken due to his limping as she was afraid that he would stumble, which he did many times along the way. Paul refused, even when Stella tried to grab the water bottle from him he held it close to his chest and turned away. No matter how hard she tried she couldn't take it off of him. In the end she started to list all the ways that Paul could drop Ken but he just stated that she could drop him in all the same ways.

"Thank you." Said Paul as Stella dropped him at his door. Stella wanted to wait for Paul to go in to his room and get settled before she went to her own but he froze as soon as she opened the door.
"What's wrong now?" She said trying hard not to sound impatient.
"I can't." He stuttered.
"What?" Questioned Stella and this time she sounded a little impatient and placed one hand on her hip.

Paul quickly thought of an excuse to why he couldn't stay in his room, he didn't have to think too hard there were a few very good reasons.

"The floor is probably still wet and the window has been boarded up." He stated. "I think I am going to go home. Please would you ring Joan to tell her to pick me up?"
"But it is mid-term!" Exclaimed Stella getting really annoyed now "You can't go home."
"Yes I can." Replied Paul looking at her "I am going home."
"You will miss all your lessons." Continued Stella "You just need to sit down and I will find another room for you."
"I am not a child." Stated Paul raising his eyebrows "I can make my own decisions."
"No you can't." Replied Stella "Most of the time you never decide anything!"

"Yes I can and I am going and there is nothing that you can do to stop me." Concluded Paul.

Stella eventually gave in, she already had Joan's number from another occasion when Paul decided that he wanted to go home midterm. That time Joan had managed to convince him that he should stay and he did. Stella hoped that the same thing would occur and rang Joan whilst Paul sat in one of a cluster of chairs in the corridor almost directly opposite his bedroom door. Paul sat with Ken in the water bottle which he had placed between his legs but still cupping the far side of the bottle with his hands. He was thinking deeply about the new tank that he needed to buy his goldfish.

"Joan is still at work but will be here as soon as she can." Said Stella holding her phone in her hand "You are lucky she was working in Bath on business. If she was in Cornwall it would have taken her six hours opposed to the two that it is going to take now."

Stella sat in the hallway with Paul who didn't say anything and just listened to the lecture that she was giving him about how he wasn't prepared to be an adult. He wasn't really listening but he pretended that he was. Joan arrived a few hours later talking to Stella before she spoke to Paul who insisted that he went home. Both Stella and Joan were unsure whether he was meaning to come back but after meeting with the university principal, it was decided that he was going to come back after a few days off which they granted him under the circumstances. They also agreed to clean up his room and investigate what had occurred. Paul refused to go back to pack his things so Joan reluctantly entered the scene. She was quite shocked by the amount of glass still left on the floor, there was still the jumble of the window pane glass and the aquarium.

Joan took Paul back to Bath with her, it was too far to take him the whole way home so he stayed in the spare bedroom of the flat that she was momentarily renting. Paul was happy once he was there and started to talk a little more. He was shown his room where he stayed for the rest of the evening. Joan couldn't even coax him out with dinner so she just left him alone. When Paul emerged the following morning he was his usual self although he was struggling with not being able to pick anything up.

"Did you say that the doctor booked you in for next week to have your bandages checked?" Questioned Joan who wondered if she would have to take him to his doctor's appointment then take him back to her flat "Paul you will have to go back that day because I can't keep running you around."
"Sure you can." Replied Paul confidently "Anyway my appointment isn't until the following Monday."
"No I can't, I have work all next week. It is a good thing it was a Friday otherwise I wouldn't be able to help you out." She was becoming stern now, she didn't want Paul to rely on her forever "I will take you back a week Monday and you have to stay there."
"But they may need to replace my bandages!" Exclaimed Paul "What am I going to do then?"
"You will just have to stay in your room." Concluded Joan "Hugh and I are going for lunch today and then to the cinema you will have to occupy yourself until then."
"How will I pick up anything?" Asked Paul worried.
"You think you're so smart, you figure it out." Replied Joan before going off to get ready.
"I thought you said that you were going to help me out today?" Said Paul.
"I was." Replied Joan from her bedroom.
"You were planning on cancelling your date with Hugh then?" Questioned Paul before he exclaimed "You had no intention of taking care of me."
"Taking care of you?" Shouted Joan coming back into the lounge, dining, kitchen area where Paul was sitting on the sofa "You should be old enough to take care of yourself but no, you turn into a complete baby when something different happens and you can't continue your routine like normal. I am tired of having to run around after you Paul after this get someone else to cater to your every whim. You are not a prince you know. Find a friend."
"I thought that you were my friend." Asked Paul.

Joan softened her tone she was very annoyed at Paul but didn't want him to get upset before she went out. She didn't trust him really to be sensible when he was upset.

"Oh Paul." She started before joining him on the sofa "You have to really try sometimes to think about a situation and before you panic, think of options that you can use. Instead of sitting in your room all alone waiting for someone to find you instead you should have called Stella or your tutor or someone to help you. Remember you should never be afraid to ask for help and I urge you to ask for it. I am your friend but I am also your sister and I can't look after you forever. As much as you don't want to hear it I have my own life to lead and I can't keep running after you when you get upset."

"I know." Agreed Paul "I don't trust anyone as much as I trust you."
"You need to learn that there are people out there which you can trust, you just need to find them." Finished Joan.

The doorbell rang, "That must be Hugh." She said getting up, grabbing her shoes before answering the door. Hugh came into the room and started to talk to Paul, they had met before but Paul was still not sure about him.

"Anyway, Paul, tomorrow I will take you out to find a fish tank. I don't think that plant is going to cut it for much longer." Smiled Joan.

Ken had been moved to a bowl instead of the water bottle that Stella had allowed Paul to keep. She didn't think that she would want to use it after a fish had been swimming about in there.

She turned to look at Hugh, "How is Camble?" She asked.
"He will be fine on his own." Replied Hugh "Unlike a lot of dogs I think that he actually likes it. Although I could have brought him here if I had known that Paul was here. You might have liked the company."
"No thank you." Replied Paul "I don't like dogs anyway."

Hugh was astounded and talked to Paul about the reason why. It was mainly because Paul said that they were dirty. Joan had to drag Hugh out of the door because they were starting to talk about other topics.

Paul didn't do much whilst they were out. He did listen to music, which was a little difficult because trying to press buttons on his mp3 player with his bandaged hands was a little tricky.

Hugh and Joan came back late afternoon. They sat with Paul and they all talked until dinner time when Hugh said that he would cook dinner. He seemed really at home in Joan's flat it made it easier for Paul to feel less awkward. Joan helped to get the ingredients out before she set up the table. They all sat around the dinner table. Joan and Hugh laughed as they watched Paul try to use a knife and fork. It was difficult but somehow he managed it.

"I heard that you have a girlfriend." Questioned Hugh raising his eyebrows.
"She is just a friend." Replied Paul "Why can't a male and a female just be friends without people thinking that they are in a relationship."
"I dunno." Replied Hugh "But it is fun though."
"What is?" Asked Paul.
"Assuming." He was very vague about this but Joan seemed to understand what he meant
"He is just messing with you Paul." Explained Joan "It is fun to wonder what it would be like if certain people were couples."

A while later Paul went to bed, it was the only part of the evening that he actually enjoyed, being alone in his room. He lay there and thought about all different things before he drifted off into a deep sleep.

39

December 2003, Nineteen Years Old

"Your feet look fine now." Said the doctor as she unravelled the remaining bandages on Paul's feet "Your hand too."

Joan had dropped Paul off a few weeks earlier for his doctor's appointment. His room had been cleared up and so Paul was to stay. The doctor said then that his cuts were not yet healed so gave them another week.

Paul smiled weakly as he looked down at his hands and saw that the bandages revealed a few small scars. He looked at them intently for a while longer than was necessary and the doctor tried her best to comfort him.

"You don't have to worry all is fine just a few scars nothing really." She said softly before adding an upbeat tone "Ok you are set to go."

They talked briefly about the pain medication which Paul had been on and then the doctor discharged him. Paul winced as he walked on his feet but the doctor realised that it was psychological, his feet had healed without scars which was surprising and she didn't understand how they could still really hurt. Paul did leave Ken in his room for the first time previously Paul had carried Ken around in the water bottle but Stella persuaded him to leave Ken in his room claiming that it would be stressful for Ken to keep being moved. She was probably right and anyway Paul believed her, so decided that it would be best for him even though he worried about Ken every time he was left alone. Paul expressed this to Stella who came to meet him after his doctor's appointment. When they reached Paul's room he started to run to get there Stella knew, like the doctor thought, that Paul limping was psychological.

"You can't carry him everywhere." She said as Paul ran over to the aquarium which was now placed on the desk to the edge of the room.

Paul sighed as he looked at his orange friend but knew that Stella was right, Ken was probably safer in his own aquarium than being carted around in a tiny water bottle. Paul was still distracted by the scars which lay all over his hands they were small but visible. Stella looked at his hands and tried to sound supportive when she said you couldn't notice them, but Paul could and it annoyed him greatly. He wasn't worried about what everyone else thought of his hands, he only cared what he thought of them. He looked at the new pane of glass that lay in between the window frame, this time the university had replaced it with double glazing. He looked around the floor and couldn't find any of the pieces of glass but for a long time after the event Paul would carefully hop across the floor and jump on his bed trying to avoid all of the areas where glass had been. Eventually Stella realised this had to stop, and bought him a large rug to place over the areas that used to have glass on them. The rug was plain, blending into the original carpet. It was hard to distinguish the rug from the carpet, although the rug was plusher than the old carpet was. Paul had an epiphany, in his mind the similarity in the rug and carpet gave him no excuse and he started to walk on the carpet as if nothing had happened.

40

June 2004, Twenty Years Old

The summer break came around and Paul was ready for it. Most of his luggage had been packed for a few weeks. Paul quickly packed the rest of his clothes the evening before he was due to leave. This time his parents picked him up. His luggage was loaded into their car and he closed the door on his doom room for the last time, as he was moving into different accommodation for the next year. He sat in the back with Ken and his aquarium carefully and securely strapped to the seat next to him. The ride was smooth and quick which was a relief, as Paul was eager to be back home and was delighted when they arrived. It was a dewy morning which he could tell was going to be a hot day. The fog was just beginning to lift drying out all the foliage gradually.

Paul slowly wiped his finger across the window in the kitchen gathering the water into one droplet. Condensation had covered the corners of the window frame and the liquid slowly ran down to the window sill as the day began to slightly warm up outside. The sun was already high in the sky and rising still.

"Paul." Said Joan seriously when she came into the kitchen she had come back home for a few weeks.
Paul didn't say anything but stared blankly at nothing out of the window, she sat down on one of the kitchen table chairs and continued "Paul, I'm engaged."
"What?" Said Paul quietly turning around to look at her he was slightly dazed.
"Hugh asked me to marry him." She said with a small smile on his face as she looked down at the ring on her finger which Paul had missed when she greeted him "We are getting married next

summer."

"I am pleased for you." He replied with a straight face they were in silence for a while before adding "Are you happy?"

"Very happy Paul." She replied with a beam on her face.

"Good." He replied echoing her smile "Then I am happy too."

"We are going to live in Bath." She said.

Joan had thought that Paul would have been unhappy about the move because she wouldn't be at home when he came back from university but she was very wrong he was over the moon, "That means that I can come to you on the weekends!"

"Sure." Replied Joan trying to sound pleased but couldn't help the half frown that appeared on her face.

Paul did really like Hugh, he was kind and understanding making Paul feel comfortable around him. Since meeting Hugh at Joan's flat in Bath, Paul had grown to like him very much. He had always included Paul in whatever they were doing with friends, even inviting him to things that Hugh knew Paul would decline attending. Hugh would invite him just because he wanted to make Paul feel included. Paul had come to stay with Joan in Bath for a few weekends, and Hugh had taken them both out a few times to different things that Paul did enjoy. Having him as a brother-in-law was defiantly a good type of change.

Hugh had been a real help to Paul, helping him to find his accommodation for the next year of university. Realistically finding a university house to share would be hard. He didn't have anyone really that he was close to, so couldn't form a group to find a student house. There *were* spaces available, as students had posted their need for extra people in their group on the university forum. Paul didn't like the thought of not having his own bathroom and sharing a building in close proximity with strangers, it wasn't really his thing. A one room flat in a block of flats was the only thing that Paul even considered. He wasn't pleased about having to share a building with other people, but he had his own bathroom which was the main thing. He made up a game and decided that he was going to pretend that he was living back in the student halls.

The next academic year was better, Paul was now used to the way that university work. He had figured out a personal and study routine which he followed very strictly. He tried to stick to his routine as much as possible, but it didn't work particularly well when an extra lecture would be added to his time table. Even knowing the week before wasn't enough for him and it disorientated him slightly. He knew he could never work on a rota or a casual job, he knew he needed to know what he was doing and when he was doing it. The confusion and the feeling of being overwhelmed was not worth it. The exams at the end of the year were ones to give him the academic part of the teaching degree that he was studying for. The next year was going to be the hardest for him yet, he wasn't looking forward to his placement year. Learning on the job was a big part of becoming a teacher and he was still unsure whether he was cut out for it or not. He didn't like the idea of working with people but being a teacher was now the thing that he knew he had to do, and didn't know how to be happy if he couldn't do that. Taking a deep breath he prepared himself for this year deciding to not think about the placements until next summer.

41

May 2005, Twenty One Years Old

The following summer came around quickly and another year of Paul's degree had gone by without Paul having an incident. It was a relief to all his family, Paul living away from the university was a worry to them all on how he was going to cope fully by himself but he managed it making both him and his family proud.

Joan and Hugh's wedding had been planned and was edging ever closer. It took place on one of the warmest days that summer, it was just as the leaves on the trees were turning a golden brown as they prepared for autumn. Paul liked to listen to the rustle as the leaves brushed against each other, and the crunch that they made when they were thick enough to walk in.

Paul was too busy thinking about university and what he would discover in the next year rather than listening to the conversation of Hugh and his friends. They were all brushing down their suits, making sure that the flowers in their top jacket pocket were straight. Paul was staring out of the window with his flower drooped to one side and his collar poked up on the other side. Hugh was a few years older than Joan they were both English teachers and met at a conference four years previously. Hugh worked at a school in Surrey a long way from the one Joan had worked at in Cornwall. Since Joan had moved to Bath a year previously, it became a more stable base, realising the opportunities that they both had there it seemed the best place for them to live.

They moved to the outskirts of the city where there was more affordable housing, and it was closer to where Joan had applied for a higher teaching position. Joan had briefly worked at that particular school a few years back and they were delighted that she applied for the job. It wasn't very difficult for them to know that she would be the right teacher for the school. They had bought a house of which was a middle terrace in a long block of houses that all looked the same. They all had red brick walls and grey rooves. There was no character to the house and the garden was little more than a postage stamp but nevertheless it was theirs and much cheaper than they imagined. They both wanted a house after both renting flats for a few years they decided that they wanted to buy something, something that was theirs. Paul had visited the house after they put in an offer and he had thought it adequate but from a personal point of view he never thought that he would be able to permanently live in a house with almost no garden.

The wedding took place outside Joan and Paul's family home in their fields behind the house. The wind was blowing gently through the decorations that were attached to the chairs. The cool breeze was a relief on such a hot day. The chairs were in two blocks with an aisle between them and four chairs to a row. There was a small stage at the front of the rows of chairs with a small painted arch, which was covered in a light blue chiffon material woven in between the trellis. The same chiffon material was wrapped messily around and the chairs to match the effect of the arch. There were a few flowers tied into the chiffon on both the chairs and the arch. It was designed by Joan, she was sceptical at first but after seeing some pictures of arrangements along the same idea as hers she was more confident. She still could have never imagined how good it would look. When Joan first saw it completed she was even more excited, it was just as she had dreamed it could be. The ceremony was performed early afternoon and there was an evening planned out with music and dancing. Paul sat on the side lines for that event not wanting to get involved. Joan had said he could bring Stella if he wanted to but for some reason he didn't want to or didn't get around to it, either way he was alone for most of the evening only talking to his cousin Jessie or his parents. As the night drew on he went up to his room and looked out at the open fields. The party below was winding down as some people had started to depart, others were staying the night in which the house was laden with camp beds for them to sleep on. Joan and Hugh were leaving to return to Bath, they had decided to keep the dramatic exit in their itinerary. Their honeymoon was going to be during the school Christmas holidays. It was taking them to the wintery landscapes of Scotland for a week, they had both wanted to go as children so decided to go together to live out their childhood dream. They laughed and joked about being snowed in a cottage that was in the middle of nowhere up a mountain or on the side of a hill. Paul didn't find their jokes very funny and continued to tell them how silly they were being but they just laughed more, something that Paul didn't understand. Paul did say goodbye to them before they left, once they were on their way the party continued for a while with those who were staying.

It was the end of the summer and Paul insisted that he went back to the university, now that Joan and Hugh had left he felt an empty feeling of being surrounded by strangers. His parents weren't happy at Paul's choice to go back to the university early. As much as they wanted him back there they didn't want him to go too. Even though Joan had moved out a long time ago, there was a new empty place in their hearts that they didn't want to get any bigger. They persuaded Paul to stay for a few more days, he didn't want to think about university much but the longer he stayed at home the more he thought about it and worried about it.

This year Paul had got a flat of his own and it made him very happy not having to share a hallway with the noise that trailed passed every night. He was now in the peace of a one room studio flat that was sat on the top of some garages accessed by a pair of external stairs. Paul didn't mind the noise of them opening and closing and the sound of people talking whilst finding whatever they needed in them. He was much more comfortable with completely his own space, he worried less as he didn't have to think about awkwardly saying 'good morning' to his neighbours as they passed each other in the hallway. His new flat was more like a small house to him it didn't feel like a flat at all. It was just him and some garages, at this point in time there was nothing better. There was no ground floor, first floor, second floor; only his floor.

It was decorated sparsely with few pieces of furniture, but Paul didn't see the point in putting loads in there because in one years' time he could be moving elsewhere. He had planned to go back home after he had finished his degree but his parents explained that he needed to get a job. The holes that they felt when both their children flew the nest had miraculously filled. They had discovered the freedom of retirement, they were happy if their children visited them but not to have them back their full time.

Paul hadn't thought much about applying for jobs or where he wanted to work or live. Whether he wanted to stay in Oxford or go elsewhere. There seemed like endless possibilities, too many for Paul to consider. He decided to shut himself off from the thoughts and the worries of something that was a year away. He was told to start thinking early about his future, but it worried him so much. To him it wasn't worth destroying his happiness in this moment, just to think about moments which could change was all too much for Paul. He couldn't risk being overwhelmed more than he was going to be as he entered this placement year.

42

June 2005, Twenty One Years Old

Paul flicked through some jeans they were all horrible, to him anyway. They had rips in the legs and were all baggy. He didn't really want to try them on but Stella persuaded him to. Paul was uncomfortable doing this 'cat walk model walk' act but he put up with it smiling through. Stella began to get excited and ran around the shop picking up almost one of every item for Paul to try on. She was constantly passing items of clothing over the top of the changing room for Paul to try on, he stared at a few of them. Once he had shown Stella a few of the outfits, all of which she had loved, Paul changed back into his clothes and emerged with the hangers dangling from his fingers and loose clothes draped over his shoulders.

"But you didn't even try these ones on." Stated Stella holding a couple of the items up.
"They didn't fit." Replied Paul trying not to let on that he was lying and hadn't even tried them on
Stella shrugged her shoulders, "I could have found the right sizes."
"It is lunchtime now anyway." Replied Paul handing all the clothes to the changing room attendant who was now swamped in a shower of colourful colours.
"You have got to update your look." Said Stella when she realised that he wasn't going to buy any of the clothes that she had picked out for him "You can't keep wearing the same shirts, beige trousers and knitted jumper."

They ate lunch at Stella's favourite restaurant, it was a sushi restaurant and Paul was sure that maybe she liked it but he certainly did not. He didn't like fish for a start let alone raw fish, Stella told him that it was different to cook fish and he *would* like it. The final straw was the cold clumps of rice that lay beneath the thin slithers of grey meat. Paul got up from his seat and walked out of the restaurant without a word. Stella just rolled her eyes and continued to eat her food.

Paul stood outside the door of the restaurant not sure where he was going to go, but he did know that there was a large library and felt that he really wanted to lose himself. Reading a book or two was the way to do it. He found a small corner in the library at the intersection of some shelving units of novels. There was a tartan tub chair on its own with a small table next to it and a table lamp placed on top. He hadn't read a novel before but had heard that they could be so interesting that one becomes engrossed in the story. He looked at the different ones on the shelves and none of them appealed to him. He decided that picking one at random, no matter how uncomfortable it made him feel, was the right way to go. He placed his hand on the shelves and ran his hand up and down the books a few times before he picked one out of the many. He started to read it and finished it by the time the library was closing, he shut the book and placed it back on the shelf.

"Didn't you want to borrow it?" Asked the librarian who had noticed that he was reading it earlier.
"I finished it." He replied.
The librarian was a bit surprised that he could have read such as large book in a short time but accepted it, "Did you enjoy it?"
"It was ok." He replied "I prefer the non-fiction books, anyway I didn't think I would understand it."
"Do you now?" She said turning off the desk lamps "Next time you can read some of those then."
"No thank you I have probably read them all before." Replied Paul not meaning to sound arrogant.
"There are hundreds of books yet to discover." Replied the librarian smiling "If you enjoy the non-fiction books then I am sure if you look hard enough there will be one that you have overlooked."

Paul smiled appreciatively and left the warmth of the library. It was dark outside but was brightly lit with the street lamps, so

R.V. Turner

Paul didn't mind so much. He thought of all the books that he had read as a child and thought whether he should have saved them for when he was an adult, but realised that the librarian was probably right. There were a lot of books left to read. He began to get excited again, he hadn't read a book on science or geography since he decided to focus on music but maybe now he could give them another go. He traipsed back through the centre of the city towards his flat, he smiled when it came into view. Climbing the stairs carefully, he opened the door to the dark flat to which he responded immediately by turning on the lights.

43

September 2005, Twenty One Years Old

Paul wasn't at all looking forward to his placement year. He had two placements lined up, which were fortunately chosen by the university, saving him the stress of having to find them. On the other hand if he was given control he would have chosen 'Paul appropriate places' which may have been better for his anxiety, which he felt thinking about the year ahead. The placements were chosen by the university on the grounds that one would have what they decided were 'difficult to control children'. Paul's first placement was an 'excellent rated' upper school which appealed to Paul slightly. He had looked at the building and found his way around the school website this, one looked promising. The other he felt was less so, as it was a 'poor rated' middle school, which he wasn't looking forward to at all. Not only was the building run down making Paul question the cleanliness of the place, but most of all he didn't understand nine to twelve year olds. He found them too young and their ideas too different, it wasn't where he wanted to end up working and as it was his last placement he had the first half of the year to worry about it.

"You will be fine." Said Stella the day before Paul was due to start at the upper school "Anyway don't get too comfortable you have the middle school next."

She smiled giving him a friendly pat on the arm to show that she was joking, but Paul didn't read the signs and assumed that it was an insult. He didn't bother asking for clarification on what she meant, so he didn't say anything and instead stared down into an unappetising bowl of pasta. They were eating lunch in the university cafeteria, majority of the students were more than happy with the food that was served there. Paul was disgruntled at every little thing and was never happy eating it, but wouldn't have wanted to have to cook for himself and pulling a face he bore through it. Stella sat for a while watching him analyse his food, but she soon got bored of his silence. She left Paul thinking about whatever it was that was going on inside his head, and honestly she didn't want to or couldn't be bothered to find out what Paul and his brain were talking about. Paul wasn't even aware that she had left until he had finished the last mouthful of his meal and looked up for the first time since he started eating. He casually looked around and discovered that he was alone. He wasn't bothered about being alone, not now anyway he was used to his friends leaving him.

He stayed in the library for the rest of the day, not having any lectures to go to, he wanted to keep his brain active and instead of worrying he poured himself into his books. He wandered the long way back to his flat by himself, when he left the university library the sun was just beginning to settle in the sky slowly drifting down. It was dark when he eventually got to his flat, since he meandered along at a slow pace. He didn't really want to stop walking, he found that it helped him think in all the good ways, and knew that when he went inside and sat down all the worry would take control of him again. He looked at his flat with less than positive eyes, it looked very uninviting to him now. He was aware that he had spent many nights happily watching something on TV or reading a book but now it seemed cold and empty. He was tired though, and without turning on the lights he went straight to the bed and laid on it. He was only meant to lay there for a while before he was going to get up and change in his pyjamas but before he knew it, morning had awoken him. His body clock must have kicked in as it was 08:00, the usual time that he would have set his alarm clock for. He was confused when he woke not remembering what day it was or where he was meant to be going, but soon the memories of the placement flooded back to him. He sighed laying his head on his pillow one last time before he slid out of bed. He showered before he changed into a smart grey suit with a matching tie. He carefully combed his blonde ginger hair flat just before he picked up his brief case, which was neatly packed with stationary and a few snacks just in case he got hungry. He was reluctant to leave the safety of his flat which now in the daylight looked more inviting and comforting to him. Nevertheless he built up what little courage he had left and stepped outside.

The upper school was in the centre of the city close to the most affluent areas. There were large houses all along the streets and there was even a gated community all prepared with large gardens and garages. Paul wandered up the street, he wasn't a money orientated person but he did enjoy looking at the modern architecture as he meandered slowly passed. Around the next corner he came up to the school's front gates they were large, blue and wide open creating a very welcoming feel. The upper school had been built fairly recently, it was modern much like the houses just outside it. Paul looked upon it and smiled, he was trying to give himself confidence but wasn't sure whether it was working. He found the reception easily as there were many signs pointing him in the right direction. He was conscious of the fact that as he spoke to the receptionist his voice began to wobble and he felt his palms sweating. He was greeted by the headmaster who shook his hand eagerly before showing him into the classroom of the teacher that he would be assisting. Paul was set up with a temporary desk in the corner of the room whilst the teacher's desk remained at the front. It was neatly placed so that he could observe what the teacher was doing and saying and understand the reactions of the students to the lessons. Paul was very happy with the position of his desk, he would rather have observed the whole time than get involved but he knew that this wouldn't be the case. Paul was introduced to some of the teachers who he would be working closely with. Most of them seemed very happy that he was there, the others turned their noses up as if a student teacher wasn't good enough for *their* school. Paul didn't notice this he strongly believed that he deserved a chance at trying to achieve his goals, absentmindedly he believed that everyone else thought this too.

The class seemed pleasant, the majority of them accepted him as a teacher not questioning his teaching methods in the slightest.

They listened to everything that he said and completed the tasks just as Paul had designed them. He was pleased with the progress that he was making, and one of the teachers told him what a good job he was doing. Paul beamed with proudness something he hadn't felt in a long time and he found that he could finally say.

"Yes I *can* do this."

It was a relief to his family when Paul explained to them what a good time he was having teaching. They were worried about him still, thinking that Paul wasn't very happy at university but as Paul began to feel like a teacher he began to believe in himself. His family were proud of him, he had changed his frame of mind towards not only teaching but learning also. He was excited to learn more about music so that he could then teach his students to become well rounded in the subject. He spent time planning his lessons and thinking about what he could teach the students in the parameters he was given. He wanted to tailor their learning so that they could all have the best chance in achieving what they wanted to achieve.

For part of his degree Paul was meant to keep a diary of the progress that he was making, what he was teaching the students and what he himself had learnt. However since he had begun teaching he had forgotten all about it. He had forgotten that he was even doing a degree and that he wasn't a fully qualified teacher yet; just as some of the other teachers kept reminding him. Paul wasn't dissuaded by their words. He knew that he could teach, and he could tell that the headmaster and the teacher that he was assisting thought that too. He didn't understand why the other teachers were not giving him the chance that he deserved. He pondered this whilst he and Stella sat outside one of Stella's favourite cafés in the city. It was the weekend and Stella was excited to show Paul the café so had asked him to come with her, fully expecting him to say no. Paul, with his new found confidence said yes, but as soon as he got there he wanted to go home. It was packed with people and there wasn't anywhere to sit at first, and they had to wait whilst other customers finished. Before the waiters or waitresses even had the chance to clean the table Stella pounced upon the next available one. The weather outside was beautiful which gave Paul some inspiration to try and enjoy himself. He watched as the perfectly formed clouds drifted over the iridescent blue sky. It glistened like the sea did when the sun rays bounced off of the waves.

44

February 2006, Twenty One Years Old

Paul never understood the phrase 'you can do it' the teachers at school would always tell him this, in reference to sports particularly, but whenever he questioned the teachers on the use of the phrase they would simply say that you should tell people they can. They thought it was encouraging to him, when inside it made him feel like a failure even when he knew and had understood that he couldn't. It made him think about Mrs Summers and how she didn't like this expression either. Paul hadn't thought of her in years and smiled when he did. She would always understand him and always treat him as if he was an individual with a unique way of thinking, whereas the others would try to get him to do all the things that all the other students 'could do'.

"But what if you can't?" He would asked them.
"But you always can." They would say "You just have to believe in yourself."
"I get more frustrated when people say you can, when you believe you can't and nobody asks you why." Paul would reply.

He would try to tell them that it wasn't *him* to go to academic competitions and it wasn't as if he didn't believe in himself, but he didn't want to put all his self-worth into something that could tear him apart if someone else told him that he wasn't as smart as he thought he was.

More importantly this was what jumped around his mind when a student stated, "I can't do this sum."
"Why?" Asked Paul he had always wanted to teach how he would have liked to have been taught and he would have always have

liked to have been asked why he couldn't do something.
"Because the numbers jump around." Replied the student.

Paul understood immediately that this was more than a student who couldn't be bothered to do his work and he knew without the proper assistance the student couldn't, and the student believed this too. It was more than the fact that the music lesson that Paul was teaching was too hard for the students. Majority of the students struggled with the theory lessons, all they wanted to do was to mess around with the instruments. All the students were learning to play the guitar, Paul had asked them to match the chord with diagrams of the fingering positions on the fret board. He had numbered each of the frets and each of the strings to make it easier for the students, although this didn't help this particular student. Paul had explained the task carefully and simply to the student before the student expressed that he understood the task but he couldn't do it.

"Why do the numbers jump?" Asked Paul.
"They just don't seem to stay in the right place." Replied the student "When I try to work out sums and stuff they just don't stay in the same place."
"Do you have any difficulty reading words?" Asked the other teacher who had overheard the conversation.
"No." Replied the student "Just numbers."

The lesson was over and both Paul and the teacher were thinking about the student.

"I am glad that someone else asks why too." Said Paul randomly.

The teacher didn't really understand what Paul was talking about so just kindly smiled at him. The teacher liked Paul and knew that he would become a good teacher as he understood the working minds of the students and tried to help them as the unique individuals that they were. The student was assessed by the SENCO coordinator at the school. Later he was given a referral and after months with the consultant he was diagnosed with number dyslexia. After that the teachers never told him 'you can' they told him that his best was good enough, and whatever he couldn't do to ask the teacher and someone would help him. He was brighter in his personality and smiled more, he was getting somewhere and it gave him hope. He was no longer going to be ignored by the teachers and he could tell the teachers why he was struggling and they would understand, whereas before they would have simply told him to 'try again'.

"It is a shame really that we have to have labels before we get noticed or believed." Said Paul.

45

March 2006, Twenty Two Years Old

It was soon time for Paul to move on to his next placement, the middle school. Strangely he had become attached to the upper school and the time that he was there flew by and every moment that he was there he knew that he was a teacher.

Paul knew where the middle school was but tried to avoid it as much as possible, it was a rundown area outside of the city, he didn't like to discriminate but it didn't appeal to him. He walked into the reception on the first day. The reception area was in a desperate need of redecoration, and he could tell that the reception staff were doing all they could to ensure that the area looked inviting and as clean as possible. He was greeted by the headmaster who smiled genuinely at him as he showed him around. He was introduced to any member of staff that they came across and then, more in depth introductions were conducted with all the staff he would be working closely with. They all were interested in asking him about his course and how he felt about working in a school for the first time.

Paul tried to answer honestly but felt his public personality coming over him and soon he was chatting as if he talked to people all the time. He wondered why the school was given a rating of poor, but then he met the students. They shouted in the class all the time and refused to listen to what the teacher was saying, let alone listen to Paul who struggled in getting his voice heard. Paul's confidence dropped during the first few weeks he was ready to give up. There was one boy who stood out to all of the teachers as the boy who seemed to want to listen and learn. Paul had noticed that he had a talent for music but because of the other rowdy students in the class he never got the chance to pursue it. During one of the practical lessons Paul quizzed the boy on how much he liked music and if he wanted to learn an instrument. The boy said how he did like music lessons but his parents couldn't afford them. Paul was certain that he could get the lessons he wanted without having to buy them himself.

"Is there a piano teacher who comes to the school?" Asked Paul when the class was over.
"Sure there is but not many students take the lessons." Replied the teacher wiping the notes off the white board.
"Why?" Asked Paul.
"They don't seem to be interested in them even the ones who could afford it." Replied the teacher.
"That isn't very fair." Replied Paul.
"No, but not everything is fair even if we want it to be." Said the teacher turning around "This is about Harry isn't it?"

Paul nodded he explained how Harry wanted to learn an instrument, and with the piano he could buy a keyboard rather than an expensive instrument if he wanted to. Even so a piano would be provided for when he had lessons, and he wouldn't have to pay to hire an expensive instrument to practice at home.

"I know." Said the teacher thoughtfully "However it isn't possible if he can't afford it."
"Can't he be subsidised by the school?" said Paul trying to figure out some way that the student could take the lessons that he wanted so much.
"I suppose." Replied the teacher "If you talk to the head he might allow such a thing."

Paul went straight to the headmaster's office and knocked on the door. The doors too were in a state of disrepair as at the corners the paint was peeling off, and the handles looked as if they had been tarnished for years. Paul was invited into the headmaster's office which was small and smelt a little damp, Paul explained the predicament to the headmaster.

"There must be some sort of help he can get." Paul exclaimed.
"I will talk to the piano teacher, if there is promise in him as you

say, then she might agree to take him on a lower rate if he is that eager." Replied the headmaster.

Paul left the office with some feeling of success and hoped that the piano teacher would agree to a certain subsidised payments, or payments in instalments just anything so that the student can at least try to have music lessons.

A few days later Paul was asked to go back to the headmaster's office, Paul felt like he was back in school again. Paul was smiling when he came out he had succeeded in his quest. The headmaster had spoken to both the piano teacher and the parents of the student and all agreed that a subsidised amount was the best option. The student was excited when he was told a smile spread across his face, as if the world had just opened up new possibilities and chances. He thanked Paul but Paul said that it was headmaster who did all the work.

"Paul it was you who saw promise in that student." Started the headmaster "It was you who achieved this for him I just helped you along the way."

Paul smiled through the whole story when he relayed it back to Stella. He had made someone feel something and it made him feel good.

"I knew you could do it." Said Stella smiling "I am proud of you, and you said that you wouldn't like it."
"I didn't much." Replied Paul "However even if it was all to help that one student it was worth it."

Paul truly believed what he had said about that one student, he felt he had really made a difference. The student now had the choice to try and that was all that mattered to Paul whether he makes it as a concert pianist or plays it for fun.

46

June 2006, Twenty Two Years Old

The concrete beneath their feet was heating up, Paul shifted his weight. It was as if he could feel the molecules in the solid moving, in the excitement of the warmth. The beginning of summer brought a heat wave causing most of the students to abandon their classrooms for the outside air, hoping that a cool breeze would wash over them. Stella and Paul were standing near the apple tree that shaded a bench that was full of people. They stood there for a while, Paul refusing to move on to find another place to sit.

"But we always sit here." Stated Paul as he noticed that there was no room for them.
"Never mind we can sit on the grass over there." Said Stella motioning to a small patch of ground that was free from notebooks or lunch boxes.
"But we always sit here." Repeated Paul stamping his foot like a child.
"It is fine Paul we can sit somewhere else." Said Stella trying to calm her voice.
"But I want to sit here." Said Paul firmly.
"You can't sit there!" Exclaimed Stella annoyed "Why do you have to always do this?"
"Do what?" Replied Paul innocently.
Stella huffed and threw her arms in the air, "You always have to act like a child when you are twenty two Paul! It is time that you started to act like it."

Paul was silent, he turned his head to the side and fidgeted his hands, he wasn't sure what he should do. Every bone in his body told him that they always sat on that bench and there was no alternative.

"You never listen to me either." Continued Stella all of her anger was beginning to come out at once, as if it had been brewing for the four years that they had been at university "I tell you things that I wouldn't tell anyone else and you ignore every single one of them. I don't understand how you don't care about the person who has cared about you for the past four years."

Paul had listened but he wasn't sure what his reaction should be, he knew that she was angry and didn't know how he should deal with it. He just wanted to change the subject, he didn't like confrontation.

"Are you coming to my graduation?" He asked.
"No." She started she had passed the point of caring most of the time she would shrug her shoulders and move on, not this time "I am not coming to your stupid graduation and I don't want you there at mine either."

She didn't feel the need to say anymore she had a glaze over her eyes, but only a glaze. Turning away from Paul she walked passed the patch of ground which had now been taken by other students. She headed for the main building leaving Paul watching as the clouds drew away from the sun to let its rays dance upon everything on the earth.

Paul was unsure about Stella's actions and decided that the best thing was to stop thinking about it. He walked away from the spot where they were stood, around the old cloisters that were sheltered from the sun and he sat there in the shadow. He sat with his knees pressed tightly together and his hands clasped in his lap. His blonde ginger hair had become long over the summer term as he had not gone back home to have it cut. It had grown slight waves but was still neat and pressed down as flat as it would go, but somehow it just kept springing back up again. He sat in the cloister until the shadows had grown long and dark. The sun had gone in and the cool night air had taken over from the hot humid day. He got up and stood up straight and with his fists gently clenched he walked back to his room with them swinging by his

R.V. Turner

side.

47

July 2006, Twenty Two Years Old

He heard his name being announced, it sounded like an echo from a dream. A dream that he could only just remember but became a muddled blur as he remembered more and more of it. Seconds passed before he realised that he was meant to go up on the stage. He stood up from his seat quickly and awkwardly before walking up to the stage. His hands were clammy and he kept scrunching them up as he climbed the oak stair case to the top of the stage. The announcer moved away allowing him to take the stand and say his speech. He stood in front of the lectern touching at the papers, which had already been placed there, with his fingers. He wiped his hands on his trousers over the pockets before starting. He didn't think that he would be nervous, he never had been before when speaking to a crowd, but now he was there he felt an anxiety that he had never felt before. It took over him as he looked out across all the faces that were looking back at him. As he spoke he felt his voice shaking, he looked down at his notes and all they were was smears of words and letters. He didn't know what to say as the letters jumbled up before him. He flicked his eyes from the audience to his notes before deciding that he could make up something new. He would make up something new.

"I came here four years ago and when I did I was, I was." He paused trying to find the right word "I was different. People didn't like it because I challenged their ideas and came up with my own. I believed I was right and I still believe I am right because that is what we should do. Believe in ourselves. That is the most valuable thing that I have learnt here. That I shouldn't care what people think of me, but I do. I shouldn't worry about it, if they don't like my ideas, but I do. I stand here before you and wonder if I had followed the crowd, who would remember my name. Who would say they knew what I liked or what I was like. It would be unlikely that even a quarter of you would know me at all. I enjoyed my time here, but I am happy to move on and leave this and all of you behind me."

His speech didn't go in the direction that he had written it, but he hoped that it made a difference to the faces that were looking at him. He turned away from the lectern before remembering something and he turned back just to say, "You live in a small white cottage on the edge of a little village in Wales. You have a brother and you live with your parents but you want to move out and live in a city where you can discover how good you really are. I have seen your art and I love it and think that everyone else should too. You twirl your hair with your fingers when you are nervous or don't know what to say next. You would like a dog but don't like to go for walks. You love to read but have never finished a book. I want to thank you for looking after me when I was acting like a child, I am sorry but I can't help it. It is who I am and will always be and I hope there are other people who are willing to help me like you. You once told me 'you just have to believe that you will do something and you will do it.' I didn't believe you then but I am trying to. I do remember things about you and I do listen. I just wanted to let you know." By the end of his speech he was in tears his words stuttered and slurred as he tried to find the right words but didn't know if he had. He was thanked by the announcer and Paul walked down the steps back to his seat where his sister was sitting.

"I want to go home now." Said Paul to his sister before he carried on walking to the doors at the end of the hall. Joan followed him out and noticed that the rest of the faces were looking at him once more before he exited the hall.

"Who was that for?" Asked his sister not understanding who his heartfelt speech was aimed at.
"For Stella." Replied Paul he had stopped crying for the most part and his voice stayed monotone.
"I didn't think she was coming." Replied Joan not understanding.
"She didn't." Replied Paul.

"Then why did you say that?" She asked confused.
"Because I just wanted to let her know." He replied vaguely "That's all."

Joan realised that it would be no use asking anymore questions. They left the campus with the sun burning above it and the dry ground cracking under it. The sky was a light blue and the flowers by the entrance door smelled as sweet as they always did and as they walked out into the air Paul noticed it for the first time.

48

December 2006, Twenty Two Years Old

"You really must get a job Paul." Stated his mother who was trying to dust around her son who was sat on the sofa staring into empty space.

Paul said nothing. His mother was getting impatient with his constant moping ever since he left university back in the summer. It was almost Christmas time and there were chances of snow on the horizon. It was a weekend but every day now seemed the same for Paul, they all seemed to merge into the next and the next.

"You left University over five months ago. You need to at least start looking for a job." She threw him the local newspaper in hope that would give him some incentive to start looking "You have trained to be a music teacher so go and find a position or a placement just something!"

The newspaper landed on Paul's lap open with the pages folded under each other. Paul weakly lifted it off of his lap and carefully placed it in the space next to him. His mother was fuming and slammed the door on her way out of the lounge. For a moment Paul kept his stare and then he looked over at the newspaper. He knew he needed to look for something as much as he didn't want to, he thought that if he looked and said that he hadn't found anything then his mother would stop nagging him.

"Find a different job Paul. It doesn't have to be a music teacher it can be a piano teacher." Said his mother.
"You need training for that." Retorted Paul.

"Then get it." His mother was being firm "Next Saturday I am taking you down the job centre if you don't find something on your own."

Paul defiantly did not want to go to the job centre. One of Joan's friends went there to ask about jobs in events planning and ended up working for a supermarket. Not exactly the road that she was expecting to go down. Paul was now sure that he could find something on his own and he had a week to do it.

Monday came and his parents both left for work. Paul had the house to himself he took a deep breath and opened the top of his laptop. He only used the job site that Joan had used and he only looked at jobs in either Oxford, Bath or Cornwall, the places that he knew. Most of the jobs were in places that he hadn't been before, and there were only a few jobs going in the town. He was stuck, there wasn't anything that he wanted to do it was all administration assistance, experience required or cashiers, experience required or waiters, experience required. It seemed like an impossible task. Reluctantly he picked up the phone and dialled a number.

"Can I speak to Linus please?" He asked.
"Can I say who is calling?" Asked the lady on the other end of the phone, luckily it wasn't Sally who answered.

After Paul had said his name and explained that he had done work experience eight years before hand she was happy to put him through. Linus answered the phone with his usually happy tone and to Paul's surprise he remembered him and the fiasco with Sally.

"You will be happy to know that Sally has retired bless her." He said before asking about Paul and what he had been up to.

Paul didn't usually like talking about himself he found it boring but he did it as he had learnt that social conventions state that people ask other people about their lives. After he had finished and Linus congratulated Paul on passing all of his University exams, Paul asked about the music school.

"Yes it is all going well thank you." He started "You play piano don't you?"

"Piano, violin, cello and flute." Replied Paul not meaning to sound precocious.

"Well we don't have a need for violin, cello or flute teacher but we do have an opening for a piano teacher if you are available?" Stated Linus.

"Ironically that is the reason that I called." Said Paul not believing what he was hearing "Although I have a music degree I don't know how to teach."

"You are a music teacher aren't you?" Questioned Linus.

"It is very different from teaching a specific instrument." Explained Paul.

"I know Paul I was only joking." Laughed Linus "There are training courses that we can send you on and for now you can come in and shadow the current teachers. Hopefully you can pick something up from them."

Paul thanked him and asked the only question that came into his head, "When do I start?"

"You can come in tomorrow if you want." Said Linus "Our music teachers work on a self-employed basis. There is a contract that you would need to sign but other than that you would work for yourself and would be able to take on private clients if you wanted. The correct qualifications are needed though so don't start this until you have them!"

"Do I get paid?" Asked Paul bluntly.

This made Linus laugh even more and he chortled when he explained to Paul that once he was qualified he would get paid. Paul was pleased with himself when he finally put down the phone. He was excited to tell his parents. Although he shouldn't have told them in an 'I don't know why you were bugging me about getting a job because I got one easy' tone as this made his parents a little less proud of him, nevertheless they were happy that he would be getting out of the house.

"I can take you in when I go to work and your father can pick you up." Said his mother.

"Or you can learn to drive." Replied his father taking a sip of his tea.
"We will talk about that later." Defended his mother "For now this should work fine. I know you are not getting paid yet but at least you are getting some experience."

The following day he was dropped outside the music school. It was half term so there were a lot more lessons packed into the day. Even though Paul knew this he wasn't expecting that many people to turn up. Most of them were young children who were running around with instruments strapped on their backs or sheet music held in their hands. Most were accompanied by their parents in some way either dropping them off or picking them up but once inside the music school, they were let loose. Paul was met by Linus who introduced him to Sam who was one of the piano teachers.

"We also use Freya but you will meet her later on." Explained Linus.

Paul felt a bit awkward as he squeezed into the small sound proofed practice room along with the student and Sam. Paul tried his best to listen to what was going on but the room was too small and he was beginning to feel claustrophobic. He tried so hard to suppress his nervous laughter and his anxiety, that he missed most of what was said in the lesson which lasted an hour but felt like years to Paul.

"That was a bit of an advanced lesson so I don't know if it was helpful or not." Explained Sam "Freya usually teaches the beginners so I think that you would be better off sitting in on her lessons."
"Ok." Agreed Paul quietly he found Linus and explained this to him.
"Don't take any notice of Sam." He said "He thinks that he is the greatest pianist in the world."
"Does he?" Questioned Paul not really understanding "That is very unlikely."
Linus laughed, "You are funny Paul."

Freya was calmer and more relaxed than Sam putting Paul a bit more at ease. She was happy for Paul to sit in on the lessons. The practice room that she used was a bit larger and there were a few more chairs for Paul to choose from. The student was a primary school aged child and her mother also sat in on the lesson.

"I hope that this will give her confidence." Whispered the mother to Paul.
"Do you?" Questioned Paul not really wanting to chat and trying to listen to what Freya was saying
"Certainly, she said all her friends can do things and she is adamant that she isn't good at anything but she is. Anyway when I mentioned music lessons she seemed keen so here we are." Replied the mother.
"That is good." Said Paul.

"Sorry you were stuck with the mother." Said Freya after the lesson was over "She can chat a lot but this was the most productive lesson we have had, usually she is trying to pep talk her daughter even though she would be fine if her mother just sat in the corner of the room and let her get on with it, anyway did you learn much?"
"I suppose." Replied Paul "I couldn't really hear much with her jabbering."
Freya smiled, "Never mind there are a lot more lessons that you can sit in on."

There was a brief silence whilst Freya organised the different pieces of music that she had got out for the student to practice. Paul was stood up not really knowing what to do with himself.

"You can play the piano if you want." Said Freya not turning around from the shelf that she was placing some of the books on "It would be good to hear how you play."

Paul decided that he wouldn't correct her on her grammar and decided instead to take her up on the offer. It was where he knew he performed best, he didn't focus on the audience and tried to pretend that he was playing his piano at home.

"Wow." Said Freya turning around "You play better than I do!"
"No I don't." Replied Paul "You play very well."
"Aw thanks." Said Freya "You are sweet the next lesson is a more advanced student they are practicing for their grade two exam."

Paul laughed briefly.

"Yeah ok, I bet you passed all your exams by the time you were twelve." Said Freya "I have heard it all before you are one of those music prodigies. What other instruments can you play?"
"It was fourteen actually." Corrected Paul "I can only play the piano, violin, cello and flute."
"Yeah only." Repeated Freya rolling her eyes.

Paul stayed at the music school for the rest of the day sitting in on Freya's music lessons. She must have been almost thirty years old as she said that she had been teaching for almost ten years. It was the only job she had ever had and the only one she ever wanted. As she put it, it was the best job in the world.

"Teaching people to learn music?" She stated "Who wouldn't want to do that."

Paul's parents were pleased that he had enjoyed his first day. He wasn't sure whether he would like to teach piano for all his working life but he was up for finding out what it was like.

"Paul doesn't like people." Said Joan when she was told "How is he going to teach people he has no patience."
"Gee thanks." Replied Paul this time it was him rolling his eyes "I think that I will be good at it, it I have my grade eight distinction."
"I wonder who told me that grades didn't matter." Questioned Joan sarcastically "Just because you have grade eight doesn't mean that you are any better than someone who has been playing for years and doesn't have a grade to their name."
"I suppose but to become a piano teacher I need grade eight I am glad that I got it when I did." Said Paul "I couldn't go through that again."
"Nervousness is just a part of life Paul." Said Joan.
"I don't like it and I don't want to put myself in any position again

when I am anxious." Said Paul determined.

"Good luck on the training courses then." Said Joan "I guarantee that you will be nervous then and when you have your first independent piano lesson and if you ever find a job as a music teacher you are going to be nervous in all parts of life and you are never going to get used to it, you just need to accept it and try your best to think logically about the situation and remember to breathe."

Paul attended some of the training courses which showed him techniques that were useful to use when teaching people to play an instrument. Paul was surprised on how short the courses were and at the end of them he still wasn't sure whether he would be able to teach someone. There was a guide to follow which he found very useful, such as teaching scales first and technique rather than diving into a piece of music. It all seemed logical to Paul and as he thought about his piano lessons, he remembered how Mrs Round had taught him to play. Then again, Paul had already started to teach himself different pieces of music. It was scales and technique that he needed to be taught really, and it was probably why he was most nervous about teaching those.

49

January 2007, Twenty Two Years Old

Joan and Hugh's first child was born on the 4th January at a hospital in Bath at 7am. The baby came into a world with the sun shining overhead and a boastful robin singing in the bush outside. Paul described the baby as 'icky' and 'wrinkly' when he first saw her and then the tears came. From the baby not Paul. That was the last straw the little tears rolling down the dumpy little cheeks wasn't something that Paul could cope with. Loud noises weren't his thing and he decided that he would be better off standing in the hallway. Hugh was in hysterics as he greeted everyone who passed by with the news of a baby girl. Little baby Sara was greeted home for the first time later that day and hadn't stopped crying since. Joan was already trying not to bury herself in the sofa in a desperate attempt to block out the noise, and Hugh was sitting on one of the breakfast bar stools with a blank expression on his face. His arms were dangling in his lap and his mouth was slightly open.

They managed to both fall asleep where they were sitting, as Sara had decided that she was bored of crying and had settled. The new parents were woken up to a loud noise coming from the cot in the corner of the room, it was 2am at least they had slept for two hours. Paul didn't understand the fuss when he came down from upstairs, he had slept wonderfully with his sound proof headphones on. He was staying with them again, mainly because he didn't want to have to go back home with his parents who came up as soon as the baby arrived. It was the weekend and so it was not a work day and he wanted to make the most of it. He decided to give Sara another chance and found her sleeping softly on her back on a large dog pillow. Paul pointed a finger and was about to prod the baby when Joan exclaimed for him to stop.

"She has been there all morning." Whispered Joan.
"That is very un-hygienic." Said Paul loudly waking up the baby who went to wailing again.
"That is the only place she will sleep." Said Joan quietly trying to get Paul to keep his voice down with a load of hand movements.
"But she is a newborn." Stated Paul as his statement posed both the question and the answer.

Paul decided that it was ok to prod the newborn now and poked her lightly just below the chest. She stopped wailing, confused probably, and looked at her Uncle.

"There." He started "Easy."

He walked away from the dog bed that was placed on the end of the sofa for Hugh's small beagle, who was more than surprised when he found a small baby in his bed. Camble was a smart dog really, he just liked to pretend that he wasn't. Paul would spend hour's dog sitting and wouldn't be able to teach him one trick but Sara could make him sit just by existing. When Camble got used to the idea of Sara he would sit by the dog bed as a guard whilst Sara was there. When it came to the time to place her in the cot he would trot by Joan or Hugh, who would carry her to the little bed where he would sit until he got kicked out by his owners. The cot was moved to their bedroom which Camble originally was banned from, but somehow he managed to stay in there until his owners were ready to go to bed.

"I liked your dog better when he wasn't obedient with me rather than him be obedient with her." Said Paul pointing at the baby who was asleep once more.

50

April 2007, Twenty Three Years Old

Paul had grown more confident in teaching students to play the piano. He was a little awkward at the start and definitely stuttered too much, but he got to understand the nervousness that students felt when they arrive for their first music lesson. Most of the students were still in first school although Paul said that he preferred to teach older students, he found it a greater achievement when their faces lit up when they managed to play a scale correctly for the first time. He had been working at the music school for a while when a position came up at a school in Oxford. Paul was both pleased and disappointed at the same time. His parents were pleased and not just because if he got the job they wouldn't have to take him to work every day. They encouraged him to apply even though he was reluctant, he filled out an application form and emailed it. His application was sent days before the closing date for the position, he was very indecisive of whether or not he should apply and the final moments of pressure ensured him that he had to. A few days later he received an email he looked at it with a frown.

"I am happy with my job do I really have to change now?" Questioned Paul.
"There comes a point where you are in a job and you are comfortable with it all the people you work with are nice and everything is the way that you like it." Started his mother "Sometimes you just have to take the risk and go for something to challenge yourself to make you feel a sense of satisfaction when you complete something and achieve what you never thought that you could, sometimes you just need to go for it."

"I get a sense of achievement from teaching students to play the piano." Retorted Paul.

His mother didn't get the recognition that she was expecting for her heartfelt and motivational speech. She had spent many times thinking about Paul's future and how she could help him to understand spontaneity and for him to feel what he wanted rather than think it out logically.

"Paul you just need to get your own life." She stated frustrated "You need to live on your own somewhere, where you can start a life of your own, where you can discover how the rest of us get along with life!"

51

June 2007, Twenty Four Years Old

"You'll do great." Said his sister straightening his tie just before she left him in front of the large upper school that loomed over him, it was intimidating making him feel more nervous than he already was.

Paul wanted to, but was somehow unable to believe his sisters encouraging words as he walked into the interview. He looked at Joan briefly before walking into the reception and thinking how he had decided that he was never going to put himself in a position to make him anxious again. Yet here he was feeling the nervous energy running through him and no matter how steadily or deeply he breathed the feelings would not be dissuaded to leave. He mumbled the words when he told the receptionist who he was there to see. She didn't seem too impressed with him but completed the request without complaint. The receptionist took him to the meeting room which was very close to the reception desk. The room was small and plain looking there was only a desk and some chairs. He looked straight ahead of him and there were two menacing looking people staring at him as he was led into the room. They both rose from their seats simultaneously, each shaking Paul's hand in turn. They all sat down and started to talk. They asked him different questions like 'why do you think that you are suited for this job?' and 'why did you want to become a teacher?' just all the typical questions. Paul tried to answer them the best he could but struggled to hide his nervousness, but they didn't seem to mind they had probably seen it before. He did start to ease as they seemed like pleasant people they talked to him like he was a person worthwhile of them taking their time to get to know. He still felt anxious when he left the interview but he did have a feeling of achievement especially when his sister said that he would have done the very best he could under the pressure.

Paul hadn't told Aunt Bess about the interview, both Paul and his parents wanted to keep it quiet from her as she would usually say something totally unhelpful. But Joan let it slip when they were eating dinner the Saturday after Paul's first interview.

"What job is this?" asked Aunt Bess munching a carrot loudly.
"A music teacher." Replied Paul proudly with a big grin on his face he really was hopeful that he would get the job and every time he thought of working at that school, he smiled.

She scoffed, her own children had gone on to be what she called 'proper respectable jobs' neither Joan or Paul listened to what she had to say about work. It was a relief to their parents that they didn't, as if their children had listened they may have given up on their dreams altogether. Paul looked at Aunt Bess' pouty, wrinkly face that showed her disapproval of him, Paul didn't care. Life is what he wants now, whether she approved of him or not.

Paul was invited back for a second interview, he was proud that he had made the shortlist but anxious about the next interview. It wasn't like his interview for University and seemed more complicated. He had to teach a ten minute lesson with preparation that he had done before hand. Even though he had worked on placements nothing would compare to the real thing and the fact that everything that he had worked for up to this point, rested on fifteen year olds. Nervous doesn't really describe how he felt as he stepped in front of the group of twenty five year ten's. He could feel his legs wobbling beneath him and his palms were becoming sweaty and as he wrote on the white board, the pen began to slip around in his hand. He did have some connection with the class even if Paul didn't notice it, they were all quiet and listening to him. None of them even giggled when he dropped the pen on the floor, it almost gave him an eerie feeling as if they were silently judging him. He got them to do a quick task on genres of music by getting them to work in groups. They seemed to enjoy that; their books were closed and there was no copying off of the board to do.

He had a good feeling once his lesson was over and the students seemed to have enjoyed it, so he was happy. The Director of Music and the Director of HR both sat in on the lesson in the end Paul ignored them and got on with the way he would like to teach. Afterwards he met the headmistress who seemed to like the way Paul talked about music and teaching. He talked and talked about why he was interested about music and why he wanted to teach. She could tell that he was really passionate about it, whereas Paul just thought that he rambled on too much about irrelevant details.

He was ecstatic when he received a phone call from the Director of HR offering him the position, permanently. His smile was carried with him for days afterwards, until the contract was mailed to him and the realisation of his commitment began to seep in. The upper school was in Oxford which was fine in some respect because he had lived there before and knew the city fairly well. Although, he would have to live there by himself, in a flat all of his own. He smiled to himself when he said the words 'by himself' in his head, what more could he want? Since that thought entered his worried brain the nervousness and doubt went away and he began to feel excited. He did remember what his mother said about just going for it, and somehow it didn't seem logical to leave everything that you were comfortable with to go after something that may not work out. But he wanted to take her positive point of view on this, no matter how hard it was for him.

"Just remember you get the holidays off so you can come back to visit." Said his mother as Paul started to sign the thoroughly read contract.
"I will have lesson preparation to do." Said Paul not looking up from the document as he dated it.
"Surely you must have some time?" Questioned his mother.
"Maybe." Replied Paul vaguely as he held up the document proudly.

His mother thought that it was her pushing Paul away that made him not want to come back for the holidays, but Paul didn't cope very well with the constant changing of accommodation when he was at University and he wanted to have somewhere where he knew where he was, and his routine didn't constantly change.

That place would have to be wherever he ended up living in Oxford that is what he thought anyway.

He posted off all the necessary details to the school and confirmation of receipt was sent by email a couple of days afterwards meaning that Paul was all set. He just needed to find somewhere to live and to him, it didn't seem that hard. Whereas his family knew how picky he was and were preparing themselves for the frustrating times ahead.

52

July 2007, Twenty Four Years Old

Joan and Hugh had offered to take Paul to look at flats and realising that it would take some time booked two hotel rooms. They wanted to find one soon as the job started in September which only gave them a few months to find something. If they looked at what was out there at least they would have an idea of what Paul could get for his money.

They wandered around a few flats that Paul said were 'acceptable' but none of them he really liked. He wanted a ground floor flat with the front door on the street, he didn't want to be in a large block of flats where there were a lot of other people. He wanted to pretend that it was a house rather than a flat. Hugh luckily spent so much time searching on the internet for flats for Paul, he felt as if he knew every corner of the city. He did find one place which he thought was perfect it took a lot of emails back and forth to the estate agent and finally they were booked in for a tour of the flat. As soon as Hugh showed Joan the picture of it she knew it was perfect. Paul did too and actually thanked Hugh for all his hard work, something Paul had never done before.

"The bathroom isn't attached to the bedroom and the kitchen is separate from the lounge. The front door opens upon the street and there are no stairs leading to the front door." Started Joan "There are small flower beds either side the path like grandma's house and there is a small open porch like our house."
"Hearing you say it sounds even more perfect." Said Paul clasping his hands together turning to talk to the estate agent about the details.

R.V. Turner

Paul moved in two weeks before his job started, but he spent most of his time at either Joan's house or his parents. His whole plan of not messing up his routine didn't start off well, as he didn't really want to start living on his own, although he would never admit it. The thought of being by himself seemed perfect but in reality it was much different.

"But you are paying rent for an empty house!" Exclaimed his mother when he turned up on their door step once again "You shouldn't keep using a taxi either! We could come and collect you from the town."

She wasn't best pleased and felt like she should keep him waiting on the front porch. The rain had really started to come down hard now, and she knew that Paul didn't like the rain. She opened the door and let him in to the warmth of the house. She wanted Paul to visit but she didn't want him to get too comfortable as she knew that once he got settled he wouldn't want to move out again.

53

August 2007, Twenty Four Years Old

"They wouldn't have given you the job if they didn't like you." Encouraged his sister "You're amazing and don't let anyone try to tell you otherwise."

Paul played with a bit of paper that he had torn off of the side of some junk mail. He was sat in Joan's house with a mug of tea in front of him, untouched. Joan was stood up leaning against the worktop clutching her tea and sipping it every now and again. Their conversation was disjointed as Paul appeared to be deep in thought, when in actual fact he was trying to block thoughts from entering his head, without success.

"Come on." Said Joan "You are going to be fine you just need to stop worrying."
"It isn't that easy." Replied Paul shredding the paper in his hands and scattering it on the table top.
Joan gave him 'a look' and immediately Paul swept the mess into his hands and placed it in the bin.

He moped around for the most part of the day until his train arrived to take him down the country close enough to home, to catch the 144 bus to the edge of the town where his parents would collect him. He was pleased to go home in some respect, but his thoughts lingered with him for too long and tired him out. He was mentally exhausted and all he wanted to do was go to sleep, as he drifted off in the bright lights of the train it rushed through a tunnel and the darkness seeped into the carriage. He was awoken by the train conductor walking over to wake him up, to inform him that the train had reached the end of the line and was now unable to take him wherever it was he was going. Paul woke up not remembering where he was, when he realised he jumped out of his seat and was relieved to find that the train had retired in the right station. He quickly rushed off onto the platform as if he was afraid that the train would start moving again and take him elsewhere. He was beginning to think that he was lucky but as he reached the bus stop he looked at his watch under the light of the lamp post and realised that he had missed his bus. He stomped his foot hard on the concrete surface sending a ricochet up his leg causing it to ache briefly. He didn't know what to do now, it was a thirty minuet bus ride to the town and a twenty minuet ride to his house from there. If he called his parents now it would be an hour after his parents had got ready to collect him, but there was no other choice. They set off at 11pm Paul was cold, tired and a little scared as he sat on a bench under the bus shelter. He listened to music on his phone for a while but had to stop as his heightened senses meant that the music blurred with the outside noises, and Paul jumped every time the music changed volume. He couldn't relax so sat there looking around himself, 12am ticked on his watch and the street lamps all went out up and down the street. Now in complete darkness he looked up to the starless sky for some comfort that wasn't there. It felt like hours more, but was only a few minutes later, when his parents arrived and Paul ran to them.

"We had begun to worry that you weren't on board when you rang us." Said his mother as she hugged him over the back seat.

Paul smiled weakly and was so glad to be there with them, for once he couldn't think of anywhere else he would rather be. That was, until he was alone in his bedroom tucked in his warm sheets and snuggled down wanting to stay there forever.

54

September 2007, Twenty Four Years Old

His classroom was a large open space, he supposed for allowing the use of large instruments. There were two sound proof practice rooms opposite the door. Paul took his first tentative step over the threshold into the room. He stood awkwardly in the doorway with his fists clenched and swinging his arms gently. The headmistress's assistant was showing him his classroom but Paul wasn't listening much to what she said. He looked around the white walls at the notice boards, which were backed in colourful paper that could barely be seen under all of the posters that were displayed. They covered each other and wrapped around themselves as the corners began to curl. Paul didn't even wait until she had finished talking, he just walked over to the first notice board and gently took hold of one of the pins with his right hand and his left hand supported the paper. He pulled the pin and watched as the paper gently folded over itself onto his arm. He placed both this and the pin on the window sill next to the board. He continued in this way mechanically and meticulously.

"Ah, I see you have spotted the students work." She said trying to ignore what Paul was doing "You can change the room if you like but we can ask the cleaners to move any furniture."

She left him in the classroom, engrossed in rearranging the notice board, but not before giving him a sideways glance. Paul was left in the room alone, he smiled when she left not because he was happy to see her leave but because he was finally on his own; to do what he wanted without those sideways glances. He finished taking the paper off of the board and started to organise it. He took out pieces that were dated a year ago and placed the best of the others on the board. He placed them in lines at an even distance all around. The work was about inspirational music artists to the students and they had all made posters of them. Paul redressed the title of the board as it was becoming torn at the edges. He placed it back on again refreshed. He didn't take any time to admire his work but continued with the other boards. Once he had finished he sorted the left over work to be distributed back to the students. He then sat down tentatively in the chair that was behind the desk. He wiggled in it before making it higher and then lower and adjusting the back rest. He was comfortable at last and started to organise the desk. There were a few pieces of stationary still left on the desk a note pad, pencils and pens. Paul immediately noticed the pens and took everyone out, he looked at the ends of them and the ones that didn't have lids went straight in the bin. The others were checked for their writing flow and for their ink level. He threw a few more away before sharpening all the pencils to the same length and throwing away a rubber that had doodles on it. All the draws were empty so Paul placed the note pad in the top draw and closed it. He looked at the draw before opening it again and taking out the note pad and putting it back on the desk. He looked at the 'in tray' that was at the side of the desk. There was a letter in it. He looked at the envelope carefully before opening it. It was a welcome letter, Paul felt a small twang of proudness so put it neatly in his top draw. There was a key in there too so Paul locked the draw with a certain satisfaction. The bell rang which was the start of morning break and for Paul it meant his first staff meeting. He dreaded it, he was sure he was going to despise it but he had to go really and then, after the staff meeting he would get to meet his students.

55

September 2007, Twenty Four Years Old

The upper school seemed to blend into the background of the town. There were houses either side of it, all modern in their outlook. The school itself was very contemporary, made out of glass and steel with large steps leading up to the doors. A tree was planted in a large hole in the tiles, either side of the steps and two long bushes were planted either side of the door itself. Every time he walked in, Paul was at wonder with the marvel of the architecture and how intricate it must be. His classroom was down a small corridor, out of the way of the busy movement of students walking up and down the halls on their way to lessons. Paul preferred it this way he wouldn't have liked the idea of having an office whose door opens upon a busy corridor. It was Monday, which meant his second staff meeting. Paul found the first staff meeting adequate, but it had been too crowded and most people ignored him anyway. Not in a mean way but they were just busy having conversations with teachers that they already knew. He was determined that at the next staff meeting he would push himself, to start up conversation with the first person that he didn't see talking to someone else.

"What do you teach?" Asked Paul in his attempt to make small talk, he didn't feel like he was doing very well and when the teacher took a slightly longer amount of time to answer his question he started to move away. He didn't notice that she was part way through a biscuit and was unable to answer his question without spitting the pieces all over him, so wanted to finish it before she started to talk.

"Modern Foreign Languages." She stated just as Paul was moving away.

Paul wasn't sure that she was talking to him at all, but he turned around just in case making eye contact with her trying to figure it out, before pointing to himself and watching her nod just to make sure. She introduced herself as Lara and after Paul had told her his name and what he taught she continued to ask Paul questions about himself, such as where he was from, how long he has been teaching, where he did his degree and so on. Paul was a little overwhelmed and started to go red in the face and began to breathe irregularly. He didn't think that small talk would be this difficult, but he found Lara was the opposite to him as she said how much she loved having her door open upon the hum of all the people talking and moving about. He stopped talking altogether.

"I'm sorry do I make you uncomfortable?" Asked Lara.
Paul smiled awkwardly.
"Oh, sorry. I usually find that it's me." She said.
"No, it is probably me." Replied Paul before walking away.
He had had enough of the staff meeting and decided that he wanted to leave and go back to his classroom so that he could just, just breathe and think. The room was too loud, there were too many people and he didn't want to have to make small talk with any of them. His technique to try to talk to the other teachers didn't work and he decided not to go to another voluntary staff meeting again.

56

October 2007, Twenty Four Years Old

Paul settled into the way that the school ran, although he had decided that he wouldn't participate in the lunchtime routine. Every lunchtime before the students were released from their lessons, most of the teachers and support staff would all congregate in the cafeteria, which was huge although it still felt crowded to Paul. Not only were there too many people all trying to get their lunch at once, he found the servery very disorganised. Before anyone was able to choose what they would like to eat they would have to wander around in the middle before they could get an overview of what food was on offer. When they had decided, they would have to integrate themselves into the middle of the conveyer of people that were already moving round, so that they could get their preferred meal. Every day since then the teachers in the music department would ask Paul if he wanted to come with them to lunch and everyday Paul would decline. He ate sandwiches that he bought from a local shop and sat in the company of himself and the comfort of his classroom. In the end his colleagues stopped asking him, as they knew what the answer would be.

During a lunchtime at the beginning of October Paul decided that he would venture out for a walk. He had an hour for lunch so was able to escape and return, hopefully, before his lesson was due to start. He had just reached the doors of the reception when he spotted Lara. He was in half a mind to go and talk to her but decided not to, and left the building wrapped up in his long wool coat. He walked along to the park, which wasn't very far away from the upper school. He usually walked through the park to get to work, it was a more pleasant way to go and it was shorter. He looked across at some of the benches that were around the field, before he chose one and sat down on it making sure that he was sitting on his coat as he didn't want to get his trousers dirty. He sat up right with his hands clasped in his lap. He hadn't been there very long before Lara marched through looking as if she was on a mission. Paul didn't bother to stop her and she didn't notice him as she rushed passed. Paul sat for about twenty minutes before he started to feel cold and was just about to go when he spotted Lara coming from the other direction. She didn't seem as focused as she was when she walked through earlier and appeared more relaxed. She was swinging her ID badge, which all the staff at the upper school had to wear.

"I thought it was you but I was in such a rush." She started when she saw Paul "I couldn't remember where I had put my ID badge. I had to go home and find it otherwise I would have to report it to Jill and as the head of the department she isn't exactly kind."
"The Director of Music seems nice to me." Said Paul.
"Oh he is, you are lucky there but Jill is another matter." Finished Lara "Anyway I have it now I thought that I must have left it at home as I noticed as soon as I got in that I didn't have it."

She asked Paul about his decision to have a walk rather than join his department for lunch.

"Actually, now thinking about it I don't think that I have ever seen you in the cafeteria." Said Lara.
"You probably weren't looking that is all." Replied Paul not knowing why he didn't want her to know why he didn't want to eat lunch with the hordes of people that gathered there.
"No I definitely have never seen you there." Said Lara "Then again, I don't go there much either."
"You don't?" Questioned Paul sounding more surprised than he meant to.
"Nah, it is a bit stressful especially when I have a lesson straight after." Said Lara "I like to make sure I am back and sometimes students like to use my classroom for study and I need to be there for that so it is more important really."
"That is true." Agreed Paul "It is very busy in there."

Lara smiled she understood, so changed the subject as she didn't want to make Paul uncomfortable again. They started talking about walking through the park to get to work every day which led to where they lived. It would seem more than a coincidence that they would live opposite each other, but that is what turned out to be true.

"I wonder why we have never come across each other before." Questioned Lara.

They then discovered that it was because Paul left for work half an hour before Lara did.

"I suppose I don't really need to leave that early." Said Paul thinking about the morning routine he had used ever since he was little.
"No fair play to you, really it is good to leave early then you can definitely make sure that your lessons are all in order." Said Lara "Then again I do like sleeping, so whatever."

She laughed and Paul awkwardly smiled. They walked back to the upper school together talking, mostly Lara was talking but for once Paul was actually happy to listen. They reached the upper school both early for their next lesson.

"Maybe if I leave fifteen minutes earlier and you leave fifteen minutes later we can walk together some time." Said Lara before making her way to her classroom.

She didn't leave any time for Paul to answer but he didn't mind, did he really want to leave fifteen minutes later?

57

October 2007, Twenty Four Years Old

The school hall was full of small tables set out with a chair one side and two the other. There were only a few teachers who had arrived already prepared for the long parents evening ahead of them. Paul was one of those teachers, as his first parents evening he wanted to make a good impression. He was sat at his table, on it was a pile of papers and books neatly stacked and a name sign saying 'Mr P Westwood' and underneath it said 'music'. Even though it was only a piece of card folded, Paul looked at it with pride his name was in bold which made him feel even more important. It felt good for once being the person sat on the other side of the table. Even though Paul was a good student at school and usually achieved what the teachers called high grades, they would always say the same thing to him, could participate more in group activities. It didn't exactly make Paul feel good to hear this, so he tried to speak positively about all his students. The beginning of the evening went well there were a few parents who filtered in and out of the hall, but later on the hall was packed. Paul only had a few appointments between 7pm and 8pm so was sat for some of the time trying to make himself look busy and feel less awkward. The last parent was at 8:10pm and he was looking forward to going home shortly after. However, the parent talked for almost twenty minutes alone before adding.

"I really need to go to the ladies would you watch the boys for me?" She asked not waiting for any answer and running in the direction of the toilets.

Paul looked at the boys. There was the one that was in year nine who he taught and two younger ones who had barely started first school. He smiled before trying to make small talk, the form of communication that he liked least.

"So are you doing anything for half term?" He asked.
"Yeah we are gow'in to see granma and granpa and we are gow'in to go to da park and feed da dwucks wif them and exploring dar woods and den we are gow'in sommear else but I can't remmer where." Replied the youngest of the boys.
"That sounds nice." Replied Paul not really catching what he was talking about.

He spent the next five minutes asking other questions that they answered in long sentences. He was relieved when their mother came and collected them. She thanked him and as anybody would, Paul said "no problem".

Paul started to pack up before anyone else could talk to him, Lara had finished for the evening and was waiting for Paul.

"Did you enjoy babysitting?" She asked with a smirk.
"Funny." Replied Paul sarcastically before adding "How long have you been waiting?"
"Only a few minutes." She replied.
"Lying." Replied Paul "You finished at 8pm why did you wait for me?"

He looked at his watch which read almost 9pm, before he picked up the papers on the desk.

"Because I could." She replied vaguely.

For the moment this was enough conversation for Paul because he just wanted to get home. He had to go back to his classroom to put some of the papers away. Once he was ready they were about to leave before Paul remembered something and went back into the hall which was beginning to be packed up.

"Why are you keeping that for?" Asked Lara.
"It is my first parents evening." Replied Paul looking at the name sign he was holding "It means something."

Lara just smiled before changing the subject to something else.

They walked back home under the starry sky, there were few people out and about which was comforting as they walked across the quiet park together. Paul waved to Lara from his front door just as she reached hers, she smiled and waved back.

58

March 2008, Twenty Four Years Old

The warm spring day left the grass dewy, even though the sun was shining brightly overhead with no clouds to block its rays. Paul walked with Lara through the park on their way to work, they were half way across when Lara sat down in the damp grass and motioned for Paul to sit with her.

"The grass is wet." Said Paul making a face.
"Then sit on your man bag, you wuss!" Replied Lara smiling.
"We will be late." Replied Paul clutching his bag and continuing on his way.

Lara got up she didn't challenge him, but she rolled her eyes before she followed him running a few strides to catch up to him. The birds flitted about the treetops at the edges of the wood as Paul and Lara walked through the rest of the park. Neither of them felt like going to work on such as lovely day, the students didn't understand the fact that maybe the teachers too would rather go outside than have to teach.

Paul refused to open the windows in his classroom, the students were sweltering. The walls somehow trapped all the heat and without the windows open, there was no way of it escaping. When the head of the department came in to speak to Paul about something, as soon as he came into the room the heat made him instinctively open the windows, the small amount that they would actually open. All the students in the class breathed a sigh of relief as they felt the nice cool air on their backs. Paul struggled with not telling the head of department to shut the windows again, but he did restrain from doing so until his class had left that afternoon. He felt safer with all the windows closed, at least that is what Lara put it down to when she found him closing all of the windows back up again.

"I just like it that way." Said Paul defensively when Lara expressed her opinions on the matter.
"Sure you do." Replied Lara.
"Why can't I just like having the windows closed just the same as why you like having them open." Said Paul "I put that down to the fact that you feel like you are in a cage otherwise."

Lara understood his point and apologised, although she still thought that there was a reason behind his behaviour.

59

April 2008, Twenty Five Years Old

"I can't believe that you didn't tell me that it was your twenty fifth Birthday!" Exclaimed Lara walking into Paul's classroom making him jump.

He was busy typing on his computer, leaning very close to the screen in deep concentration.

"We could have done something, like get a meal or something." She continued walking up to his desk
Paul smiled awkwardly, "Thank you but no."

He continued to do whatever it was he was doing before Lara entered his classroom. He expected that this answer would be a message for her to leave him be, but she continued regardless.

"Come on now let's do something tonight?" Said Lara "We could go to the pub."
"I don't drink." Replied Paul.
"You don't have to drink you could get an orange juice." Said Lara.
"Majority of orange juice is from concentrate." Said Paul looking at her as if it was obvious "There is no way to guarantee that it isn't."
"Um ok." Started Lara slowly "I could get a pizza and we could watch a movie."
"Lara no. I don't want to go to the pub or to have pizza or to celebrate at all. My family did what I asked why can't you." Questioned Paul looking up from his computer once again.
"Because everyone should have a special day." Argued Lara "But fine never mind whatever you want."

She curtsied sarcastically pulling a face before she walked out of the classroom.

"It is *my* birthday!" He shouted out after her before smiling himself as he settled back into his work.

60

April 2008, Twenty Five Years Old

"I don't think that people understand how stressful it is to strive for perfection every day, in everything knowing that it is not possible." Said Paul trying to explain his feelings to Lara.

They were sat on the bench that Paul insisted that they always sat on. He didn't like the look of the one by the play park and the one in the woods was covered too much with graffiti, and it made him uncomfortable. *Their* bench was on the edge of the field by the entrance to the park. It wasn't the best position because Paul jumped every time someone walked through the gate, but it was better than the alternatives. They had just walked back from work together, the Easter holidays had just begun and the school had broken up early. All the teachers took advantage of this and disappeared off as soon as the students did. It was a very warm day with the sun shining its very brightest and the flowers that had already emerged from their winter slumbers expelling their sweet smell onto the scene.

"Oh Paul." Started Lara softly "You make everything sound so pessimistic. You first need to understand that your best is your own kind of perfection."

Paul interrupted her, "No I mean in every moment for example if I was going to work on Thursday to make it perfect I would wear my blue and grey striped socks, my grey trousers with my white shirt and blue jumper. I would have cereal for breakfast and a glass of fresh squeeze orange juice."

"Why not regular orange juice?" Questioned Lara.

"Because most orange juice is made from concentrate." Started Paul.

"So?" Asked Lara not understanding the problem.

"So it is made from water and an orange juice powder taking most of the goodness out of it." Replied Paul "Anyway that is not the point."

"But that is exactly the point." Replied Lara "Was that conversation 'perfect'? I mean did you anticipate that I was going to ask that?"

"No but once you did it was pretty easy to anticipate that you didn't know anything about orange juice." Replied Paul seriously.

Lara laughed, "You are impossible!" She exclaimed "You know that don't you?"

"Actually, all through university people said that." He replied but realising after he had spoken that Lara's question was rhetorical, so he smiled as if he was being funny.

"I don't think there is anyone in the world just like you." Said Lara not meaning it to sound mean.

"I could say the same about you." Replied Paul raising his eyebrows "Come on lets go the sun is going in."

"You go ahead." She said "I am going to stay here for a bit."

Paul didn't know whether Lara wanted him to stay or not, so anticipating that there was a decision that needed to be made, he figured that if he just stayed where he was, he didn't make a decision because if he hadn't posed the question he would have been sat there anyway.

"You not going?" Asked Lara looking at him with friendly eyes.

"No." He replied "I am staying right here."

"I am glad." Said Lara lingering before she finished what she was going to say "Thank you."

61

April 2008, Twenty Five Years Old

"This is nice." Said Lara standing in front of a mirror holding a top against herself "Don't you think?"

Paul looked at the geometric pattern and raised his eyebrows.

"You are right." Said Lara "A bit too much."
"This one is nice?" Asked Paul picking out a plain light blue shirt.
"Yeah." Replied Lara "It would look good on you."

Paul smiled pleased with himself. Lara chose another top and Paul nodded when she said how nice it was. Paul was beginning to enjoy himself and so was Lara as they started to pick out outfits for each other. All the clothes they picked were clothes that they would each usually wear, until Lara chose a t-shirt for Paul and alarm bells rang in his ears. It was as if Lara could hear them clanging against each other because she quickly put it back.

"No I will try it on." Said Paul dragging it back out of the rack.
"No Paul you don't have to." Replied Lara trying to put it back but Paul was certain that he wanted to try it on, Lara gave in "Ok but only if you pick out something for me."

Paul was made uncomfortable suddenly by the thought of having to decide what clothing someone might like. He was comfortable when finding similar clothing to what she usually wore, but finding something based on his judgement was a little overwhelming. Then again, Lara personally liked the t-shirt she chose not necessarily on Paul but she thought that he might like to try it on.

"These." Said Paul pulling out a pair of Chelsea boots from one of the shelves.

Lara looked at them, she usually wore the same pair of worn canvas shoes. Paul noticed that she wouldn't wear any other shoes, she had a few stored in a stand by her front door but they all looked fairly new. They also didn't look like the shoes she would wear, although there was a pair of brown boots with a fur trim that Paul thought that she would have worn at least when it was wet.

"Ok." Said Lara "They probably look better on anyway."

Paul put them back and said the same thing that Lara did when he didn't want to try on the t-shirt.

"No come on now, I have to play too." She smiled as she sat down on the stool and kicked off her shoes, which lost a bit of the rubber sole as she did. The neat chestnut brown boots complimented her dark skinny jeans she stood up cocking her head to look at them. She wandered to the full length mirror and gazed down at the boots.

"Do you like them?" Asked Paul.
"Yeah." She started softly "I think they will do."

She smiled a cheeky grin as she swapped back into her own shoes. She told Paul to go and change whilst she was busy tying her laces. Paul went to the changing rooms and swapped his crisp white shirt with the t-shirt that Lara had found. He looked in the mirror and didn't see himself. He emerged to show Lara, she smiled with the difference of just seeing him in a different style of clothing.

"I don't think it goes with my trousers." He said looking down at the brown suit trousers that he was wearing.

He looked up at Lara who had her hands clasped, Paul knew what she was getting at and nodded slowly. She ran off into the shop as Paul suddenly had a wave of déjà vu, but knew that it was just a moment going into the long term memory instead of the short term memory so he passed it off. Lara returned with a slim pair of jeans, for a moment Paul thought that she would come back with a pair of ripped jeans that he wouldn't have liked. He tried on the whole outfit and involuntarily smiled at himself in the mirror when he showed Lara. She looked at his glowing face and smiled to herself with the feeling that she had done something good. They bought the clothes that they had found and Paul even left the shop with the light blue shirt. The sun was shining overhead drying up little puddles of the previous day's rainfall.

"Do you think clothes make you feel different about yourself?" Asked Paul swinging his bag gently as they walked along the pavement.
"I think so." Started Lara gathering her words "I feel better in certain clothes than others."
"But they are just pieces of material." Replied Paul not understanding why "They can't change who you are."
"No but they can make you feel better about yourself." Replied Lara nodding her head gently "Making you feel more confident. I find I perform tasks better in clothes that I am comfortable in."
"It sounds like you have written a paper on it." Exclaimed Paul laughing.
"It is good to hear you laugh." Said Lara seriously looking up at him.
"I laugh sometimes." Replied Paul.
"Yeah but it isn't real is it?" She questioned.

Paul stopped her they stood in the street briefly, but Paul said nothing even though he had opened his mouth as if he would. He closed it again and continued walking. Lara knew from the silence that she was right. Paul was quiet a lot of the time and just recently he had begun emerging like a butterfly. He was still the same Paul correcting people on impulse, but he had learned that his emotions didn't need hiding. He just wasn't ready to show them yet, especially to Lara. She linked her arm around his expecting him to pull away but he didn't move as she gently brushed her arm with his.

62

June 2008, Twenty Five Years Old

"Are you here for your passport?" Asked Lara when Paul came into her classroom with an eager face.

He had the previous day off and was waiting for a package to arrive at the school, he had been waiting weeks for it to arrive and asked Lara to look out for it just in case it came whilst he wasn't at work.

"How did you know it was a passport?" Asked Paul accusingly thinking that Lara had opened it.
"It says 'passport' on the envelope!" Exclaimed Lara handing it to him.
"Oh." Replied Paul reaching for it and quickly but carefully opening it "Don't you hate passport photos."
"I am sure it is fine." Replied Lara "Show me."

Paul showed her the passport, his photo was like any other passport photo with the light background and the straight face.

"It is fine." Replied Lara.
"But I look so boring." Replied Paul giggling.
"That is how you look every day." Replied Lara with a straight face.

Paul looked at her to try and work out whether she was being serious or not but when the broad smile began to grow across her face he knew that she was joking.

"Mine looks like that." Began Lara "Actually I think mine is worse, I was giggling the whole time it was being taken."

She started to laugh remembering the day her passport photo

was taken. It was taken by a family friend and she kept on making Lara laugh, not on purpose but it turned into a big joke.

"Are you off to anywhere then?" Asked Lara wondering if Paul was going off on an adventure.
"No." Replied Paul putting the passport back in the envelope.
"Why do you need a passport for?" Asked Lara.
"ID." Was the short reply.
"ID for what?" Asked Lara beginning to get tired of having to ask all the questions.
"I need photo ID for collecting parcels that get delivered to the depot." He replied.
"But you get all your parcels delivered here." Questioned Lara.
"Only important things." Replied Paul "I don't want to clog up the school's mail system with my parcels."
"How considerate of you." Replied Lara smiling gently.
"No really it is a lack of efficiency, if I have my parcels delivered to the reception because then they have to deliver it to my pigeon hole and if it doesn't fit then it is really a faff." Explained Paul "They could be spending their time doing other things than sorting my post."

Lara nodded her head in agreement, but she believed that Paul was trying to be considerate and he just didn't want to appear that he cared. She didn't want to tell him this though, so just went along with what he said.

"I'm going to France in the summer." Said Lara.
"I figured as much." Replied Paul.
"What? How did you know?" Said Lara.
"Everyone goes to France." He said "Bye."

He walked out of the classroom leaving Lara confused and baffled, so just like any other meeting with Paul. It was a sunny day outside and the windows were open as much as they could go to filter the air that was beginning to heat up in the room. Lara's classroom was on the first floor where as Paul's was on the ground floor so he could get away with keeping the windows closed just as he liked it, for a while anyway.

63

July 2008, Twenty Five Years Old

The summer holidays came round quickly, all the students were excited for their seven weeks holiday. The summer was looking promising, the sun had been shining for weeks without rain and the days had been warm and were getting warmer. The students had gone home and the school seemed deserted, a few teachers were still about finishing their work or marking recent pieces of homework. Paul was in his classroom enjoying the quiet atmosphere. He was going back to Cornwall for a few weeks in the holidays and he was excited for it. He wanted to be back with the wind in his face and whipping all around him. The warm sun bracing against the hills causing one side to be hot and the other to be cool. He thought of the walks he could have along the cliff tops, but then he thought about the tourists and his smile turned into a frown. He stopped his typing slowly dragging his hands away from the keys. He was planning to go in to work for a few days in the following week to finish off his marking. His parents were away for the next week so he would go to Cornwall when they returned.

Paul and Lara walked back to their flats together after they had finished their work, the sun was still shining brightly in the sky causing a soft glow. As they walked through the park they noticed a lot of children still in their uniforms playing in the play park. Their parents were gathered around the edges talking to each other, holding little rucksacks and little jumpers. They were all clearly excited that their summer had started and the children were gathering in little groups to discuss their plans for their holidays. It seemed like an age now, until the new school year started; forty nine days to go.

"Do you remember being their age?" Said Lara wistfully.
"Of course I do." Replied Paul as if it was a stupid question to ask.
"I remember playing with my friends all day every day for the whole summer." Started Lara "We never went on holiday when we were kids but I didn't mind, it meant more time for exploring."
"Was it fun?" Asked Paul wondering what it would be like to be playing with friends as a child because Paul never really had any.
"Yes it was." Said Lara "But you don't need to worry about that, there are plenty of memories just as good that we can make together."

She smiled at him but knowing that Paul would probably be happy to just stay in his flat.

"I am going to France for the first two weeks but after that we can do whatever you want." Said Lara trying to make Paul feel better even though he didn't really mind not doing anything.
"I am going to Cornwall for the third and fourth week and then to Bath for the fifth week." Said Paul.
"Sure we can meet up after then?" Questioned Lara she was slightly upset by the fact that there wouldn't be much time for them to spend together but she didn't let on to Paul.
"Yes." Said Paul looking at Lara smiling "We can do whatever you want."

Lara smiled at him she wasn't sure whether she believed him or not but felt like she wanted to. They reached their flats but were still talking, rather Lara was still talking. Paul as usual was trying his best to listen to her but not inputting anything of his own.

"I'm cooking pasta for dinner." Said Lara she didn't even have to wait for a reply.

Paul struggled with cooking and didn't really eat anything, he wasn't exactly hungry but he felt like a meal would make him feel better. Lara cooked tagliatelle with a tomato based sauce, she talked mainly about the meal such as the fact that she didn't have any parmesan cheese and only had cheddar.

"Do you know how much parmesan cheese is?" Exclaimed Lara as she dished up two bowls.

Paul shook his head and tucked into his bowl as soon as Lara had placed it down on the table. They ate their meal mostly in silence, they ate quickly and afterwards Lara had some ice cream but Paul refused until he saw how good it looked and then he decided to have some. He smiled contently as he scoffed the vanilla ice cream. Lara had put chocolate shavings and some chocolate sauce drizzled over it.

"You really must learn to cook yourself." Said Lara licking her spoon "You can't just live off microwave meals for the rest of your life and I am defiantly not going to cook for you forever." She joked as she went to put her bowl in the dishwasher.

Paul sat looking at his bowl as she said this and worked out that she wasn't going to tidy his bowl away. Reluctantly he placed his bowl in the dishwasher and then washed his hands putting hand gel on afterwards.

"Thanks for dinner." Said Paul as he edged towards the door.
"You're welcome Paul." Replied Lara getting out more ingredients Paul watched as she got out flour, sugar, butter and eggs placing them on the work surface.
"Why are you making cakes?" Asked Paul figuring out what she was making.
"Because they taste good." Replied Lara "I thought that you were leaving?"

Paul paused for a moment he did like the cakes that Lara sometimes brought into work for the staff to share.

Lara realised that Paul wasn't leaving and looked at him, "Do you want to make them?"
"With you." Added Paul not wanting to make the cakes all by himself.
"Sure." She replied.

She talked him through the process of creaming the sugar and the butter together, then adding the flour and eggs. She added chocolate chips to the mix and Paul continued to stir the mixture in his awkwardness he spilt the flour and had become upset over it, no matter how many times Lara told him that it didn't matter. Paul put the mixture into the cake cases in the tins and Lara quietly giggled over the massive inconsistency of the amount of mixture in each one. They placed them in the oven and watched them slowly rise.

"Are you going now?" Questioned Lara raising one eyebrow "Don't worry I am not making anything else."

She handed him a little box with a few of the cakes in it. They had tried them and liked them which made Paul pleased on his first attempt at cooking.

"Do you want me to show you how to cook anything else?" Asked Lara once Paul had crossed the street.
"No it is ok." Replied Paul "If I want I can learn it all on the internet."

Lara smiled watching as he went into his flat the lights turned on as soon as he was inside. They flickered off and on again as he made his way through each room. Lara closed the door on her own warm home shutting out the darkness that was just descending on the town.

64

August 2008, Twenty Five Years Old

"Did you enjoy France?" Asked Paul enjoying the sunshine as they sat on the bench in the park.

There were a few families gathered in the playpark but they were far away and Paul didn't seem to mind them so much now.

"It is nice that you are taking an interest!" Exclaimed Lara happily munching on an orange.

Paul tried very hard not to show his annoyance at the loud sound that it made whilst she was eating it.

"Not really, it is just polite." Replied Paul grimacing.
"Anyway it is nice for you to pretend." Lara joked flicking some of the pith from the orange onto the ground.

She explained how her and a few friends went for excursions in the south of France and then gradually moved up to Bordeaux where they got the ferry back to England. She explained in detail where they went and Paul was trying not to show how bored he was with her stories. It was probably because he couldn't relate to them because he wasn't there.

"I don't really like Paris much." Explained Lara "It is a bit over rated most people will probably disagree with me but it was much like London."
"How could it be any different?" Said Paul bluntly "All cities have the same basis although the architecture does change."

He went on to explain the types of architecture in France and how they differ to other cities. Lara listened patiently until she was given a gap to continue telling Paul how they went down the side streets and found a small restaurant. She seemed very excited whilst she talked about the restaurant because of this Paul let her interrupt him.

"I assume that it didn't occur to you the reason why the restaurant may be down a side street." Started Paul but he realised that this made Lara annoyed so he stopped talking.
"It was lovely anyway." Continued Lara quietly "All the staff were very friendly always making sure that we had enough drinks and everything."
"I find that annoying." Said Paul aloud seemingly meaning to think it.
"What?" Questioned Lara thinking that it was about the restaurant again.
"I don't like it when staff from restaurants and cafés check to make sure that your meal is ok." Complained Paul "If I didn't like it don't they think that I would tell them?"
"Maybe *you* would." Said Lara "But most people don't like to tell people when they don't like something and it is nice that they asked us if we wanted more drinks."
"You are more likely to buy one if they ask you." Replied Paul.

Lara ignored his argument and continued to tell him how they went to an observation point and looked out across a town to the sea, and how they stayed up late so that they could see a different town lit up. She told him how beautiful it was but assumed that he wouldn't understand.

"I understand beauty." Retorted Paul "Towns have people in, though the architecture would be beautiful if people didn't plaster graffiti on the buildings or stick gum everywhere."
"What about natural beauty?" Asked Lara "If we went to some mountains or went for a walk in the countryside would you say that was beautiful?"
"We will have to find out won't we?" Replied Paul softly before continuing "Anyway it depends on the fields."

65

November 2009, Twenty Five Years Old

Lara's classroom opened onto the large open hallway along with the four other language classrooms. On the door of the classroom it said '4MFL' meaning classroom four, modern foreign languages. Her desk was at the far end of the classroom, in the corner by the window alongside the interactive white board and a regular white board next to that. Around the room work from the students had been stuck up on notice boards that were backed with coloured paper. Paul sat on one of the student chairs in the empty classroom, he appeared as if he was a student ready for his lesson but the teacher didn't bother to show up.

"Ready for a lesson?" Asked Lara walking into the room. Paul didn't bother to turn around with his reply but waited until Lara had walked in front of him.
"What?" Replied Paul misunderstanding.
"Let me teach you." Said Lara eager to try to teach Paul a language.
"There is nothing that you can teach me!" Exclaimed Paul slightly angry.
"What do you mean?" Asked Lara trying to stay calm.
"I can speak over ten languages, one of them I made up myself." Stated Paul sounding disappointed in himself
"Why are you sad about it? I don't mind." Said Lara "Maybe you can teach me a language that I don't know."
"There is nothing that anyone can teach me." Said Paul sounding self-centred and big headed but not meaning to.
"I am sure that there is something that you don't know." Replied Lara.
"I doubt it." Said Paul "But it can't be helped. I am going to lunch

now."

With that Paul walked out the room leaving Lara smiling and she couldn't help letting out a slight giggle. It was a laugh that showed genuine care of Paul, rather than laughing at him. He made her smile more often than not. She noticed the little things that he did. She thought them sweet and individual as if no one else in the world would do what he did or said what he said. The other teachers did accept him, but there were certain things that he would do like say something that sounds like a joke but he said it in a way that showed he was serious. Lara just accepted him.

66

January 2009, Twenty Five Years Old

"Mistakes happen Paul it really doesn't matter." Said Lara softly putting her hand on Paul's shoulder.

He didn't shrug it off like he usually did but let it linger. He needed comfort, he didn't fully understand why but he knew he needed it.

"I don't make mistakes." He replied with a wobble in his voice.
"I don't like it when you get upset Paul." Said Lara "I would rather you never come to the cinema or anything with me if it meant that you wouldn't get upset."
"Why would you say that?" Asked Paul.
"Because some people are worth it." She replied.
"Worth what?" He questioned.
"It doesn't matter." She said softly with a smile before continuing in a chirpy tune "Come on then otherwise we will be late for work." She jumped up but Paul didn't come with her.
"The film last night was rubbish anyway." Continued Lara "You wouldn't have enjoyed it."

She marched over to him and grabbed his hand which he pulled away immediately.

"Good." She said beaming "I am glad that I have Paul back again."
"But I didn't go anywhere?" He looked quizzical.
"Once again, never mind." She said under her breath.

They walked together under the dark clouds that were gathering. They continued talking right up until they were in Lara's classroom and Paul sat down at one of the desks leaning his arms on it.

"You never get upset about the things that I do, or don't do." Said Paul innocently.
"I do." Replied Lara softly but shortly.
"What?" Questioned Paul "I didn't know."
"You wouldn't." She replied quietly before speaking louder again "It doesn't matter Paul. I have told you that before."
"What upsets you about me?" Asked Paul.
"Are you sure you want to know?" Replied Lara raising an eyebrow.
"Yes." Replied Paul "Because then I can be better."
"You don't need to be better." Replied Lara "Because then you wouldn't be you."
"Tell me." Insisted Paul.
"Ok, I don't like it when you conveniently forget about us meeting up." She started before Paul interrupted.
"I thought you didn't mind?" Questioned Paul.
"I do mind, but I don't like you getting upset even more." She said before continuing "I would like to dance in the rain with you or go out in the snow, sit on the grass and eat a meal in a restaurant. I want to walk with you in the woods, not on the path. I would like to go on holiday with you so we can experience the world together."
"Would you like to get married?" Stated Paul abruptly.
"No, Paul I don't want to get married to you." She replied.
"In general." He replied.
"Oh, um I don't know I suppose so." She replied vaguely "Would you?"
"No. I just hurt people." He replied as Lara listen to him say this she thought she heard a little sadness in his voice, but she didn't know how this was true as Paul didn't often show passive emotions, they were usually intense and unbearable to both Paul and the people around him.

He started speaking in his usual tone again, "What would your marriage be like?"
"Um, truthfully? I am sure it is like everyone else's." She replied adding quickly "Not that I have thought about it much."
"Truthfully." He replied surely.
"I would like someone who is caring, not just about me but caring

about people in general. He would make me laugh and I would feel his heartache and he would feel mine. He would enjoy spending time with me as we shared what we loved to do. We would like different hobbies but somehow they connected us. We might have children but it wouldn't break us if we couldn't have them and after twenty whatever years of marriage we would never part because we, as humans, have the ability to love someone forever and that is exactly what I would like to do." Said Lara.
"I never knew you felt all of that." He replied disappointedly "I didn't think you thought about all of that."
"People are more complex than you think or than they appear. Thoughts and feelings change quickly and emotions can be hard to read." She replied.

Lara had sat down next to him where they stayed in silence for a while. The sun streamed through the windows onto the wooden table tops. Paul stretched out his hands so that they were in the sun. There was a contrast to the cold table top and the warmth from the sun's rays.

"If normal people get married then I want to get married to." Concluded Paul.
"There are no normal people. All people are different and bring their uniqueness to the human race, you don't need to get married or eat in restaurants or dance in the rain. Your normality is real and is normal to you. My normality is real and is normal to me. It is no different to other people's normality and yet it couldn't be more different." Said Lara.
"Words confuse me." Said Paul meaning spoken words especially when they are about everyday life.
"I know Paul." Replied Lara.
"How do you know?" Asked Paul "I didn't know your feelings."
"Some people know other people's feelings because you feel closer to them than they do to you. Some people just find it hard to understand emotions in general and it is all ok Paul you don't need to worry about it. I understand."
"How did you know I was worried about it?" Continued Paul.
"I know because you worry about everything." She replied "I don't want you to worry Paul. I want you to feel calm and secure in

everything you do but I know that may not be possible as much as I want to try."

67

February 2009, Twenty Five Years Old

The holiday diary was Paul's next achievement. He enquired whether Lara would allow him to read hers, she did question why but Paul just answered, "Educational purposes for social development."

"Sure you can read it." Said Lara pleased with this answer and handed him a light green leather bound book, it was bulging at the edges where she had glued in receipts and photos that she had taken "There is nothing personal in it, just the stuff we did."

Paul started reading the pages which were colourful with some doodles that Lara had drawn.

"Do you have to make them so..." He paused for a moment "So crowded."

Lara laughed at the back handed insult, "No it doesn't have to be *crowded* you can make it whatever you want as long as you write the words, you're good."

"Thank you but I don't think that you can make that judgement." Replied Paul misunderstanding Lara's use of the word 'good'.

Thus Paul decided to go on holiday, but didn't tell anyone about it. During February half term he took a few days to go on holiday and decided that he would start small. He chose Wales as his destination, it was not too far away but far enough that he would feel that he was not at home. He travelled down to find that the picture of the nice small cottage that he had rented, was actually a rundown barn conversion with a partially fitted door and the windows which seemed to just stick open. His smile dropped a little when he saw it, but decided to venture further inside. It was the pool of water in the middle of the bed which was the last straw. He searched around for another place to stay, by this time he was cold and the rain had started. He did think about going home because no one knew that he was on holiday and no one would know he didn't even make it one night away. For some reason Paul wanted to make it work, he tried to find another cottage for rent that week by leaching off of the Wi-Fi in a little café where he only ordered water. He didn't find anywhere and had to cast the net out a bit wider, meaning the bed and breakfasts. Paul never really liked the idea of staying in a room in someone's house even if it was a big house, he still couldn't be alone. He found somewhere which had two nights instead of the four nights he was originally planning to stay, but he took it anyway. A nice warm bed was all he wanted now. He was greeted with smiles from an elderly couple who moved around well for their age, Paul guessed eighties, but then again Paul was never very good about guessing things with people.

"Now if you want to have any extra blankets please let me know before 10pm. I will be in the lounge until then and you are welcome to join us. There is a couple and a gentleman staying here too and they often join us to watch the television in the evenings." She started in her thick Welsh accent "Breakfast is at eight and will you be requiring dinner?"
"No thank you, I won't be requiring any meals." Replied Paul.

The thought of having a meal cooked by a stranger wasn't a very comforting prospect and would suit himself with packet food. Although drinking tea was going to be hard to give up for two days. After the landlady left Paul decided to write in his diary.

"After being greeted with the disappointment that was cottage number one. Cottage number two shouldn't have such a high bar to reach. A bed and bathroom would be welcome and that is what I have got. It isn't an en-suite but I will just have to make it work. It is nice and warm, although now in my bed it is 22:30 and wish I had asked for that second blanket. There is a fire in the corner but it is definitely off limits I can see the soot falling down from it now, even by the low light of the bedside lamp next to me. I am trying not to think of who else has slept in this bed, even though the sheets feel clean it will never be enough to wipe of the memory of all the hundreds of people who have laid here. Lara's diary said that they went to restaurants, cafés and bars, I will just have to stick with wandering around and trying not to get bored. I am finding it hard to be tired, even though when I finally arrived here all I wanted was for the landlady to leave me alone so that I could go to bed. The more she kept talking the more I had to pretend to listen and in the end you become bored of pretending and actually start listening to at least have an intelligent conversation of sorts, I wouldn't call talking about the weather and how this rain differs to the rain last year or last Christmas or last summer an intelligent conversation, but nevertheless I tried."

"I am sat in my room it is only lunchtime, but I am bored so decided to come back and write in my diary. There is not much to say really after waking up every half hour last night I am tired, although over tired might be the word because I don't feel sleepy. I should do a study on my sleep patterns to regulate the way I sleep. I sneaked out of the front door this morning, so the landlady didn't coax me in to have breakfast. I wandered around the sleepy town that I found myself in, but after getting mud on my shoes and it starting to rain I decided to call it a day, so ended up alone in my room. It seems pointless really because I might as well have been in my flat back in Oxford. The Wi-Fi here is poor as I chose a more than average Wi-Fi zone this one is more like between poor and very poor. The mobile phone service is not that great either. I sporadically get texts I have one from my mother telling me to visit them even though I know that they don't mean it, and one from Lara wondering where I am. I just told her that I am at home taking a few days off and not to bother me. She usually doesn't because she knows I won't be any fun. Then again I wouldn't say that I was fun, and thinking about it now I don't know why she is even friends with me. I need to remember to remind myself to ask her this question when I get back."

"Second sleepless night and I am thankful that I am leaving today. I can't stand another night here. I am so bored I should have asked someone to come with me. I definitely never thought I would think that. I did try to enjoy the company of the others downstairs, but they were getting involved watching a game show. I knew all the answers obviously, but tried my best to keep my mouth shut until one of them exclaimed that Africa was a country. Then I really got involved. I went up to bed around 21:00 as I couldn't stand to watch another game show with them. I wasn't tired but it was the best excuse to leave. Home today. I still have two days to go and the weekend but never mind at least I will be home."

"I arrived home yesterday it was a tiresome journey as the trains were delayed, and even though the whole of the carriage I was in was empty, the only other person in there decided that he wanted to sit next to me. I looked at him and then at the rest of the carriage but he didn't get the hint and continued to smile. It annoyed me. I have decided to continue to write a diary, I don't know how long it will last but apparently most people do this so I suppose that I should too."

Lara was reading the diary, she was lying on his sofa and Paul was trying not to get annoyed at the fluff her socks were producing or the fact that she was squashing his nicely plumped cushions. Since she let Paul read hers, he decided to repay the favour and the following weekend he handed her the work that he had tried to so elegantly write.

"I don't think that many people keep a day to day diary. Even if they did I don't think that they actually keep up with it for very long." She said flicking through the rest of the empty pages.
"This is very confusing." Stated Paul "What should I do then?"
"Do whatever you feel." Replied Lara "You want to write a diary? Then write a diary. You want to paint a picture? Then paint a picture. Do whatever it is that makes you happy not what everyone else is doing. Don't be a sheep."
"But I like sheep." Said Paul "I wouldn't want to be one though."
"It is a metaphor." Laughed Lara "You don't have to write stuff just because everyone else is doing it and if you do want to write make your own style, don't push yourself to string together a perfect sentence. Most of my diary is just shortened sentences that would probably make no sense to anyone else but me."

"I understood it." Stated Paul.
"There we go I clearly write better than I thought." She smiled at the half attempt to give her a compliment.

Thus was the end of Paul's diary writing, every now and again he would look through his half-finished journal and decide that he better write something in it. Then he would read the first few pages and relive his very short holiday. He would close it and then place it in the bottom of a draw so he never had to lay eyes on it again.

68

April 2009, Twenty Six Years Old

"Is the grass wet?" Asked Paul scrunching up his face.

Spring had arrived in Oxford and the little park was surrounded by fresh flowers in all different colours. Although the ones around the play park were decidedly limp from all the trampling they received from little feet. Lara rolled her eyes and said nothing she wasn't going to give up, she wanted him to sit on the floor.

"Fine, I shall just sit on my coat." Said Paul throwing his coat down this was a bit unexpected and Lara wanted to mess with Paul just a little bit.
"What about grass stains?" Questioned Lara in a low voice raising her eyebrows.
Paul quickly grabbed his coat from the floor, "Suit yourself." He said walking across the newly dewy grass.

Lara stayed where she was when Paul realised this he turned around. She raised her eyebrows once more. Paul opened his mouth as if he was going to say something but decided not to.

"So, when you get to work. Who's going to get the milk for you tea?" She questioned knowing that she was winning.

Paul thought about it for a moment before turning back and throwing down his coat ad sitting on it. "Fine." He said looking grumpy.

"Now, now." Petted Lara not entirely trying to comfort him she added, "You have made me very happy today."
"You manipulated me. How do you know, I may have decided not

to have tea today?" Said Paul annoyed.
"You always have tea when you get into work." Stated Lara "Tea that is not too weak, not to strong, tea that is perfect. One cube of sugar, if there are no cubes then you 'borrow' one from my department and just enough milk to make it go a caramel colour."

Paul smiled in awe. He always loved listening to things she remembered about him and he always tried to say something back. Although this time he wanted to say that something that he hadn't been told but what he thought was true about her.

"You eat porridge, at all times of day all winter because you say it helps you think in the cold weather, but really you use it to cover up how sad you are when the evenings become darker." He replied.
She was speechless, "How, what, why would you think that?" She said when she had found her voice.
"Because it is true." Paul replied in a matter of fact tone "I know you, now. I never understood before but I try, really try to understand you."
"Why?" Asked Lara.
"Because I know how much it means to you." He said "Although I don't know why."
"Oh Paul!" Exclaimed Lara putting her arm around him hugging him.
"Now, now. None of that." Said Paul with a slight smirk of embarrassment.
Lara released her grip and Paul got up, "Work?" Asked Paul to which Lara nodded. She watched him walk away slightly before she got up. She stood amongst the spring flowers that grew between the spaces in the grass. The dew had begun to dry up and she could feel the dust beginning to gather.
"I will tell you why." She started before adding quietly "Eventually."

She ran up to join him as the early morning sun was just coming to its full strength making the world feel more like summer than spring. It was true that Paul didn't like getting any milk from the catering department. As he was always the first in to his department, it was often up to him to get the milk which turned into

Lara's job. The catering department was down a flight of stairs into a cafeteria, they were always busy moving this way and that. Paul found it chaotic there was no order to the way that they were doing things, and walking through the labyrinth made him feel small and because they didn't know who he was. He was afraid of being kicked out, as if he was someone who just wandered in because they needed milk. Lara offered to go for him, it was only meant to be once, but never again had Paul needed to step foot in the catering department or the school cafeteria for that matter.

69

April 2010, Twenty Seven Years Old

"His is a fragile world." Said Joan "A simple change in the wind can blow him over. His mind is always full of everything. He said to me once 'my head his buzzing with a million bees but when they sleep at night I miss them.' I didn't understand him then, but why would I when hearing this from a seven year old. Now I understand him and I honestly want you to understand him too."
"I understand him." Replied Lara softly "Really you don't need to worry."

Joan was trying to protect Lara, she knew that Paul could be awkward but she didn't want that to stop them. Joan was trying to say all she could about what she understood of Paul. She didn't know Paul as much as she thought. Paul would do anything to make sure that Lara was happy and would never push her as far as he had pushed some people. Joan didn't yet understand this.

"Sometimes I feel that he would blow away in the lightest wind." Continued Lara "I am sure he is tougher than we think."
"He is resilient but I think that is more because he teaches himself to be rather than an actual attribute to his personality." Replied Joan.
Lara laughed, "We sound like we are psychoanalysing him!"

Joan laughed too. She had often tried to figure out what was going on inside Paul's head, when he would do or say something not to the norm of children or adults his age. He always did seem young for his age, and all the teachers would say that he was a late developer mentally, which was ironic really because his knowledge was always far beyond his years. Paul would, like a toddler, throw a tantrum if the slightest thing was moved on his desk. His desk in his classroom included.

"What are you talking about?" Asked Paul when he entered the kitchen.

Joan was about to say 'nothing' like people usually say, then you know that they have been talking about you, but Lara answered first.
"You." She said smiling at him.
"Doesn't surprise me." He replied not taking the bait.

Joan raised her eyebrows she didn't think he would say that. He used to get really annoyed when people would talk about him even if it was for good reasons. Unless he was in the conversation he didn't like it.

Paul asked Lara if she would like to meet his sister, although he said it more in the way of 'would you like to meet my niece' and that meant going to his sister's house. They travelled by train, it was a pleasant enough journey the sun was shining through the clouds instead of behind them. They had the seats that Paul wanted and he had the aisle seat just the way he liked. Lara didn't mind she preferred to have the window seat. They had a block of four seats to themselves so shoved their bags on the other two. There were plenty of other seats around, obviously it wasn't the right day for a mass visit to Bath. Joan met them at the station and they arrived back later in the evening to her house. They were only staying for the weekend but it was a nice trip for them to take together, at least they thought so. All four of them sat round the kitchen table talking until Paul got bored and went to check on Sara, who was looking at some pictures in one of her books. Joan and Hugh's house was open plan they found it easier to keep an eye on Sara. It also meant that she could sit in the lounge instead of messing about where they were. Hugh went off with him mainly because it was way past Sara's bedtime and he wanted to see if Paul could pursued her to go to bed. Paul succeeded to the surprise of no one, Sara and Paul had a bond that was more like brother and sister than uncle and niece. Though she did listen to everything that he told her whereas with her parents she tried to get away with everything.

"Sara's a cute kid." Said Lara generically.
"She is a handful!" Exclaimed Hugh "Only three years old and already an attitude."
Lara laughed kindly before stating in a polite way that she was tired and was going to bed. There was only one spare room so Paul had to go on the sofa. They didn't own a camp bed or anything like that, so the sofa was the next best thing although Paul did try to protest but they all figured that he would. They did manage to convince him that it was polite that the guest had the spare room.

"I am a guest too." Replied Paul "I don't live here."
"You are here more than you would like to admit and anyway you are family, it isn't rude if I asked you to sleep on the sofa, but it is if I ask Lara." Said Joan.

The next morning Paul was greeted with the cheery Lara who had a good night sleep and had the nerve to ask Paul how his night went.

"It was a sofa, how do you think?" Said Paul rudely.
"Fine if it means so much to you have the spare room." Said Lara folding her arms.
"Really?" Questioned Paul.
"No of course not!" Exclaimed Lara trying not to laugh "I am not giving in to everything you want Paul."
"Why not?" Questioned Paul.
"You are my friend not my child." Stated Lara.
"Yeah you start treating him like a child and he will think that he is one." Stated Hugh.
"That is rude." Replied Paul.
"I am family." Said Hugh raising his eyebrows "I am allowed to be."
"True." Nodded Joan joining in the conversation.

Paul huffed before going into a different room which was hard to find when your bedroom was the place where everyone congregated. By dinner time he had shaken off his bad mood and he started to complain that he had wasted a lot of time being annoyed.

They Said That I Was Brainy

"I didn't realise you were this difficult to live with." Said Lara who was in hysterics as soon as Paul started to complain again.
"He was." Said Joan trying not to join in the laughter which was echoing from Hugh also "Correction, is, he comes here a lot now."
"You do?" Questioned Lara.
"No I don't." Corrected Paul.
"You do!" Exclaimed Joan "In your last year of university you were here almost every other weekend."
"I don't like people ok!" Exclaimed Paul who decided that he would take Camble out for a walk.

It was drizzling but Paul wanted to get away from people in general and that was the only way to do it, that or hide in the bathroom.

"He does get overwhelmed poor dear." Said Joan shaking her head.
"I know." Replied Lara gazing out the window in the direction that Paul was walking in.
"I wonder if he will ever get used to it." Said Hugh.
"He is twenty seven years old." Replied Joan "I think it would be hard for him now."
"I don't agree." Said Lara "He had done so many things that he never would have, I think he deserves more credit than we give him. For us something like reading aloud to a crowd is an achievement, but for him not getting annoyed that his paper was put in the right pile instead of the middle pile, is something that we should be proud of him for."
Joan looked at her, "I never thought anyone would understand him better than me but obviously you do."

70

October 2010, Twenty Seven Years Old

"People don't talk enough don't you think?" Suggested Lara as they were walking to work.
"People talk too much." Was the blunt reply from Paul.
"I knew you would say that." Said Lara.
"If you know everything that I am going to say then why do I say anything at all?" Said Paul "QED."

They walked in silence for a while, as they reached the park it started to rain gently at first but then began to pour down. Lara was carrying an umbrella but didn't open it. Paul looked across to her and then tried to grab the umbrella but Lara wouldn't let him.

"No." Said Lara firmly pulling the umbrella away from him "Dance in the rain remember!"

Paul didn't appear too pleased with her but watched as she twirled around. Paul pulled up the collar of his long coat and stuck his hands in his pockets. He felt the water trickle gently in the gap of his collar. The rain splashed up on the ground sending mud up Paul's legs he looked down at them and then looked at Lara who had stopped to watch his reaction.

"I need to go and change." He said.
Lara laughed, "No you don't, now come on."

She held out her hand to him, it lingered there for a while whilst Paul was making up his mind.

"Home." He said and turned around and started to walk back the way they had come.

They Said That I Was Brainy

Lara ran after him and walked backward directly in front of him putting her hands on his shoulders. He didn't stop so she continued to try and stop him.

"This is one moment." She started "One moment, you can't fix it or change it because this is what it is. Nothing more nothing less and if you walk away now you will never have this moment again, you walk one way and I walk the other."
"Then you walk the other." Said Paul.

Lara stopped still whilst Paul walked passed her she turned and ran after him again.

"Here." She said handing him the umbrella "You will need this."

She continued to walk her way to work without him. Paul stood in the rain watching her go and then he looked down at the umbrella in his hand. He pressed the button and it popped up, for a moment he thought that the rain had stopped.

"Come home." He said gently "Please, otherwise you will get wet." Lara smiled at him, "Thanks for the sentiment but did it ever occur to you that I like the rain?" She said it sarcastically but knew that Paul wouldn't understand.
"I will walk with you in the rain on the weekend or after work but if I don't go home now and change I will be late." He started "If I go in wet people will stare at me."
"When have you ever cared what people think?" Asked Lara.
"Always." Replied Paul.

Lara was quiet she looked into his face it was pale and his eyes were wide and full of worry. He was scared his routine had been changed and he was lost without a map to guide him. Lara understood this so turned with him and they both started to run. Paul had put the umbrella down as it was difficult to run with. They both went to their homes and changed and when they emerged the sun had come out as did a rainbow over them. The rain had stopped and there were puddles all around them as they walked back through the park they could hear the rain drops fall from the trees. They reached work ages before they needed to be there and Paul was relieved, he gave an obvious exhale of breath when they walked through the door.

"I am going to hold you to that promise." Said Lara waggling her finger at Paul before she walked off in the direction of her classroom.

Her hair was still damp, although she had attempted to dry it. It left little wet patches on her clothes but she covered them up with a jumper that she had put in her bag. Paul was nervous still, as he edged slowly towards his classroom. He sat down at his desk and looked at his attire.

"Wrong." He said aloud "It is all wrong."
"What is wrong?" Said Lara, she had come back to get her umbrella.
"Wrong shoes, wrong trousers, wrong shirt, wrong tie, wrong jacket, and wrong socks, wrong." He said leaning back in his chair.
"I say you look lovely." She said with a smile getting her umbrella that he had put on his desk in his nervousness "Please believe me."

She left him with his thoughts and no matter how hard he tried he couldn't believe her. He didn't do anything before his first class turned up, he tried his best to get through the day and when he was back home he slumped on his bed. He was mentally exhausted and fell asleep. When he woke up he was confused, he looked at his attire and wondered why he hadn't changed it.

"What?" He said aloud sitting up on his bed he had a mental block and either didn't want to remember or actually struggled to remember his yesterday.

There was a knock at the door Paul absentmindedly opened the door and then walked away.

"You look like you are drunk!" Exclaimed Lara looking at him.
"What?" Asked Paul looking around him "I am confused though."
"Yes I can see." Said Lara "Come on you need to get dressed."
"What is the time?" Asked Paul "What day is it?"
"Come on you can't be that confused." Said Lara but noticing that he was she continued "It is Saturday you were wearing the wrong

They Said That I Was Brainy

clothes yesterday and it is dancing in the rain time."

Paul was thankful that it wasn't a work day, he sat on the edge of his bed and put his head in his hands.

"Please Paul." She said "You promised."

Paul did remember the promise but tried not to. Lara wouldn't let him and he ended up getting dressed in the wrong clothes for the day for the second day in a row, on account of the weather.

"When you wear this you will always be wearing the right thing." Said Lara pointing to his face.
"I assume that you mean my brain rather than my face." Said Paul.
"Did you just infer something?" Asked Lara surprised.

Paul was as just as surprised as Lara, he was speechless but in a good way.

"You just taught me something." He said "Thank you."
"You are very welcome Paul." Said Lara "Anytime."

The sky had turned blue and a rainbow had appeared over the horizon, the rain was still coming down and there was something wonderful about the way that the sun had shown the delightful things that the rain could do.

71

March 2011, Twenty Seven Years Old

Paul and Lara were walking to the reception desk together. They had just been supervising outside play on the playing fields. Lara had a parcel delivered and could not stop talking about it. They greeted the receptionist before she had to go to the cupboard to find the parcel. Lara followed her to a small room around the corner. Paul stayed where he was, not noticing the other receptionist who had just arrived and was unpacking her bag. She moved about like she was dancing until she sat down in the chair and looked at Paul.

"Hi Paul how are you?" She asked with a sunny smile moving her bag under the desk.
"Fine." Started Paul his eyes were darting around the room trying to find something to distract him but there wasn't anything "And you?"

She talked about how good she was feeling and how nice the weather was, until there was a lull in the conversation and her voice just trailed off into silence. Paul stood there not knowing what else to say whilst the receptionist looked at the computer to log on but realised her colleague was still signed in. Not wanting to interfere she turned away and mouthed something to herself before beginning to shuffle some paper in front of her.

"That's a nice orchid." Said Paul noticing the flower on their desk.
"Yes it is isn't it?" Said the receptionist "It is a new one."
"Do you find that they last long?" Questioned Paul he didn't know why he kept talking because he really couldn't care less about the flower.

"Oh, about five or six weeks." Started the receptionist "But we find that it is hot above the radiator so they don't last as long as they should."
"Do you water it?" Asked Paul trying to not make it sound like a definite statement.
"Of course once a week." Said the receptionist as if she had the knowledge of a lifelong orchid grower.
"Now we know why it doesn't last very long." Joked Paul raising his eyebrows.

The receptionist found it very funny and was still giggling when Lara and the other receptionist returned.

"What's this?" Asked Lara smiling after seeing how happy the receptionist sitting in the chair was.
"Paul said the funniest thing." Replied the receptionist finding her words.
"It was a very random conversation." Replied Paul.
"We like random here." Replied the first receptionist who was packing up to get ready to go home.
"Afternoon all." Said Paul when he and Lara left together.

"That is nice you made her smile." Said Lara.
"It was a very random conversation but for some reason I couldn't stop talking." Said Paul.
"Maybe it is because you liked it." Joked Lara.
"Don't be absurd of course I didn't." Replied Paul seriously.
"Then why did you keep talking?" Questioned Lara.
"Trying to make small talk I suppose." Reasoned Paul.
"But you hate small talk." Exclaimed Lara.
"I know." Stated Paul shortly.

72

March 2011, Twenty Seven Years Old

"It's hard to put into words what it is like sometimes." Started Paul.

His head was crammed with his many thoughts like a whirl pool, he could never find the right words to explain what he was thinking, and looking at her with worried eyes he tried to put this into words.

"I seem to say that a lot without actually saying anything but there is no other way to start." Continued Paul.

Lara looked at him with her ears and eyes open to what he had to say. Paul didn't even know himself what he was trying to say but Lara already knew and understood. Her hands were placed on the grass beside her and then pulled it up rubbing her fingers together.

"The grass is wet." Said Lara.
"What does that matter?" Replied Paul annoyed that she wasn't actually listening to him.
"A few years ago you would have refused to sit here. Even on a coat or something but now you are sitting here without worrying about it. Look how far you have come Paul." Lara continued.

Paul thought for a moment absentmindedly placing his hand on the wet grass, it was as if he needed to know for himself that the grass was wet. He felt as the water droplets rolled between his fingers and burst as they slipped off his hand and back to the grass.

He smiled and added, "Do you have any hand gel?"

They Said That I Was Brainy

"At least you don't carry it around anymore." Laughed Lara who hadn't got any.

Paul then reached in his pocket and pulled out a clear bottle with a green liquid in it.

"Only joking." He smiled waving the bottle of hand gel in her face.
"You are even making jokes now then?" She questioned.

They stood up from the grass, the early morning meant that there was no one else about and they had this expanse of green all to themselves. They headed for the trees the other side and through to the concrete jungle beyond. The park in the middle of the city was the solace that Paul needed to bring him home. Although every time he walked through it he kidded himself into thinking this and deep down still yearning for the miles of fields to the coastal clifftops of *home*.

"Do you like the city?" Asked Paul swinging his long arms stiffly by his sides
"Yeah sure." Replied Lara "Why don't you?"
"No I do." Said Paul "Actually that is a lie, I don't know why I said that."

He paused as they dodged a group of people walking the other way.

"Don't you ever just want to be alone in miles and miles of open space?" Continued Paul once the people had passed them.
"No not really. I don't like the idea of being alone." Said Lara
"Yes I can tell." Replied Paul slowly as he tried to find the right words to finish the conversation before they went to their classrooms "Would you like to see?"
"What? See what Paul?" Lara had become preoccupied with searching in her bag for something.
Paul thought about what to say next, "Nothing." He replied with an awkward smile.

He walked in the direction of his classroom. Clearly Lara hadn't noticed or didn't care where Paul went to, as she didn't turn to see where he had gone when she had finished searching her bag.

She just continued to her classroom at the opposite end of the building.

73

March 2011, Twenty Seven Years Old

Camble wagged his ginger tail as he merrily bounded along the pathway to the park. Paul looked at his little tongue that bounced slobbering his now greying white fur.

"Why are there dogs?" Asked Sara who was walking beside Paul.

She was wearing her favourite blue puff coat with her green leggings and new trainers. The blue was beginning to fade but whenever someone mentioned buying her a new one she would cry until they promised not to.

"Why are there people?" Replied Paul raising his eyebrows at her.

She looked at him with a serious straight face that showed that she wasn't impressed with his answer.

She wagged her little finger at him, "No, no that isn't right."

She didn't finish what she was going to say as the swings came in view and she raced over to them without another word. She called for Paul to push her whilst he was busy tying the dog to the fence. Dogs weren't allowed in the park and Paul didn't want to have to keep an eye on both the child and the dog. Sara was four years old now and was enjoying every minute of it, she would look up to people who were older than her and vowed that she would stay four forever.

She loved to feel the wind as she was pushed higher and higher on the swing, she would keep calling for the swing to be pushed higher, but it never did go as high as she believed. The park was empty when they arrived, it was lunchtime which would explain why. It was a cold autumn day and everyone else was having lunch inside but Sara wanted to go to the park and Paul didn't want to go when there were other people there. He decided on lunchtime and Sara said that she would be hungry so in the end they decided to have a picnic. Sara agreed eagerly but when half a box of raisins flew onto the floor she wasn't so amused. They walked home just as it started to rain, the wind had stopped and the droplets of water came straight down. Paul preferred this type of rain to the spitting type, if he *had* to choose but he still wasn't a fan. Sara on the other hand enjoyed very much jumping in the puddles and getting Uncle Paul's trouser legs wet. She couldn't jump very high and was more of a large step than a jump, but the water still flicked everywhere. When they returned to the house Paul offered to play a game with her, but all Sara wanted to do was to hear about when Paul was a child, when he used to walk for miles along the fields in Cornwall.

"I don't like Bath." Stated Sara grumpily.
"Why?" Asked Paul "It is a very nice city."
"It doesn't have any baths." She replied seriously.

Paul was going to explain about the Roman Bath's but decided that it was best not to and started talking about how she was going to be starting school soon. She didn't seem very pleased and only stated that she didn't like the idea of learning.

"What can they teach me that I don't already know?" She said colouring in a dinosaur.

This time Paul couldn't stop himself, he started telling her how he enjoyed learning even if he didn't enjoy school.

"Ok I will enjoy the learning." She started "I won't enjoy school though, even if it looks like I am, I am just pretending."

Joan and Hugh arrived home late afternoon just before dinner time, Sara rushed up to them chattering all the way. Paul left shortly afterwards. He had come a long way to babysit but it was for an important reason. Sara wanted so desperately to move house and she might soon get her wish. Joan had been offered a job in Devon as the head of the English department. It was an opportunity that they didn't want to miss out on. Especially if it meant moving back to the countryside.

74

April 2011, Twenty Eight Years Old

Paul started to see less and less of Lara, it wasn't that she was avoiding him or that they had an argument Lara was happy for Paul to be around, but Paul wasn't. Her new boyfriend was not someone that Paul thought he would like to meet. He seemed hard to describe and Paul didn't like that. He took Lara to work almost every day, as he seemed to have moved in to Lara's flat meaning that Paul walked alone to work. Every day Lara would say she was sure that he would be happy to take Paul too.

"Wouldn't that be weird?" He asked.
"Why?" Replied Lara.
"It just would be." Said Paul "I am fine walking to work."

Paul went back home to visit his parents during one of the holidays. They were pleased to have him home, but weren't sure why he was back. He never usually came back when there were holidays, he would probably go to visit Joan instead. They started to wonder whether something was up, and his mother enjoyed trying to find out what he was thinking so decided to ask him personal questions which he didn't enjoy.

"Have you stopped spending time with your friend?" Asked his mother "Lara."

She said it as if Paul had more than one friend, or was hopeful that he would have. She left it open for him to discuss whether he had other friends, but the pause had meant he didn't want to talk so she added the name to encourage the discussion.

"Just because I don't physically spend time with her doesn't

meant that she is not my friend." Stated Paul.
"You text her then?" Asked his mother.
"Yes." Replied Paul.
"A lot?" Questioned his mother.
"All the time." Said Paul, he looked out of the window which showed the sky full of clouds ready to expel their rain on the surface of the Earth.

They were sat in the kitchen which seemed unusually bright when the day outside was dim, and Paul thought about all the reasons for this so didn't listen to the rest of his mother's questions.

"Why do you think that Lara messages me all the time?" Asked Paul still looking out the window.

His mother didn't know what to say, but had heard about Lara's relationship from Joan who had thought that Paul was upset about it, but she still didn't know what to say. She tried the generic answers instead.

"Maybe she misses you being around?" Said his mother "You used to spend a lot of time with each other."
"We have nothing in common." Replied Paul.
"You don't have to have anything in common to get along with someone." Said his mother "You just feel more comfortable around some people than others."

Paul seemed to take in what she was saying, but didn't offer any insight into what he was actually thinking. Paul did feel comfortable around Lara, he hadn't thought about it in that way before. Lara always said things to him that everyone else didn't say and he liked her even more for it. Then again if it came from anyone else he probably wouldn't like it but from her, that he was ok with.

75

June 2011, Twenty Nine Years Old

Paul didn't visit Joan when Jerry was born. He was still working and didn't think that he could cope with another baby in his life. Sara was older now which made conversation better, but thinking about having to do the whole process over with Jerry didn't give him enthusiasm to visit them too soon. He was born in June just before the end of term so it wasn't long before he had no excuse, and had to go.

"How is Lara?" Asked Joan.
"Fine." Replied Paul shortly "I am sure anyway I haven't seen her in a while."
"You work with her." Stated Joan a little confused "You live opposite her."
"Just because you work with someone doesn't mean that she is around, she is in a different department." Said Paul.
"I know but you two used to be good friends always walking to work and everything do you not even do that anymore?" Asked Joan.
"She gets a lift to work now." He said.
"Is it because she has a boyfriend now?" Asked Joan.
"Yes." Replied Paul "It would be different if I actually liked him."
"Maybe you just need to give him a chance." Replied Joan.

Paul wasn't impressed, he had made up his mind about him and didn't want to get to know him like Joan was suggesting. He looked at baby Jerry who looked helpless lying on his back in his cot. He was sound asleep with his little arms lying curled up around his head.

They Said That I Was Brainy

"He seems to be easier than Sara was." Stated Joan deciding that she was better off changing the subject.
"I wonder what he will be like when he grows up." Replied Paul wistfully.
"We will just have to wait and see won't we." Said Joan smiling at the prospect of watching both her children growing up "I don't think that he will be like Sara though. He seems quieter already."
"He is just thinking." Said Paul "That is all."

At that moment Hugh walked in with Camble who, instead of jumping around the cot like he used to sometimes do with Sara, he lay beneath it quietly hoping to protect Jerry from his bad dreams.

"There are so many changes that they will face." Started Paul again.
"That is what life is." Replied Hugh sitting down on the sofa "But a lot of change is good."
"I wonder what decisions they will make, and whether they will be the right ones." Said Paul.
"They will just have to decide that themselves." Replied Joan realising that Paul was no longer talking about the children and rather the life decisions that he was making "There are some decisions where they would just have to believe that what they are deciding to do will make them happy."
"It is really difficult to know." Stated Paul.
"Yes, but you just have to choose one and hope that your choice is best." Said Hugh "You always have a choice."

Sara had been playing in her room, but after a while she became bored and decided that she would go downstairs and find out what the adults were up to. She lightened the mood as she bounded in holding one of her soft toys. She jumped on the sofa between her parents, and after the deep and thoughtful conversation that they had just been having, they were thankful for a breath of fresh air from the little girl who was happy just to enjoy every moment and not worry about what her future held.

76

September 2011, Twenty Nine Years Old

Paul's feelings of Lara's boyfriend were confirmed, at least to him when her boyfriend tried to set him up with someone he knew. Lara seemed to like the idea, if only he had been better at reading body language, but Paul was adamant that he was not going to go. When the date came around Paul skipped to Devon for the weekend to escape the pressure that surrounded him. Joan and Hugh welcomed him as did his niece and nephew. He was colouring with Sara when Joan started to question him on why he had come, especially without telling them.

"I just wanted to come that is all." Replied Paul who continued to listen to his niece tell him why she was colouring the grass orange.
"Paul, what if we were on holiday." Replied Joan.
"But it isn't the school holidays." Replied Paul as if the question answered itself "Anyway I like the countryside, I don't want to be stuck in the city forever."
"I know but you can't keep running away." Replied Joan before Hugh came into the room.
"It was over a girl, Joan." He concluded.
"Why does everything have to be over a girl?" Replied Joan looking at him with a smirk on her face.
"It doesn't, but this time it is a girl." He said "So who is she?"
"It isn't Lara is it?" Chirped in Joan "Has she broken up with her boyfriend?"
"No it isn't Lara." Replied Paul feeling uncomfortable.
"Ah ha!" Exclaimed Hugh "So you admit it is a girl."

Paul took a deep breath and then quickly told them about the date to which they both said that he should have gone.

"*I* didn't want to go!" He exclaimed loudly before walking out of the room slamming the door and making poor Jerry cry.

Sara didn't seem to notice and kept on talking about the splashes of colour which seemed to spread across their various sections on the page. After a while she went to the spare bedroom where Paul was and she knocked on the door.

"Knock, knock it's me!" She exclaimed in a squeal before opening the door.

Paul was stood looking out of the window when Sara sauntered over to him, but being too small she couldn't look out. Paul looked down at her and smiled before fetching a box for her to stand on. She gazed across the fields and made a comment about how they go on forever. Paul didn't correct her.

"You know." Started Sara slowly "I think grownups are meant to go on dates."
"Is that so?" Replied Paul wondering which of the grownups downstairs said that.
"No." Replied Sara "Actually I was just copying what mummy said."
"What do you think?" Asked Paul.
"I dunno." Replied Sara before thinking a bit "I think that you should do what you feel."
Paul chuckled, "You are wise for a five year old." He said before adding with a sigh "If only I could believe you."

77

February 2012, Twenty Nine Years Old

Lara and her boyfriend had broken up about four months ago. Lara wasn't very happy for a while and Paul did his best to cheer her up. It had taken a while but Paul and Lara had finally returned to the friendship that they knew, they were both happy in the familiarity of each other's company.

"I wish you would have told me about him." Said Lara quietly as they sat in the park one Monday "You didn't like him from the start."

Paul had his usual stance with his hands clasped in his lap, Lara was sat close to Paul but sitting more relaxed than he was.

"I was judging him because he took you away from me." Said Paul seriously before adding "That does sound a bit selfish."
"Why didn't you tell me?" She replied.
"Because I thought you were happy." Said Paul "I didn't want to get in the way."
"I did miss our walks and stuff." Said Lara.
"Marry me." Said Paul stopping Lara mid-sentence.
"You don't mean that." Said Lara trying hard not to smile.
"I think I do." Replied Paul confused.
"No Paul." She replied "We both aren't ready for marriage yet."

She took his hand in hers and they sat there in a comfortable silence for a while. They listened to the birds singing, it was almost spring time and they were all returning to the woods around the edges of the park. It was still cold though and they were both huddled close together on the bench all wrapped up in their coats.

They Said That I Was Brainy

"When I am ready." She started slowly "I will let you know, and I hope that you will be able to say yes as easily then as you are able to now."
"So you do love me?" Questioned Paul.
"Paul of course I do." She replied "I wouldn't be the person I am without you."
"I defiantly wouldn't be the person I am." Agreed Paul they both laughed before he continued "I know I can be difficult sometimes and you are very brave for sticking by me."

They both laughed again before deciding that it was probably time that they went back to work. Their lunchtimes always went quickly now, as they sat eating their lunch in the park together. They walked back to the upper school and the scent of the growing flowers seemed to drift around with them. The sun was shining brightly trying desperately to warm up the world and turn winter into spring.

78

November 2012, Thirty Years Old

People usually wonder briefly about those that they knew at school, wonder about what they are doing, where they are and if they are happy. Paul didn't. He didn't think about people he use to know as to him most of them were only acquaintances anyway, and would they ever think about him? If he ever did wonder about someone that he hadn't seen in years he knew that he could contact everyone that he had ever met by a click of a button if he ever should wish to. He didn't worry about not knowing where that kid who got an A grade on that French paper back in middle school was, or if that girl who was good at sport ever did get signed for that football team.

The internet was always there for Paul, if he ever did decided that he wanted to stay in touch with anyone. Although, Paul didn't have any social media. Although he did prefer to communicate with people electronically the idea of social media didn't appeal to him. He was very much in the mind-set of the best way for him to enjoy his life was for him to enjoy it himself. He didn't feel the need to share what he was doing, just so that other people could judge him on it.

Stella was one of those people who had every messaging system, and still insisted that it wasn't enough. Between every break at university she used to look at her phone and check all her different messaging sites. She usually read something out to Paul, who either wasn't interested or didn't understand the reference to what she was talking about.

Paul meandered aimlessly through the rainy shopping high

street, Stella and her messaging systems were far from his mind. It had been pouring with rain and the water from the rain clouds was left lying on the ground accumulating into large puddles. Paul tried his best to avoid them, but because he wasn't concentrating he stepped straight into a large deep puddle that went up to his ankle. He looked down at his wet foot and shook it carelessly before continuing on his way, just before stepping into another puddle with the other foot. He was annoyed now and was desperate to find some new shoes and socks that he could change into. He was reliving the dancing in the rain episode a few years ago. He went into the first shop he found that sold shoes. He moved down the aisles of new and fresh shoes but not really finding anything that he was looking for. They were either the wrong style, the wrong colour, had the wrong fastenings or had a price tag ending in a nine. As he was scrambling to the back of the shelf to find a pair of shoes in his size, he noticed a low laugh that sounded familiar. He didn't think much of it at first and continued to move the smaller sizes out of his way. A few seconds later there was a voice calling him, it sounded just like the laugh and he knew that it was familiar. He turned around in the direction of some of the seating used by people who were trying on shoes, and there standing in front of it was Stella.

She was with another girl, whom Paul assumed was one of her friends, she was trying on some heeled shoes whilst Stella kept looking longingly at some sandals obviously thinking about the summer. Paul briefly thought about pretending that he didn't recognise her, but didn't think that he could make it to the door in time before she began calling him again. So instead he awkwardly smiled but said nothing, he tried to go back to looking at the shoes.

"Paul it is so great to see you!" She exclaimed walking over to him and giving him a hug which Paul tried hard not to shrug off.
"You didn't come to my graduation." Stated Paul with a straight face it was the only thing that he wanted to remember her for now.
Stella's smile drooped a little she didn't think that Paul would start their conversation off like this after not seeing each other for almost eight years, "Yeah but that was years ago."

"Even if it had only been a few days you still didn't come." Replied Paul not wanting to continue the conversation any further he added "I should get going."
"You just got here come on let's go and get a coffee or something." She started happily again not wanting to let him run out on her.
"I am meeting Lara." Stated Paul not thinking that Stella didn't know who Lara was.
Stella's face dropped a little, "So, who is Lara?"
"My fiancé." Paul replied smiling.

Stella strained a false smile and nodded her head slowly before Paul made his escape forgetting about his soggy shoes. He was just happy to leave that shop which he probably wouldn't go in again, just in case Stella was there. He didn't want to have to go through that conversation again. He was annoyed but more at the fact that he was just settling into his new routine and didn't need a face from the past trying to wiggle their way into it. That is the way that Paul saw it anyway. He ignored the puddles as he walked through the few people that decided to brave the weather, rather than be like most of the people and take shelter in the shopping centre. There was a small drizzle in the air which started to come down as Paul was half way to where he was heading. He didn't mind so much because he just wanted to get to where he was going, a little bit of rain wasn't going to stop him now.

79

November 2012, Thirty Years Old

Paul reached his destination and stood in front of an old sandwich shop. He was a bit confused why Lara would want to meet in there. From the outside the paint was beginning to peel around the sign which was on the front of the shop. The shop was small and the sign was beginning to show its age with rust poking around the corners and the paint was starting to chip around the door. He didn't understand why Lara liked places like that, but he accepted it all the same. It was in a prime location being in the centre of the town and it seemed to be popular, despite the shabby appearance from the outside. The inside was something of an astonishment, at least to Paul. It was light and airy with sparkling floors and the tables and seats looked as good as new. Lara was sitting at the back of the shop, if Paul had a choice he wouldn't have even looked in the place but as he began to look around him he was glad that he had given it a chance. There were some posters of historical events on one side of the shop, and on the other were posters of films which were inspired by the historical events. Lara had told him how the appearance of the place didn't matter, the sandwiches were good and that was all that she cared about. They ordered their food after Paul had joined her at some bar stools which were in front of the back window looking out over a river. It had risen to the top of its banks due to the deluge that was running down into the river. The wildlife was enjoying it with the ducks trying to swim against the current and the swans who decided that they were going to move their nest further up the bank.

Paul told Lara what had happened and how he met Stella in his quest to get to the sandwich shop. He was expecting Lara to be on the angry side of the emotional scale or annoyed at the least. He didn't really know what exactly she would say or act but he didn't expect her to laugh like she did before saying, "Typical."

"Typical?" Questioned Paul "It is not a very probable thing, that you would meet someone like that."
"No I mean it is always when you are not looking for someone that you find them." Said Lara not explaining properly "It is the same with stuff you can't find. When you are not looking for it is when it always turns up."

Paul wasn't sure how to reply and kept pondering this point in his head trying to figure out the mathematics behind it, even he got boggled with all the information and didn't think of anything to say. Through their silence they could hear the water in the river gathering in little groups heading out towards the sea. There were a few people on the small bridge over the river, they were looking down at the swirling torrent beneath them but they moved on quickly and another group of people did the same. Their food was brought to them and they started to eat it enthusiastically. Lara said that cold weather always made her feel hungrier, whereas Paul said that it was just an excuse for her to eat more food.

"I love you." Said Paul trying not to spit out the mouthful of lettuce that he had just taken he carried on munching loudly on his sandwich although he couldn't hear it himself.

It wasn't a very Paul thing to say, although Lara didn't seem too surprised at it.

"I know." Replied Lara seriously carefully taking small bites as though not to make a mess.

Paul hadn't taken this view and although usually he was clean and tidy there were bread crumbs all over his seat, the floor and the table that they were eating at. Once he had noticed this he cleaned up the mess on the table and on his chair. He swept it all neatly onto his plate. They finished their sandwich and after Lara had sung the praises of the person who made them, they began their walk home. The drizzle was coming down now in steady streams of rain.

"Thank you for asking me to marry you." Said Paul.

"You don't have to thank me." Replied Lara.

"But you might not have asked me." Stated Paul.

"But I did." Smiled Lara looking at him grabbing his hand before he had any choice to pull it away from her.

80

December 2012, Thirty Years Old

Paul wasn't the type of person to tell anyone anything, where other people would have considered things important to tell someone Paul didn't understand what the big deal was all about. He causally told his sister that he was getting married whilst he was eating dinner with them. He hadn't even thought of the reaction they would give when they were told. He just thought it was normal and it should be accepted without disbelief. Sara had gone round a friends for tea, but Jerry was being his usual self and started to kick his legs under his high chair in protest of something or other, and so started complaining. Joan was dumbstruck by the news and in her amazement she didn't answer her son who began to complain even more. Hugh lent over to him making faces and funny noises with his mouth and Jerry began to laugh again, to show his excitement he began to chuck his food around. Hugh rushed to take the pot of mashed carrots away from him. Paul started talking about how funny children are until Hugh interrupted him and tried to get him to talk about his engagement again.

"I didn't know that Lara and you were in love with each other!" Exclaimed Joan.
"I don't tell you everything and I didn't know until a few months ago." He said.

Joan and Hugh were eager to hear all about it and for once Paul was happy to relay it.

"He proposed to her, the boyfriend." Started Paul "She was happy for a while before he decided to break it off with her. I didn't want to ask her what was wrong because I didn't want to understand incorrectly, so we spent a lot of silent walks to work together before she decided that she didn't want to go to work altogether. She took an extended sick leave, I have never felt so lonely when she stopped walking with me. We had finally returned to where we were before *he* entered the picture, I didn't even think that I could feel lonely but I realised that she was the reason that I was happy there. She was my routine and it broke when they got together, I felt it even more the second time. I couldn't take her not coming with me so I went to her house and after sitting on the door step for an hour it started to rain and she let me in. We didn't talk at all the whole time I was there and as I was going out the door she exclaimed "I can't have children." She was in floods of tears and I didn't know what to do. We ended up hugged in the rain and I felt only a little awkward. I knew that I was the only person in the world that could love her like I did. I didn't have any comforting words to say but I hugged her back and I think that it helped."

Hugh and Joan were listening intently to what he was saying, Joan was continuing to think about how much Paul had changed. Had he though? It was a question that he kept asking himself when people had told him this. He didn't think he had changed but developed the more he got to know, the more he thought about things other than himself. He decided that there were things more important than making sure that he put his bag in the same place in his classroom, or used the same cup for coffee and another for tea. It didn't matter that he still did these things, to him all that mattered that he understood what was actually important to him and what were just habits of things that used to be important to him.

"I haven't changed." Said Paul as if he could read Joan's mind "I am the same person, the person I was all along I just needed Lara to show me."
"I can't believe that he broke up with her just because she can't have children." Started Joan.
Hugh silently shook his head in agreement with her before saying, "Love is meant to expand through all possibilities, it sounds to

me like he fell in love with the idea of them and ended up with a different reality. No matter how much you love someone you will never change them physically or their personality, the person that you fall in love with at the beginning is the person that you are in love with through your entire life."

"I think that is the most profound thing that you have ever said." Stated Joan smiling, lightening the mood that had taken a deep and thoughtful tone.

They went onto discuss the wedding but Paul stated that they were happy to be engaged, and they had decided to continue being engaged for as long as they possibly wanted. When Paul walked out of his sister's house he was greeted by a bright sun painted on the front of a blue background.

81

July 2013, Thirty One Years Old

"What do you want to be when you grow up?" Asked Paul.

He was babysitting for Joan and Hugh, as he was staying for a few weeks during the summer they thought that he might as well make him useful.

"I want to be just like you." Replied Sara smiling sweetly whilst finishing off a very messy painting.
"No Sara you want to be just like you." Replied Paul.
"Everyone says that." Replied Sara "Say something original."
"Watch what you say." Replied Paul wagging his finger.
"Why?" Asked Sara.
Paul didn't know what to say he didn't think that she would talk back to him, "I don't know but remember I am your Uncle not your friend."
"You are my friend." Replied Sara "Then again so is Camble."
"Great." Replied Paul "I am as good as a dog."
"No." Said Sara "You bring me food instead of eating the food I have."
"You talk a lot for a six year old." Stated Paul.
"That is what my teacher says." Said Sara "I tell her that I have a lot to say."
"Is that right?" Questioned Paul.
"She doesn't believe me." Replied Sara.
"I am not surprised." Stated Paul.
"I thought you were my friend?" Questioned Sara.
"I am." Replied Paul.
"So you admit it you are my friend." Corrected Sara "Anyway you are meant to be on my side if you are really my friend."

"I am on your side." Replied Paul trying to get her to understand "Sometimes you have to admit that you are wrong."
"I am never wrong." Said Sara.
"You do realise that you have painted the grass orange." Replied Paul looking at her painting.
"I like the colour orange." Said Sara.
"Does the grass?" Asked Paul.
"It is a different planet." Said Sara.
"Which planet?" Asked Paul.
"Saratopia." Said Sara.
"That isn't a real planet." Replied Paul.
"Does it need to be?" Said Sara.

Paul thought about this for a moment, he hadn't 'imagined' for a long time. He stopped playing with toys when he began to focus on music, because at that point it was important to him. Now he felt that he should imagine his own planet, where his action man could fly around without having to think of strings in the atmosphere. Sara didn't have any action men, but she did have a soft toy elephant and cow. When Joan and Hugh came home they found them playing in their imaginary world, with Paul as the elephant and Sara as the cow. Jerry was asleep for most of the evening and when he woke up he wanted to play Sara agreed handing over the much loved cow. Shortly after she got bored and snatched the cow back, Jerry didn't mind because he was asleep once again. Camble was curled up beside him Jerry unconsciously reached out with his little hand and clasped some of the ginger fur between his fingers.

82

October 2013, Thirty One Years Old

Paul wasn't really interested in castles, history was never his best subject at school and he would rather live in a modern building than an older one. But there was that day in October when Lara asked if he would come with her to an old manor house with gardens and woodland walks. Paul looked forward to the walks as he read about them prior to their visit and they were set in a backdrop of rolling hills, and a view to the coast. Lara was more interested in the building, which was fully furnished with information about the family that lived there, all of the information that didn't interest Paul. They arrived in the morning just as a few clouds rolled over the sky blocking out the sun briefly. It was meant to rain, not that it dissuaded Lara but Paul wasn't so sure. They started the walk first just in case it did start raining, they trudged through some mud from the previous day's rain. Although Paul sort of danced through it, trying his very best not to get his shoes or clothes muddy. They entered the wood which had tall trees before a large expanse of water, as they got closer they realised that the water was mostly covered with weeds and apparently there were crocodiles in the ponds in England. As they walked round they discovered more and more plastic wildlife before coming upon a small robin, which was in fact the first real wildlife they had seen in an hour of being there. Lara was busy taking photos so it took them a while to get round the large pond, Paul didn't know why she was taking so many photos because he didn't believe that it was that photogenic. Lara took some quick snaps of Paul which he complained about because he didn't like having his photo taken.

"Are you disappointed?" Asked Lara as they waited in a small queue to buy tickets for the manor house.
"I don't know." Replied Paul honestly.

Lara paid for the tickets and was absorbed by the decoration in the room. They wandered up and down the halls, to Paul's relief it wasn't a guided tour. They spent longer in there than they did on their walk and Paul seemed to enjoy it more. The rooms were decorated tastefully and not tacky at all, it was delicate and not full of a lot of furniture but enough to make it look lived in.

"What did you think?" Asked Lara when they were on their way back.
"I don't know." Repeated Paul.
"Come on Paul you must have an opinion." Exclaimed Lara.
"I just think that we could have gone to the local park for a walk." He said.
"Were you ok going in the house?" Asked Lara.
"Yes that was fine but I did find the walk disappointing." Said Paul "Especially since I read so much about it."

They went to the coast while they were that close by, it seemed silly not to. They arrived in the crowds of people who gathered near all the facilities, and they ended up walking and walking to find a little patch of beach all of their own. It was funny that the beach was as busy as it was because the weather would seem less favourable to most people. Only a few people passed them as they sat on a large rock looking out to sea. They did walk up to the sea which was splashing back and forth making the beach smaller and smaller as it did. Paul wouldn't take off his shoes but Lara was wading through the shallow of the waves with her trousers rolled up, although it didn't seem to matter as the splashes still got her clothes wet. It was windier down at the coast, though the rain held off. Paul could feel the wind pick up and they had to shout to each other to get themselves heard. They began to walk back and they noticed that most of the crowd had dissipated, it had just started to rain but Paul didn't say anything like Lara expected.

"Do you want to walk this way?" Questioned Paul pointing to the other direction along the coast.

"Really?" Asked Lara thinking he was joking.

"Really." He replied looking at her and smiled he took her hand another thing that Lara didn't expect him to do and he led her along the beach.

They walked for as long as they liked, coming back along the cliff top as the tide had come in too much for them to return by the beach. The rain stopped and as they were on their way back, the sun came out from behind the clouds causing a beautiful rainbow to appear in the now blue sky.

"Thank you." Said Lara softly.

A small smile appeared across Paul's face which showed slight embarrassment.

83

August 2014, Thirty Two Years Old

Paul agreed to try the whole holiday thing again, Lara persuaded him to give holidays another chance saying that a holiday is always better when you have a friend go with you. This time the holiday involved a plane, something Paul wasn't keen on. He got claustrophobic easily and being his first flight his nerves rose and rose. They arrived at the airport with a lot of time to spare as Paul was playing everything by the book. There was a bit of a crowd forming of all the other travellers who were early also and Paul was feeling anxious again.

"Why do they ask you to get to the airport three hours before your flight, when the bag check in only opens two hours before your flight?" Stated Paul as they waited at the front of the queue.

They decided to queue anyway, even though the bag drop hadn't opened yet, some of the other passengers followed their lead and started to queue up behind them. Eventually the bag drop was opened and they were soon free to escape and they headed towards security. Paul panicked as he rushed to take off his bag and placed it in one of the large grey trays which was pushed towards him, by a not so happy looking member of staff. He wasn't sure what he really had to do, even though he had read multiple manuals on traveling by plane. He had ensured that he placed all of his liquids in his main suitcase in the hold, just in case he got stopped and told off for having them. Lara tried to ensure him that as long as they were not over the limit in amount and placed in a plastic bag he would be fine, but Paul being Paul was erring on the side of caution. Even following Lara's lead didn't help, she breezed through the security gate as if it was nothing, whereas

Paul still felt like a criminal, even though he hadn't done anything wrong.

"That was very stressful." Said Paul when they were picking up their bags on the other side of security.

He looked around the vast expanse of shops which lay before them, selling all different types of merchandise. He was also surprised by the amount of people still wandering about, he was astonished by the number of fights which depart every day and turned his adventure into a learning experience. They waited in one of the many cafés before making their way to their gate.

It wasn't until Paul sat down in his seat did he start to relax and as soon as the plane started to move his heart started beating faster and faster. Paul's eyes were squeezed shut when the plane took off, it was a rare occasion where he held Lara's hand. Even as the plane levelled, Paul was still holding Lara's hand his ears were ringing despite the numerous sweets he had been chewing on.

"I won't be doing that any time soon." Said Paul as they got off of the plane.

His palms were still sweaty and his heart rate was still refusing to go down. Walking to the bag pick up his legs were wobbling but somehow managed to stay up right.

"You have to on the way back, remember." Giggled Lara as she grabbed her bag.

She was sympathetic really, but found it funny that he didn't remember the flight home. They finally emerged, after collecting their bags, in the warm sunshine and fresh air of the outdoors.

"You are going to love my grandparent's house." Started Lara as they waited for their train "South of France near to the coast and the house is on a small bit of land. All of your favourite things."

Paul had to admit that it did sound good, although he was nervous about meeting new people, staying somewhere different and he could not stop thinking about that plane flight home. Lara's grandparents were French and didn't speak much English.

R.V. Turner

It was a good thing that Paul had learnt those languages so long ago. He was rusty and in his anxious state did forget words and muddled others together. Paul found it very tiresome trying to work out what they were saying to him, especially if Lara had left the room momentarily. As then he didn't even have her to translate the words that he forgot, but slowly and surely Paul began to get back into the rhythm of speaking another language. Lara's grandparents were very patient with him, not rushing him on what he said or when he was trying to find a word. They would just sit there silently encouraging him to find in his head what he was trying to say.

Paul had stopped complaining of the hardship of speaking another language, and it felt good to get back into the swing of something that he used to know. It was a good feeling, especially as he knew that Lara's grandparents appreciated him being able to talk to them. Getting to know them wasn't as hard as Paul had thought, once they had started talking neither of them wanted to stop. They spoke about the old days and how so much had changed, about Lara growing up when Lara's family moved to England. Even though Paul knew some of what they told him already, for once he was happy to sit back and listen as it was told to him again.

Paul and Lara had the guest bedroom, which was nice and airy the floor boards were polished and it was very minimalist on the inside. Paul found the room satisfactory, and exclaimed that the lack of puddle in the middle of the bed already put this holiday on top. He briefly relived the damp and depressing cottage that he almost stayed in, in Wales.

Paul sat on the bed, it was long past the time that he would have usually gone to bed. Later in the evening the cousins had descended upon the grandparent's house all to meet Lara and her mystery friend. Lara had made him leave the window open all night, even though she knew Paul didn't like it. The duvet was pulled up neatly placed across his chest, with his head laid squarely in the middle of the pillow. He couldn't sleep. Lara was snuggled in the duvet on her side, and was just about to drift off into a state of rainbows and puppy dogs when Paul decided that he wanted to talk.

"So why did you decide to move to England?" Asked Paul.

"I didn't my parents did." Corrected Lara trying to wake herself up "I just came along for the ride."

"You had a choice to stay in France?" Questioned Paul.

"Of course. I could have stayed with my grandparents." She said rolling over on her side to look at him "But I wanted to go, it was a new adventure and I was nine years old! I wanted to go. I learned English at school and my mother is English and my father spoke English, it wasn't as if there was going to be a language barrier so we just went."

"Why?" Asked Paul.

"Because we could." Said Lara "When my parents went to America I decided to stay in England. I wanted to go to university and that is exactly what I did."

"You made all of those decisions and my biggest decision is whether to have aloe vera hand gel, sensitive hand gel or hand gel for dry skin." Said Paul.

"And those are the decisions that *you* have to make." Started Lara "They are the ones that you have got to say, 'today I am going to have' and then just choose, without thinking too much about it. That's what I do. France or England, England or America."

"But it was your next adventure." Said Paul.

"No it was their next adventure." Said Lara "My next adventure was living independently, working two jobs so I could afford to stay, figuring out where I was going to live the following year, deciding that I wanted to teach. You knew that you wanted to teach or at least do something to do with music. I didn't."

Paul decided that he wasn't going to write a diary this time, his main reason was that Lara was writing one which would have everything they did in it, so there was no need for him to write one too. He also couldn't be bothered. They went Monday to Friday and they managed to cram in as much sightseeing, as they did visiting Lara's family.

The following evening, majority of the family went to a local restaurant, owned by Lara's aunt and uncle. It was very traditional and the décor made a pleasant mood, even for Paul who was relaxed. His meal was chosen for him, which he was dubious at first but it did take out the stress of choosing something. He was delighted with their choice and was finished far before all of the other diners.

"So when are you two going to get married then?" Questioned the eldest of Lara's cousins.

He was about the same age as Lara, and was even taller than Paul making him a bit intimidating. He was in actual fact a gentle giant who had grown up on a farm and talked about animals all the time.

"Not yet." Was the vague reply that Paul gave.
"Do you have anything planned?" He asked.
"No." Said Paul "I don't think that Lara wants a white wedding anyway."
"Are you sure?" He questioned.
"Absolutely." Replied Paul.

He had never thought about wedding arrangements before, for some reason the wedding didn't cross his mind. Lara had never really talked about it before.

"Why have we never talked about plans for our wedding?" Asked Paul.
"To be honest, I didn't want to scare you off." Replied Lara.

They were sitting outside under the stars of the velvet sky, and the moon was shining brightly in front of them. It was getting late and both of them were beginning to feel tired but neither of them want to leave the other alone.

"You wouldn't have done." Replied Paul.
"Are you sure?" She questioned "I didn't want you to over think having to stand in front of all those people."
"Honestly, what would you want our wedding to look like?" Asked Paul.
"I don't really know." Said Lara "Although, Joan's wedding always sounded nice."
"Is that what you want?" He asked.

"As long as you are there, and our families are there I really don't mind where it is." Said Lara before she continued with a smirk on her face "As long as I get to wear one of those long white dresses."
"You can wear what you like." Said Paul.
"What do you want to wear?" Asked Lara.
"It depends what day it is." Said Paul with a straight face but he couldn't keep it up for much longer and slowly the corners of his mouth started turning up and they both started laughing and joking about their wedding.

It was a whirlwind of a trip, for Paul at least. He actually enjoyed himself the whole time, to the delight of Lara who was eager to take him back to France in the near future. The flight home was not so stressful for Paul, although he still didn't like going through security. He knew what was going to happen on the flight, but still held Lara's hand the whole time. They walked down their street and it felt like they had never been away. Lara was sad that they weren't on holiday anymore, but Paul was happy to be home.

84

December 2014, Thirty Two Years Old

"I didn't think that you would want to marry anyone." Said Lara as they ate dinner at a small restaurant in the centre of town, she was drinking a fizzy drink and the sound of it made Paul wince.

Even though it was a small restaurant, it seemed popular it had a very unique appearance and for some reason people were attracted to it. It had become more popular than the owners had imagined, and now it blended in with the rest of the restaurants in the town. It was no longer a special place for people who want to eat something different and enjoy it in peace and tranquillity. Everyone had discovered its secret, and business was booming. The cold air outside was barred from the warmth that was within. The restaurant was heated, not only with the cosy log fire and boiler but also with the bustle of the many people that filled the walls of the restaurant to bursting point. There were a few various rooms on different levels of the restaurant, but every single one was full of the chatter of the different people who sat at the tables, which were packed with the delicacies that the Italian restaurant had to offer. It made it hard for Paul to hear what Lara was saying, who seemed to cope with the noise fine. Whereas Paul heard every sound at the same volume, and couldn't turn any of them down. Lara continued to slurp her pasta as she waited for Paul to answer her question, and Paul tried very hard not to get annoyed with her, unfortunately *that* noise he could hear fine. He was already frustrated with the noise and as the volume grew he curled his toes, instead of walking out of the restaurant to escape.

"You don't think like me, how would you know?" Replied Paul slowly cutting up his pizza into small pieces before tentatively

picking one up with his fork, looking at it before placing it in his mouth.
"True but you never seemed interested in any of that stuff." She concluded.
"Just because I never told you that I was interested, doesn't mean that I wasn't." Replied Paul quickly adding "I do have feelings you know?"
"You don't show them enough." Said Lara with a smile "Then again sometimes you show them too much."

She looked down at her spaghetti which lay in a pool of tomato pesto, surrounded by little pieces of cheese that hadn't properly melted into the dish. It didn't look appetising anymore but she continued to eat it, because it tasted lovely and to waste it wouldn't be right.

"I will try harder." Replied Paul conclusively continuing to eat the little pieces which didn't much resemble a pizza anymore.
Lara smiled appreciatively, "You don't have to change but if you let me know what you were feeling that would be good."
"Nice." Replied Paul "That would be nice. Good is what or how you are, but how you are feeling would be nice or pleasant."

Lara shook her head and resisted the urge to tell him to stop correcting her, but she had said it often enough without making a difference. It had become Paul, everyone else said to her that she should tell him not to do that but she would reply, "He is my fiancée not my child."

"It takes me a while sometimes to know how I am feeling or what I am feeling and why." Said Paul "I need to understand why before I tell anyone otherwise my feeling may be wrong or I may have misunderstood it."
"Paul I understand that, I have always understood that." Said Lara placing her hand on Paul's "Come one let's talk about something more upbeat."

Paul jumped at the chance to tell her about a telescope that was being built in some country for the purpose of finding out what dark matter was. Lara smiled politely and listened to most of what he was saying before talking about the culture of a country that she had just learnt about, which Paul was trying to pretend to listen to, although he didn't seem to be doing such a good job.

They didn't finish their last dish until the restaurant was closing up, and by the time they were leaving the restaurant was almost empty. There were only a few people left at the bar, one who appeared to be the owner, and a couple sitting alongside him. They were laughing as if they were old friends and it began to make Lara uncomfortable, as if they were no longer welcome.

"You worry too much." Said Paul.
"So do you." Replied Lara.
"True." Agreed Paul "You do a better job of hiding it than I do."

The meal was paid for and at 11pm the dark star lit pathways of the town were almost deserted. They wandered along the cobbled side roads and up through a housing estate the other side of town. Their flat was in the fourth street back from the town, it was Lara's flat. It was bigger than the flat Paul lived in and ironically cheaper. They had started to save for a house but were not entirely sure why as, there were no houses around the area that they would be able to afford, and they didn't think that either of them wanted to move away from the area. They had worked at the same school for almost seven years and felt used to it. They didn't want to change so they just wanted to save, in case one of them were given a better offer, although they couldn't think of anything better than what they already had.

Their flat was dark against the night sky as they approached the blue front door and as soon as the door was clicked away from the latch Paul switched on the lights. Their little flat beamed brightly outwards against the backdrop joining with the stars floating overhead. They closed their door on the world outside, focusing on their world inside. They sat on the sofa and watched TV but continued to talk over the background noise. It was early hours when they had finished talking about whatever they could and Lara yawned. Paul urged that they stopped talking immediately and went to bed. Lara made sure that they left certain lights on just as Paul liked it and shutting the doors just as she had always done. The flat had been combined with two completely different personalities they made a new tradition which they could both share.

85

Summer 2018, Thirty Six Years Old

The sun on his face comforted him as he leaned backwards into the soft sofa. He tilted his head and looked over at the small fish tank in the corner. Lara had done some redecorating, too much of Paul's objection, and the fish tank was not left untouched. She had written Ken's name neatly over part of the glass with special glass pens. She had coloured it in and had drawn a few pictures around the edges. Paul smiled, he actually liked the redecoration but wouldn't admit it. It was a nice touch as Lara had made Ken her pet too, which made Paul smile even more.

The way the sun came in the window reminded Paul of when he was at school. Year two, November 1990, his desk was luckily placed near the window. He often turned his chair to face that direction rather than the direction of the teacher, much to her annoyance. He began to think more and more about his school days, different things that made him laugh, cry and angry. All of the things he remembered most and wanted to remember, and all of the things he as much as he wanted to forget, he couldn't. As he thought, he was reminded of a day when he was six years old. It had stuck with him through his entire life because he took the words said to heart, for all the wrong reasons. He had heard the phrase twice in his life and he heard it for the first time when he was six years old. He remembered being sat in the classroom trying not to zone out when the teacher was talking, but didn't really succeed. He had turned his chair towards the window and lost himself looking into the woods beyond the playing field. He was thinking about dinosaurs before the room suddenly went quiet, and he realised he was meant to be paying attention. He turned just before the teacher handed him a piece of paper. She knew that he hadn't been listening but had stopped bothering to get annoyed with him. The teacher was handing each student the scores of a recent spelling test, but because Paul knew how well he had done he cast the piece of paper aside. It fell into the view of a little girl sitting at the next desk along. She peered at the paper, trying to be sly, and started to whisper to the person sat next to her. Paul never did know whether the other student was interested in what she was saying, but she started talking to him anyway. Paul knew that they were talking about him, and listened to hear what the one sided conversation was about. He understood what they were saying, but he didn't understand the way they were saying it. It was only when he was talking with Joan and it cropped up in conversation that he understood. Joan had become annoyed with what they had said concluding that they were being unkind to Paul. She never properly explained to Paul the reason that she was annoyed with them, and from then on Paul believed that they were being mean to him.

"Paul got full marks on the spelling test." Said the little girl, not waiting for an answer from the person she had commandeered to be in her conversation she continued "But he would, wouldn't he, cos that kid is proper brainy."

"Yes I am." Said Paul aloud to himself "So what."
"What was that Paul?" Asked Lara who was sitting on the sofa beside him leaning up against the soft arm with her legs outstretched over Paul's legs.
"Nothing." He said smiling "Nothing at all."

That was the moment that made Paul feel as if the world was finally ok with him being Paul Westwood. He had always believed that it was wrong to be as smart as he was, and that it was the reason why he never fitted in at school and why the other students were always mean to him. He blamed his intelligence for everything, even when Joan tried to explain to him that being smart wasn't a bad thing.

He had always tried to fit in, to not be noticed by his peers as if he could sail through school as the invisible person. It never worked out the way that he had planned, as Joan would continue to tell him that he was ever growing into the best version of himself and should be proud of who he was. It was hard to be unique in a world that didn't accept him for who he was, and as he struggled through his school life he never understood that the best thing about being unique is standing out. To Paul it was never easy to show who he really was, as the criticism that he received for showing his real personality was hard for him to bare. Sitting alone in his bedroom he would fight with his brain trying to convince himself that it was everyone else's problem if they didn't like him and not his own. Like most of the children his age who were battling with the same issues, he would never believe this and continue to blame himself for his own personality and try to change it.

It had been thirty years since Paul was that six year old trying to be like everyone else. It had taken that thirty years for him to realise that he didn't have to prove himself to anyone. He looked around him and realised that for him, life had turned out just the way he wanted it to be. Instead of focusing on what that little girl said all those years ago, there was something much better that he could think about himself. Even up until his adulthood Paul had always wanted to be 'normal' and fit in, and now it was Lara who was convincing him that he was and always will be the best version of himself and for once, he finally began to believe the words that she said to him.

"Be your own kind of normal Paul." Lara had said "It is who you are, what you are and the best thing about you."

Printed in Great Britain
by Amazon